ECHOES

G J Mowat

Dedication

To my parents, Dick and Mildred

You were the best!

And to Terry and Alex

With love

About the Author

G J Mowat is a retired nurse and midwife with military nursing experience. Born in Yorkshire, she spent her formative years in central Africa and has since traveled extensively. She lives in Cambridgeshire with her husband and son. This is her first novel.

Table of Contents

Dedication iii

About the Author iv

GEORGE 2

TILLY 11

ALICE 14

WILLIAM 20

THE PLAN 27

THE NURSE 43

A NEW BEGINNING 48

THE WARDS 55

MARRIAGE 60

NEW BEGINNINGS 62

The Courtship 68

THE CHILDREN 71

NANCY 75

THE RAILWAY 81

HENRY 82

CHARLOTTE 98

THE FAMILY 107

REALITY 110

THE DIAGNOSIS 116
DOMESTICITY 119
DISASTER 126
WAR MONGERING 136
ISOLATION 141
CHANGE COMES 146
WAR AND REUNION 154
DECISION 167
FRANCE 1916 175
CAPTAIN LASCELLES 183
EN ROUTE 185
NELL 194
NEILAN 197
THE CASUALTY CLEARING STATION 204
MOBILISATION 223
JACK 234
THE HOME FRONT 239
BEYOND EXHAUSTION 246
RESPITE 253
SEPARATION 263
STIFLED 268
LEAVE 271
BATTLE SHOCK 278

THE SPECIALIST 286

PHILIP 289

THE JOURNALIST 294

WIMERAUX 304

DISCHARGE.. 311

ECHOES 314

2016

I never really felt that hospitals smelled of anything much at all. Clean, yes, but not the pungent smell of disinfectant that so many complain of. Is it possible to inherit a memory do you think? Can inherited memories reverberate through the years and come to settle where they are supposed to be? I ask because I have just such an inherited memory of just such a smell from somewhere deep in my brain, of another time, another place, yet way before I was even born. I can see the pristine white corridor of a hospital and the clinical atmosphere in my mind's eye, and I can even hear the rustles of my starched apron as I walk briskly towards a polished double wooden door with porthole windows, which I know leads to a ward……

GEORGE

1916

He is shaking very badly. He had a haunted look on his face, frightened, and persecuted. His wide feral eyes were alert and dashing about his face expecting goodness knows what. He's curled upright in the foetal position with his back to the wall scanning all the exits to the ward. He was breathing heavily, wounded, and hurting. I approach slowly and sit softly on the bed at his side.

"Hello," I say gently, "My name is Tilly," and I hold out my hand as if to shake his, but he doesn't take it. He cowers backwards as though I have struck him. "Let me help you?" I suggest in a quiet calm voice, and I place both of my hands gently in my lap. We look at each other as the noise and bustle of the ward go on around us. There is only him and me. He's young, maybe 16 or 17 – too young to have been in a battle, to have seen what he has seen: the horrors of war, blood, death, and destruction, and, not to mention, the searing cold and trauma of losing friends. They were too young to even be at the Front, but I know many of these young boys lied about their age, fearing they would be "missing out", and that it would all be over before they were old enough to join up. He was brought into the ward in the early hours of the morning, and he hasn't moved his position since then. He has declined all help so far and won't be washed, touched, or reasoned with.

Food has been offered, a cup of cold tea sits at his side untouched, and still, he sits in his battle-stained clothes curled up and oblivious to every attention so far.

"I wonder if you could do me a favour," I ask him, and wait. He looks at me with wide haunted eyes.

"I could really do with a hand with the tea trolley, somehow, I have to get drinks out to the men on the ward and as you're one of the only ones who can walk, I wondered if you would help me. Push the trolley. I mean. I can do the drinks, but it's quite heavy with the tea urn on top, and you look like a strong lad..... Will you help me?"

He looks unsure but meets my gaze, and there is a flicker of something as I stand up. I put out my hand to him, and to my astonishment, he takes it. His grip is strong as he rises. He's tall. I direct him gently to the tea trolley behind us. He grips the rail as though his life depended on it, probably to stop his shaking hands, and off we set. I try not to draw too much attention to him as we proceed steadily down the long ward stopping at each bed to dispense hot tea and a word of comfort and cheer to the men. It's not really my job to give out the teas. I can't usually be spared from my nursing duties, but I have a brother of a similar age and the doctor attending to this poor boy thought he might respond better to a female, a nurse with a more sympathetic manner than some of the ward orderlies who had attended him since he was scooped off the battlefield and brought here during the night. "Bloody shirker," they said, "nowt wrong wi' him", "Bloody head case."

He didn't appear to have any physical injuries. Though his uniform was caked with dry mud and blood, somebody's blood – but there was definitely something wrong with him.

He pushed the trolley behind me as I dispensed tea. There was conversation and banter down the ward, and the men responded in kind.

"What's your name?" I asked him again as we neared the end of the round, "I can't keep referring to you as "This Lad!" – come on, what your Mam calls you?"

I try to keep it light and conversational, glancing at him only occasionally so as not to frighten him off. The lads on the ward shouted encouraging comments and offers of "a fag", but he ignored them. He kept his eyes firmly on me and hung onto the trolley like grim death to stop himself from shaking.

"George," he said. It was almost a whisper, but I heard him and smiled. I touched his hand lightly. "It's alright, George", I said, "You're safe now."

2016

His face is in repose. Still and quiet with all the chatter of a busy hospital ward going on all around us. I feel somewhat encapsulated within a bubble. I can hear it in a muffled sort of way, but none of it seems quite real. The operation went well, apparently. Now we wait to see if a miracle really has happened. Has the dreadful shaking stopped? Will he be better? Patience and time will tell.

1916

"It's a battle shock", the doctor said as he stood at the window of his office looking across the hospital compound. He had called me in to discuss young George a few days later. No one really knew what to do with him. He wasn't physically injured, but his mental frailty was all too clear to see. After the tea trolley incident, he had slowly allowed me the liberty of persuading him out of his filthy clothes and helping with the washing. His young body was lean and fit and, for all intents and purposes, undamaged. Initially, he shied away from physical contact. But I would hand him the warm washcloth, and slowly and gently, we removed the grime of the battlefield. He still looked haunted, and he still shook. But as I handed him a clean set of hospital clothing, I commented that they were "not exactly Saville Row", and a shy smile lit up his face.

Slowly over the next few days, he started to eat. In every spare minute I found during the day, I would seek him out and take a cup of tea for each of us. We would sit on the bench outside the ward in companionable silence. I knew it would be folly to push him before he was ready. On one such occasion, my hand brushed his as I stood up to resume my work, and he grasped it, causing me to look down at him. His eyes swam with tears.

"I can't go back, Tilly," he said, and my heart lurched in my chest. "I want to go home."

The men in the ward were a hard lot, many of them recovering from dreadful injuries and waiting for their "ticket to Blighty". The banter and the camaraderie had seen many of them through tough times. They didn't understand George at all. He shied away from their briskness and declined every attempt at inclusion. He could have been a son to many of them, but his self-imposed distancing began to wear thin with the men. Patience and understanding were not qualities the British Army held in abundance.

"What's wrong with him, Nurse?" they would ask.

"You know I can't discuss that with you any more than I can discuss with him what's wrong with you!" I would reply. George began to have nightmares. He began to scream, shout, panic, and cry during the night. This endeared him to the men even less and necessitated a move to a more isolated area. I volunteered to stay with him during those times and to provide what comfort I could. Occasionally he would allow me to hold his hand. One particularly dark night, when even I seemed unable to reach him in any way, I instinctively began to sing softly, as my mother had done to me when I had occasionally suffered nightmares in childhood. I sang of home and love and family. Familiar, safe tunes are known to children everywhere. Slowly the dawn began to break, and the murmurings of life about the field hospital stirred. I began to realise that George was quiet, still, and sleeping. I touched his head and stroked his hair as a mother would have done, and he didn't shy away. Tears began to cascade down his cheeks onto the pillows, and he looked so young. So very like our Richard – my own brother at home – just turning 16 and forbidden by our father to join the Army despite every argument and protestation presented to the contrary.

I must find time to write home to Rich, to tell him about George. Our mother lived in fear that he would lie about his age and join up anyway. The recruiting sergeants were not too particular about the legalities at his time. My three older brothers were all in France with The West Yorkshire Regiment. When, with some trepidation, I announced my own intention to join the British Expeditionary Force as a Red Cross Nurse, I expected the worst. My mother, I found, should never be underestimated and, contrary to all expectations, applauded my decision to put my Nurse training to good use.

Sister Poulter arrived to relieve me for breakfast, and I wearily made my way to the mess hall. The smell of sizzling bacon and a hot mug of tea did much to lift my spirits. I smiled as one of the ward orderlies commented that the lads on the ward had slept soundly, knowing that George was elsewhere and as quiet as he had been for some time. I fell into my stretcher cot, exhausted, knowing that it would only be for a few hours until the next intake of wounded would arrive.

By mid-afternoon, we were full at it, triaging the wounded, stripping them of filthy clothing, washing and dressing wounds, helping in the operating theatre, dispensing medication, and whatever comfort we could. The ward orderlies provided the strength to lift and turn the injured and to attend to their bodily functions. Food and drink arrived for the men, and still, we worked on helping to give them sustenance and as much relief from pain as was possible, mostly painfully inadequate. Darkness had fallen again before I even had time to think about George. Sister Poulter was still triaging and organising extra beds and linen. I caught up with her to ask about George.

"He's gone," she said, barely giving me a glance and gesticulating to an orderly to feed a man at her feet. I caught her arm, capturing her attention for an instant.

"Gone where?" I asked

"Home," she said, pulling her arm away impatiently, "to England".

Days became months, and the work in the hospital was relentless. Winter was approaching, and the chill in the early mornings turned the landscape around us into a white, misty, and rather surreal vista. We began to wear socks and vests and thicker stockings. The little pot-bellied stoves in the wards and huts were lit and tended around the clock. Thank the Lord we were not short of fuel to burn. Extra blankets were added to the beds, but we were never really warm. I have never liked the cold, and the thought of breaking ice on the water in the washbowl filled me with horror. It's amazing how resilient we are when we have to be, for within months, it was just part of the daily ablution regime. My Mum was sending knitted hats, scarves, gloves – even some fingerless ones – all adding to my impressive selection of knitwear. I shared my gifts with my fellow nurses, and we were glad of them during the few times we were able to curl up on our cots during off-duty time. We would catch up on sleep or read when the light was good enough, reply to letters, or just chat with our fingerless gloved hands wrapped around a mug of tea as the snow fell outside. A covering of snow made everything seem new, and it was with renewed vigour that we braved the cold, donned our uniforms and ventured forth once more to attend to our duties.

I often wondered what had happened to George. I liked to think he was safe back in the bosom of a loving family. His age alone should preclude his further participation in the war, so I hung onto that as hope for his future. Sister was vague and elusive, so I was determined to ask Colonel Forbes, the doctor who had been looking after him, at the earliest opportunity. By the time that came around, the Colonel had been posted, and I began to despair of ever getting any answers. Sometimes as a nurse, a special bond can develop with a patient. More than just care and compassion, when caring for their physical needs and dealing with the banter. I liked all my patients (well, maybe not Corporal Bunsen – he of the disgusting spitting habit and trying to get the nurses to wash his groin) but most of them.

Mostly they were so grateful to be out of the front line and, however badly injured, it was preferable to that. George had been special. Maybe because he could have been my brother but also because he was so young, so little understood, and vulnerable as a result. I had never heard of "Battle Shock", and I was determined to find out what I could about it and what had become of George.

TILLY

I had wanted to be a nurse for as long as I could remember. My brothers dreaded being ill and having to submit to my enthusiastic attention. They were washed, swabbed, bandaged, and fed – whether they wanted it or not – to within an inch of their lives! Mum said it was a sure way of combatting any shirking. Unlike any of their classmates, they were only too ready to return to school and away from the ministrations of "Nurse Tilly"! The family dog, Fluker, was often sporting a bandaged head or leg, but he didn't mind as passers-by would frequently stop to give him a kind word or, even better, a treat! The cat wasn't so compliant and beat a hasty retreat at the first inkling I was on my rounds.

By the age of ten, I could do a spiker bandage, administer a poultice and tie up a sling. Our local doctor was a kind man and encouraged my childish attempts. As I grew older, he asked Mum if I would like to help out at his clinic. I leapt at the chance, as by then, I was sixteen and had started to think about becoming a Nurse. I hadn't said anything to my parents. I knew they couldn't afford it, but nevertheless, I had been down to the library to investigate the options for training and what was required if ever a miracle was to occur. I knew Leeds had a large Infirmary, and being the nearest big city to us, that seemed like the solution. The librarian was the older sister of my school mistress and happily chatted away with me about the big city and her own adventures of visits in her youth. One of the books had a photograph of a Nurse Probationer at The General Infirmary at Leeds, and I made up my mind then and there that one day I would wear that uniform. I had no idea how I would manage it, but with all the confidence of youth, nothing was insurmountable!

I lived for the days when I would skip down to Dr Swanson's practice and help out at his clinic. Mrs Swanson was a nurse and had had to give up her profession when she married. She recognised in me a kindred spirit. On the day I had arrived, she kitted me out in one of her own voluminous, white, crisp aprons. Even though it wrapped around me twice, I felt wonderful and just like a real Nurse. Over the next few months, I spent as much time as I could be spared from home at the surgery. Mrs Swanson was a large motherly woman of the "no nonsense" type who ruled her home and surgery (and Dr Swanson) in an organised and efficient manner. She showed me how to take temperatures and pulses, clean and dress wounds after first properly washing my hands! I became efficient at making up dressings and using the sterilising equipment. I cleared up vomit and blood and worse! I washed floors, sorted and sterilised instruments, and acted as an assistant when Dr Swanson was stitching up wounds. I loved it and willingly did all that was asked of me, soaking up knowledge like a sponge.

Mum could see how much it meant to me, and she would take on some of my chores at home so I could spend more time at the surgery. How much my father knew of my activities at his time is difficult to say, he simply couldn't understand why a girl would aspire to any other existence than being a wife and mother. I didn't argue with him as I realised it was pointless. Besides, my dream was just that, a dream. We couldn't afford the fees for me to train as a nurse, and that was the reality.

I hadn't banked on my mother, though!

ALICE

My mother, Alice, came from a well-to-do family who had disowned her when she married Dad. Her father was a builder who owned his own business. They lived in a large detached house on its own grounds in a very middle-class area of Malton, a moderately small town in the county of Yorkshire. She had been educated at home, by a Governess, together with her younger sister, Nancy. My Grandmother was a formidable Lady, by all accounts, though I never knew her. Tall and elegant and rather cold. She sat on a number of Committees, mostly of a charitable nature, though she showed very little charity to her own two daughters at home. Grandfather was rather in awe of her, according to my mother, who had no doubt it was her mother's decision to "cut her off without a penny" rather than her father's when she had fallen in love with someone outside of her own social class and, therefore, considered "quite unsuitable" by her parents.

My father, William, is a lovely man, despite his old-fashioned ideas about women! He is kind, caring, and full of fun. He was a cleaner of steam engines on the Railways when he first encountered Mum. He used to watch her and her sister, from a distance, when they were escorted by their Governess, sometimes by their parents, as they boarded the train to Scarborough or York or Leeds. Mum was oblivious to him at this point until one day, she accidentally dropped her reticule, and he was the one to retrieve it.

“I fell in love with her there, and then” he would tell us, and she would blush and say “, what nonsense!” wafting a tea towel at him and bustling about to cover her discomfort. Dad would often grab her around the waist and dance her around the kitchen, causing us all to giggle. We often joined in by linking arms around them both in a big family hug.

As they grew to adulthood, they continued to occasionally encounter each other at the Railway Station, exchanging shy smiles. One Day dad slipped her a note, asking her to meet him after church the following Sunday. Mum had no idea how she would be able to engineer such a meeting. But she was attracted to the tall, good-looking young man with laughter in his eyes, and she was surprised to discover how much she wanted to find a way. Her sister, Nancy, didn’t miss much, and when Mum asked for her help, she was only too willing to devise a scheme to separate the parents from Mum to allow a clandestine meeting. On the pretence of an urgent meeting with the Vicar to discuss her Confirmation. This came as a pleasant surprise to her parents, even if they were somewhat baffled by her sudden change of heart. Mum was dispatched home with the carriage driver who would return for them in due course. Once they were safely gathered in the vestry, Mum dismissed the driver on the pretence of enjoying a walk home instead. William was waiting for her at the Lynch Gate, nervous but exhilarated. Mum said she had felt ten feet tall. The relationship grew slowly over the next year, always having to meet in secret and through writing letters to each other. Once Mum was sure of her feelings for William, she decided to be honest and open with her parents. It did not go down well.

William had presented himself at the house dressed in a borrowed suit, clean but a little threadbare in the rear of the trousers! His boots were polished. He asked to see Grandfather and was admitted to the drawing room to await his fate! As he waited for Grandfather to appear, he remembered a loud, ticking clock. The room was richly furnished in the Victorian fashion, a large aspidistra on a stand in the corner. The fire was welcoming and warmed the bottom of his borrowed trousers as he stood nervously waiting. Mum remembers hovering about the kitchen, unable to concentrate on any one thing, getting in the way under cooks' feet. She remembers feeling physically sick.

Grandfather Wharton entered the drawing room. William had never met him before but had often seen him in the company of other rich and influential gentlemen, most often at the railway station.

"How can I help you, young man?" asked the imposing-looking gentleman.

"Good afternoon, Sir. My name is William Dobson. Your daughter Alice and I have become friends, and I have come to ask your permission to walk out with her."

He held his hand out, and to his relief, it was taken and firmly shaken. Grandfather seemed puzzled as he scrutinised the young man closely, raising Williams' levels of apprehension even further.

"I recognise you, Dobson. You work at the railway station, if I am not mistaken?"

"Yes, Sir, that is correct. I clean the engines, but I intend to be a driver one day."

"How do you come to be acquainted with my daughter?" asked Mr Wharton conversationally.

William relaxed a little and explained how they had met and formed a liking for each other.

"She is a very fine girl, Sir, and we would like your blessing to begin courting."

Grandfather Wharton was a man of few words who thought deeply and with careful consideration, but he knew, however honest and honourable William Dobson was, his wife would never accept a union between him and their carefully educated and socially prepared eldest daughter. He was not an unkind man and thought it best to nip in the bud any expectation of such a union.

"I'm sorry you have had a wasted journey, Dobson", he began, "but I'm afraid it is quite out of the question. I would ask that you cease all contact with my daughter, and we will say no more on the subject."

Father said he felt as if all the breath had been sucked out of him as he automatically shook the hand offered before him.

"I wish you a good day, Mr Roper will see you out" with this, he turned briskly and strode decisively out of the room. The clock continued to tick loudly, and the quiet claustrophobic room began to close in on William. Roper, the Butler, was standing with his back to the open door, silently indicating that William should leave. The feeling of breathlessness as though he had been punched in the chest was acute, and now, he felt as though he was walking through treacle.

The front door of the house was closed behind him. He stood facing the gravel drive and garden beyond, bereft and unsure of what he should do next. A movement in his peripheral vision reconnected him with the present as Nancy flitted onto the gravel, keeping close to the house and gesturing to him to come towards her. Once in reach, she grabbed his arm and pulled him back the way she had come and round the side of the house close to the wall.

"I'm guessing that didn't go well?" she said as they stood with their backs to the brickwork. William was stunned and quite unable to speak.

"Alice has been called to the study to meet the parents, and you are going to the greenhouse to wait for her. It's the gardeners' afternoon off, so you shouldn't be disturbed. I'll get her there so you can say your goodbyes. I'm really sorry, William. I wish it could have been otherwise. You'd have been a rare addition to this dour family!" she smiled at him, gave him a little push and headed back inside via the side door into the kitchen.

The greenhouse was hot and humid. The tomato plants looked healthy and fruitful, he thought. He could hear a bee as he sat down on the bench and put his head in his hands. A hand placed softly on his shoulder caused him to look up, and he rose quickly to his feet, enveloping Alice in his arms. She sobbed into his shoulder as they held each other tightly. Time seemed to stand still, and he wondered how he could ever be happy again.

"What will we do?" she whispered eventually, her face still buried in this shoulder. He gently took her face in his hands and searched her eyes, for he felt her pain as much as he felt his own.

"I love you, Alice Wharton", he said, "I can't imagine life without you, and if you feel the same, I will find a way". At this point, he lowered his handsome face towards her tear-stained lips and kissed her. The passion between them was tangible, and the kiss became ever more urgent. William pulled away suddenly, holding her at arms-length, but his eyes were sparkling and full of love.

"My goodness Alice Wharton but you'll have me forgetting myself if you kiss me like that!" and he began to laugh, easing the tension. She responded in kind and moved back into the protection of his arms, holding him tightly around the waist. Slowly he drew her down onto the bench seat, and they sat side by side, closely holding hands, totally wrapped up in each other, the disappointment of the day fading with the hope of better things for the future.

WILLIAM

William let himself into the cottage feeling battered but determined. His mother was sitting at the side of the fire, sewing a patch repair into a pair of his brothers' trousers.

"Hello, Love," she said as she looked up. His face told her all she needed to know. She rose, putting down the stitching and opened her arms to him. Like a child, he fled into the safety and comfort of them, and she stroked his hair and patted his back softly, murmuring.

"There, there", just as she had done on numerous occasions throughout his life. She eased him slowly into his fathers' chair opposite her own, stoked up the fire and filled the kettle. Whatever the upset or trauma occurring, celebration, companionship, or counselling, none of it occurs in any household in the British Isles without the sustenance of a hot cup of tea. She handed him a mug, took her own and sat back down. Nothing more was said, but she knew he would speak in his own good time.

William was her eldest, and her pride in him had not diminished over the years. He was handsome, yes, but more importantly, he was bright, smart and kind. He had a wicked sense of humour and had always been a great help to her. His brothers and sisters adored him. They came from a mining family, but after an accident had ended his fathers' mining career, they had moved lock stock and barrel to a farm in the country where an uncle was the farm manager. Apart from the health benefits, William Senior had adapted readily to the outside work, and his love for and ability with the horses had developed into his being asked to manage the stables. The thought of her children not having to go down the mines had felt to Fanny like a message from heaven. William had a passion for the Railways and, on leaving school, had found himself a job as a cleaner. He had quickly become indispensable to the Station Master. His bright, sunny outlook and hardworking, flexible attitude ensured he was soon promoted from sweeping the platform and generalising repairs of the station to cleaning the engines. His ambition was to drive the Steam Engines, but first, he needed to serve time as a Fireman on the footplate.

"I can't live without her, Mam," he said as he finished his tea and put the mug down on the hearth. "I need to become a Fireman, so I can earn more and have more to offer her."

"Are you sure, love?" said Fanny "she's from a quite different world, and if her parents forbid it, you'll have a very hard road to follow."

"I know, Mam, but I love her, and she loves me, and we will be together. There won't ever be anyone else for me. You do like her, don't you?"

Alice had been to the cottage on a few occasions and had tea with his family. She was a looker all right, tall and slim with long auburn hair tied loosely in a ribbon in a plait which reached down her back almost to her bottom. Her face was beautiful, and she had charming manners, always bringing Fanny a little something to say “Thank you” for having her. A little posy of garden flowers, a few sweetmeats beautifully wrapped in a neat little tin, or a delicate linen handkerchief embroidered by Alice herself. Not of much use in a working household but pretty and thoughtful, nevertheless. Her eyes sparkled when they fell on William, and despite her reservations, it warmed Fanny’s heart to see him so happy. Her reservations she kept to herself, other than voicing them to her husband.

William Senior was a brusque direct Yorkshireman with a kind heart and enough sense to let his clever wife organise his life and that of their children. He listened quietly but intently to her concerns in the companionable warmth of the kitchen as he puffed on his pipe, nodded and supped his tea.

“Happen, he’s bitten off more than he can chew this time”, was pretty much his only comment.

“Yes, love, I like her” Fanny smiled as she picked up the mugs and headed for the sink.

“Get some potatoes from the pantry for me, Will?” she asked, and preparations for the evening meal were underway.

The family meal was as usual noisy with each of the children trying to outdo the others, news of their day, school, friends, and the disliked Sunday School teacher….

“Right, mardy cow”, ventured Arthur, the youngest.

"Excuse me, young man!" chipped in Fanny, "You mind your manners! She may be mardy, but she is most definitely not a cow!" and they all laughed.

"What's up with our Will?" Mildred asked her mother quietly; she was next to him in age and his favourite sister

"Leave him be, love", replied her mother. "He's got things on his mind." Will excused himself and left the table.

"Is it Alice?" Mildred persisted as Will lifted the heavy latch and closed the door behind him.

"Will you leave it be, Mildred! He'll tell us when he's good and ready!"

Once the meal had been cleared away and the kitchen set to rights, Mildred found William cleaning his boots whilst sitting on the backdoor steps.

"Mam says to leave it, Will, but you know how nosey I am..........what's up?" she sat down next to him on the step and put her hand on his arm.

"Alice's Dad has forbidden us to see each other anymore," he said without looking up and continuing to brush his boots. Milly had never seen him so dejected. Will was the strong one, always cheerful, game for a laugh, ever ready with a helpful suggestion, and always available with a hug. She felt strangely at odds to witness his misery and his own vulnerability.

"What will you do?" she asked as she rested her head gently on his upper arm. They sat quietly for a while, then he put down his boots and the brush, straightened up, and put his arm around her shoulder, causing her to lean in against him.

"I don't know, Milly. I have nothing to offer her. How can I ask her to leave all that she has and all that her family can give her to throw in her lot with me? For this?"

Suddenly Mildred's head snapped up. "Now, just a minute, Will Dobson! There is an awful lot worse than "this", and she cast off his arm and stood up, hands on hips.

"We have a cramped (I'll give you that!) but comfortable home, and more love in our family than she has ever experienced for all her lahdy dah upbringing!" warming to her subject, she made him smile by listing all the good in their lives he'd lost sight of over the course of the day.

"There are only three in a bed… and no bedbugs! We have our own "Po" under each bed, and we get to have a bath once a week, one after the other, whether we need it or not! What's not to love?" By now, they were both laughing, and his spirits had started to lift.

She was right. For all her joking, they really did have a lot to thank God for. Parents who loved and supported them, employment, food on the table, a roof over their heads, each other, and good health. He started to feel ashamed he'd been feeling sorry for himself, and as he began to feel increasingly positive, he made up his mind to speak to Mr Briggs, the Station

Master, tomorrow and get himself a job as a Fireman with every intention of being a Driver within the year.

Alice read his short, secretly smuggled note with joy and hope. He loved her, it said, and although he had told her this, it was still thrilling to see it written down. She was not to despair; he had a plan. She hugged the note to her and tucked it safely inside the bodice of her dress. For the first time in days, she smiled and looked in the mirror at the reflection of a pale, tear-stained face, blotchy dark eyes from lack of sleep and hair which resembled a bird's nest. She set immediately to rectify the situation, and when Nancy knocked on her door to accompany her downstairs for tea, she was tidy, calm, and composed. Nan had been so supportive, she hated to see her elder sister so unhappy, and she liked William. He made her laugh, and he was good company.

"Come in. Nan," Alice said as she opened the door to her bedroom. "I've had a note", shutting the door behind her.

"I know," said Nan. "I brought it! What does he say?"

They talked for a short while, and Alice hugged Nan and danced her about the room in her excitement. "You'd better not appear so happy at tea", counselled her sister smiling

"Even Mother might suspect a change in the air!" as if to emphasise the point, she lifted her pert nose up into the air sniffing haughtily in gentle mockery of their mother, Adelaide. Laughingly they linked arms and descended the staircase to take tea with their parents. Alice felt confident things were about to change now that William had a plan. She would wait and trust and pray.

THE PLAN

The early days of spring had heralded a change in the weather. Gone were the bitter winds from the north and ice on the pond in the mornings. Warmth had arrived, and once the morning had taken hold and the sun had developed in brightness and strength, Alice felt a warmth on her back as she entered the kitchen garden with her trowel and gardening gloves. Mother did not approve of her gardening; it would ruin your hands! But that in itself was an added attraction. Alice found it relaxing and balm to the soul as she knelt down at the edge of the herb garden and began to weed and prepare the beds for this year's crop. Pulling up weeds gave her great satisfaction. She felt she was rooting out the old and preparing for the new in more ways than one. The sun on her back was soothing, and the quiet stillness of the garden provided her with time to reflect on the events of the past few days.

She hadn't realised the depth of her feelings for William until presented with the possibility of losing him. Her heart had felt broken, and to be honest, it had come as a bit of a surprise. The time she had spent since in self-imposed isolation had clarified her feelings and resolved not merely to accept her fate but to fight for what she wanted, what she needed.

Alice realised she had always felt at odds with her parent's plans for her future. All young women of a certain age and class were expected to marry well, be mistresses of their own households and provide their Lords and Masters with offspring. The candidates paraded so far for her inspection were all well connected and from good families but uninspiring, dull, and she rather suspected were victims of a certain amount of inbreeding. Having a good seat on a horse was not at the top of her list of necessities for a life-long companion. Qualities of strength, inside and out, kindness and a good sense of humour were part of what she admired about William. The fact that he was also tall and good-looking was an added bonus. She was not naïve enough to think the difference in class was of no consequence, but she worried more about whether his family would accept her than whether hers would ever accept him. That door, she knew, was well and truly closed. Adelaide Wharton had made her position crystal clear, and that was an end to it. The Dobsons, Adelaide had pontificated, were a perfectly respectable family, as far as she knew, but working class and therefore quite unsuitable for a union with her own family.

"Well, mother, you are going to be challenged about that," thought Alice as she straightened up, sat back on her knees and inspected her handiwork. The beds were cleared and dug over, ready for planting. New beginnings. She collected her tools together and made her way towards the shed at the end of the greenhouse. Bert Hardy, the Wharton's gardener, was potting seedlings and looked up as she placed her bucket on the worktop.

"Mornin' Miss Alice looks like the start of spring."

“Yes indeed, Mr Hardy!” she replied with a smile. “I’ve put the weeds on the compost heap”, and she set about cleaning her tools.

“Very kind of you, Miss”, replied the old gardener. “Will you be planting the herbs, as usual, this year?” Alice looked at him and smiled again, a more distant look in her eyes.

“I don’t know yet,” she said, “we’ll have to wait and see.” Hardy raised an eyebrow at her.

“Right, oh Miss Alice, I’m sure you’ll do what’s best.”

Mr Briggs held up his hand, “Now, Will, before you say another word, you know I hold you in high esteem – just let me speak, will you? I’ve been meaning to have a word about your future.”

That stopped William in his tracks. He was standing in the Station Master’s Office wearing his dark blue overalls and holding his cap in his hand. He had asked to speak to Mr Briggs the day before and had his speech all prepared. How he needed to better himself, he was a hard worker. He loved the Railways and how one day he wanted to become an engine driver. His agitation was apparent. Alf Briggs was nervous. Will had worked at the station for eight years. He grafted hard, did whatever was asked of him and never complained. In all honesty, Alf Briggs took him for granted, and he knew it. The lad was now twenty-two, he would want to move on, and Alf wasn’t too sure how he would manage without him. When Will had asked to see him the previous day, it had provided Alf with just enough time to work out a plan.

"It's about time you were a Fireman, young Will", said Alf, and Will was stunned.

"And in good time, I'm sure you'll make a fine driver. Now, what do you think about that?"

Will sat down heavily in the chair indicated and looked up at Mr Briggs.

"But that's exactly what I wanted to talk to you about. How did you know?"

Alf had no idea but wasn't about to admit that to the lad. He had taken the wind right out of that pair of sails, and he was feeling rather smug.

"So, you agree with me, do you? You want to progress in the Rail Industry?"

"Yes, Mr Briggs, I certainly do", smiled Will, and he held out his hand to be shaken. Alf Briggs took it as Will stood up, relieved not to be losing his best worker. Over the next few days, they worked out the logistics, timescale, and a slightly increased pay packet. William Dobson felt like the luckiest man on earth. He had taken the first step, and it had been easier than he could ever have imagined. He couldn't believe his luck.

"Cook tells me you've been helping in the kitchen", ventured Adelaide as she passed Alice her plate at dinner.

"Yes, Mother, I find I like cooking."

Her mother looked astounded.

"Really?" she commented in a most dismissive tone. Alice was determined not to rise to the bait as she applied herself to the meal. She really did like cooking and not only thought it would be helpful in her future life, if not essential, but surprisingly Alice was finding it creative, enjoyable and immensely satisfying. Cook had recognised her talent and enthusiasm and was nurturing it. Already Alice had mastered bread making, soups, and simple baking. She found kneading bread released a lot of tension, and the realisation made her smile! She grew to love the warmth and bustle of the kitchen, the good-natured banter and teasing and finally, the satisfaction of the finished dish. The staff had been wary of her at first, but she had mucked in, kept her head down, and suffered scolding for her mistakes along with the rest of them, and once they realised she genuinely wanted to learn and work hard alongside them, respect began to grow.

"I made the soup tonight," she said, and Adelaide looked up in surprise. It had been a rather delicious leek and potato soup. Adelaide was impressed, but she hid it.

"Just don't get in the way of the staff, dear. You would do better learning more about the household accounts," she sniffed. Her father caught her in the doorway as she was retiring for the night. "Excellent soup, my dear!" He said with a wink and a smile.

Contact between the two people was minimal. Alice was closely watched over and escorted by her mother, and Adelaide scrutinised the post. They saw each other at Church on Sundays but were not permitted to speak. Nancy couldn't bear it. She was the only glimmer of hope in those first few months. What few notes had survived had been down to her ferrying them discreetly between the two.

"Oh, come on, Mum, she needs some form of exercise" Nancy faced her mother in the parlour,

"I'll be with her, and we can take the horses over the moor. She hasn't been out for weeks!"

Alice had never been as keen a horsewoman as her sister, but the possibility of a degree of freedom was rapidly changing her mind.

"Don't be vulgar, Nancy, and please don't call me "Mum". It is so common. I am your mother!"

"It's such a lovely day, Mother. I'm sure I would enjoy a brisk ride out", chipped in Alice.

"Oh, very well, but you are to avoid the Railway Station or any contact with that boy!"

The two girls turned and moved in a dignified manner out of their mothers' hearing. Once the door was firmly closed, they could barely contain their excitement, racing each other up the staircase giggling and hushing each other as they headed with all speed to Alice's bedroom in order that she might change quickly into her riding habit. As Nan was already attired in hers, she took the opportunity to race back down the staircase to organise another horse to be saddled for her sister. Alice was a competent horsewoman, but Nan was a natural. They both rode astride, except when in their Mothers' company, and now the opportunity of laughter and freedom had them spurring their horses into a gallop once out of the impressive gates. They arrived at the glade ruffled, panting, and flushed. Alice took off her hat and shook her hair free. It was taken up by the wind and blew wildly around her face. The freedom was intoxicating. She had an overwhelming need to see William. "All right!" laughed Nan "We'll wheel around the town from the far side. We might make it in time for his morning break! I'll keep Alf Briggs talking. He has an eye for a bit of horse flesh. You know ……." She teased in a knowing way.

"He has the occasional flutter on the gee-gees I hear! Not that Mrs Briggs would know anything about that!"

Alice felt the excitement mount in her chest, and she had squadrons of butterflies in her stomach as they approached the railway station. Nan directed her to a small enclosed field to the side of the tracks protected by a drystone wall. Alice dismounted and led her horse through the five-bar gate. The field was empty except for grass, and the sunlight was dappling through the trees. Alice found a secluded spot, sat down and waited.

Miss Nancy Wharton breezed up to the Railway Station on the back of her beautiful Hunter and scanned the yard for Will. The sun was almost at its zenith, and there was barely a cloud in the sky, the warmth of spring fresh in the air. Snowdrops were being engulfed by crocuses, and daffodils were tight in bud in their earthenware pots on the station platform. She tied Thunder to a post in the yard, making as much noise as she could in an attempt to flush out her sister's intended.

"Halloo, Halloo!" she called out, and sure enough, Mr Briggs appeared, donning his jacket and setting his cap, advancing towards her.

"Miss Nancy, good morning. How can I be of assistance?"

"Hello, Mr Briggs", smiled Nancy, exuding charm.

"My horse is in need of a drink, and I think he may have picked up a stone in his shoe. You wouldn't be so kind as to have a look for me, would you? I believe you know a fair bit about horses yourself, Mr Briggs?" Alf Briggs beamed with importance, delighted to have had his opinion sought by an admired horsewoman. The lads in the yard couldn't help but notice the kerfuffle and welcomed a break from their usually mundane chores. Nan was trying to catch Will's eye whilst guiding the Station Master in the opposite direction. She indicated that Will should come closer.

"Now, where's this fine horse, Miss Nancy?" Briggs was keen to impart his expertise. Nan gestured in the direction of Thunder and made as if to follow but held back suddenly, checking her boot heel as she paused to allow Will to approach.

"You go on, Mr Briggs, I'll be right with you", she shouted as she gave Briggs a gentle push, reaching for Will's arm as she, to all intents and purposes, used him for support as she inspected her boot. Without looking up, she whispered to him intently.

"If you hurry up, you'll find Alice on the other side of that wall", indicating with her head the general direction of the field.

"Don't be long", she warned. "I can only keep Briggs busy for a few minutes", and she hastened off to discuss serious horse matters with the Station Master.

Will was instantly flooded with emotions, nervousness, excitement, fear, and apprehension as he glanced over at the drystone wall. His feet were taking him across before he even realised he was moving, and within seconds he had vaulted over it and almost landed on top of Alice. She squealed in surprise and delight. She looked ravishing. Her eyes shone, her skin was clear, and softly blushed pink. Her thick auburn hair was loose and wild about her shoulders. His breath caught in his throat, and he found himself speechless. As she sat back upright from being so close to being landed upon, she smiled at him and said:

"Hello Will", he thought then that he would die if he couldn't have her and they fell into each other's arms.

He couldn't kiss her enough. The feel of her and the smell of her was intoxicating. She returned his kisses and embraced him with equal passion and thought she would never want to be anywhere else. He realised he was covering her face in soot and engine grease, and his attempts to wipe it clean with his large, red spotted handkerchief started them both off laughing. Telling each other of the love they both felt suddenly made the realisation of their situation only too obvious and the time spent together so fleeting.

"I have to get back, but I have so much to tell you," said Will. "How can we meet? We need to make plans."

Alice straightened her hair and clothing, but she couldn't stop smiling.

"I love you, Will Dobson", she said, and she touched his face. He held her hand to his lips,

"Nan will help us," she said "get a letter to her. She'll ride by the station about this time tomorrow". He helped her up and embraced her to him, kissing her hair.

"You are my life now, and I won't let you down" with that, he kissed her again hard on the lips and vaulted back over the wall, leaving her both happy and sad at the same time. The ride home gave her much to think about, least of all how she would explain the sooty marks on her clothing if she should encounter her mother! Nan readily agreed to collect the letter. She had more freedom than her elder sister, and her prowess as a horsewoman meant she rode out most days without a comment.

William began working as a Fireman on the footplate of the steam engines, which took him further away from the town than previously. However tired he was at the end of the day, he usually managed to add at least a few lines to his next letter to Alice. He kept it in his pocket in case he should come across Nancy, so it was often unsigned when Alice received it. She didn't mind that, and she treasured every word. Will stood on the footplate of the engine, thundering down the tracks with the wind and steam blowing through his hair. The driver sat perched to his side, leaning his arm on the sill at his side, hand on the whistle as Will loaded another shovel of coal for the furnace. He found himself laughing at the joy of it all, the work was hard and dirty, but he felt alive as he shovelled coal into the boiler. The fire burned brightly, powering the engine, and two blasts on the whistle caused him to look up – the driver was pointing out of the cab, signalling Will to do the same, the noise preventing any form of conversation. Will's eyes followed the driver's finger, and to his astonishment, he caught sight of Nancy thundering alongside at full gallop on Thunder, laughing with joy and gesticulating to them. He joined the driver at the gap and waved back vigorously. On the spur of the moment, he had an idea. He picked up a lump of coal, wrapped it up in an oily rag, took the paper wrapping off his sandwich and used it to envelop the letter he had in his pocket, tied both together with a piece of string and hurled them out of the cab towards the girl on the galloping horse. She quickly realised what he had done and acknowledged it with a thumbs up and a wave. He saw her slow down to dismount and retrieve the letter as the train continued on its unrelenting way. He returned to his duty and continued to shovel another load of coal into the fire. He felt a warm glow inside, knowing that Alice would be reading his letter tonight.

Walter Wharton stood with his back to the fire, hands deep in his pockets. The room was warm but oppressive, the curtains were drawn even on the light spring evening, and he sensed there was an atmosphere building which was not to his liking and likely to cause disagreement and upset. Walter was no lover of upset. He valued order and respectability, even if it was predictable and safe. He would rather have been anywhere else at that moment, but his wife had prevented it. Adelaide sat ramrod straight at the table, her face a hostile mask, hard, determined and unforgiving. Her Victorian attitude to dissent would override her very real, if deep-seated, love for her two beautiful, if wilful daughters. Only a few hours earlier, Adelaide had truly believed the worst had passed, and the sordid encounter between Alice and the Dobson boy was at an end. Now, this.

Walter had been a passenger on the train that afternoon. He had witnessed their youngest daughter galloping and laughing alongside the speeding locomotive. Her obvious exhilaration in the activity, riding astride, and then slowing in order to retrieve an object thrown at her, had caused him considerable discomfort and embarrassment in the company of his business partners.

His admiration for her riding skills had swiftly been buried. The other Gentlemen had been discreet enough not to comment if they had witnessed the encounter, but Walter wasn't risking it. He shook hands rapidly with his companions and hastily exited the station without a comment being made. He had regaled the whole sordid episode to his wife on his return home over a cup of tea and now wished he hadn't. Adelaide was incensed. She caught Nancy as she was tripping lightly down the staircase, having delivered the letter to Alice.

"Get out of that riding habit, young lady, and present yourself with your sister and whatever it was you retrieved from the field this afternoon. Your father will see you in the drawing room." She turned swiftly and swept away down the hallway like a ship in full sail.

Nan's stomach turned over. She fled back up the stairs into Alice's room, not even bothering to knock. The look on her face spoke volumes. But she recounted what had just happened, and they hugged each other for comfort.

"It's alright, Nan, go and change. I'll think of something, and don't worry. It's not your fault. I'm the one who is really in trouble." She tried to smile as she guided Nan towards the door.

"Oh, my great goodness!" she thought as she slumped heavily down in the chair. The letter had been of a chatty nature, updating her on his new job, his family, his love for her, and that the dog had recently had a litter of puppies. Hardly revolutionary. It was also smeared with oil and coal dust which gave her much satisfaction as she handed it to her mother in the drawing room.

"I apologise for defying you both", she began before either parent had the chance to say a word.

"I love William Dobson, and I intend to marry him as soon as he asks me", she spoke calmly and with determination standing bravely before her parents. Adelaide looked as though she was about to explode, having dropped the oily letter onto the table as though it was contaminated. Walter held up his hand to forestall her immediate diatribe. He was a reasonable man with a measure of sympathy for his eldest daughter. He had allowed his wife a free hand in the bringing up of his girls. Perhaps he should have been stronger and had more say. He realised his daughters were both feisty, strong-minded women –after all, they took after his wife! He didn't doubt Alice's feelings, but this was a mismatch. His wife said so. Alice simply couldn't be a working-class housewife, she hadn't been brought up to it, and Adelaide would never accept it, which would make his life a misery.

"It's disappointing that you have persisted with this relationship, my dear", he began ", when your Mother and I are so opposed. You have betrayed our trust, and now you have involved your sister in your complicity."

"Oh no, Father", interrupted Nancy ", I offered, I like William, and they love each other."

"Be quiet, Nancy!" spat Adelaide "what do you, or they, know about love? There is more to marriage than love. There is the ability to provide for a family, respect, mutual interests, and social standing in the community."

"I don't care for social standing, Mother. I agree with you that marriage is more than just love but love is the beginning. Building a life together and facing life's challenges together is also what marriage is about. I don't want to defy you in this. I truly believe that William and I have a future together, and we would like your blessing. But if that is not possible, I am of age, and I will leave this house to be with the man I love."

"Bravo, Alice," said Nan as she hugged her around the waist in support.

"Nancy, go to your room. I will deal with you later," said Walter. He looked immensely sad, his shoulders slumped, and he appeared to have aged ten years. Adelaide rose and joined her husband beside the fireplace. Nancy left the room.

"This relationship cannot work, Alice," she said "you have never done a day's work in your life, you have no household skills, he has no home to offer you, and how will he support you on what he earns? I don't dislike the boy but be practical. Your upbringing has not equipped you for the life he has to offer. What use will you be to his family?"

"I do have skills, Mother. I can cook, I can garden, and I can manage household accounts. I'm healthy and strong, and I can learn. What's more, I want to learn. I want to feel useful – something I don't feel in this house." with this, she swept out of the room, pausing briefly in the hall to take a deep breath. She caught sight of herself in the mirror over the dresser. Mother was right. What use could she be to a working-class family? She would be more of a hindrance at first, but she was determined to learn. She would make a good wife and, God willing, in time, a good Mother. She would prove to them both that they had misjudged Miss Alice Wharton.

THE NURSE

Dr Swanson relied more and more on Tilly's help. His wife had begun her instruction well. She was bright, interested, and quick to learn. It was rare to have to show her twice. She also had a lot of common sense. With four brothers at home, he supposed that was something she had had from an early age. Tilly's willingness to be of assistance and her warm and cheerful disposition would make her a fine nurse one day. She was also performing tasks under his instruction well in advance of her tender years. He had no doubt about her ability or dedication. He had known her and her family all her life. In fact, he had delivered her when the Midwife had already been out on another call. He would be sorry to lose her, of that there was no doubt. Mrs Swanson had taken him aside only last week and spoken to him, at some length, about Tilly's future. He had to admit he'd been avoiding the subject, but now he'd had time to reflect and seriously think it through. He knew she was right. Tilly would be eighteen in July. She wanted to train to be a nurse, he knew it, and he had the ability, the means, and the moral obligation to help her. He would speak to her parents.

Tilly took off her apron, washed her hands, tidied her hair, and put on her coat.

"I'm off now, Mrs Swanson unless there's anything else you'd like me to do?"

"No love, you get home now. I'll empty the autoclave, and thank you again. Those bandages have never been so well-rolled!"

Tilly smiled as she clicked the surgery door closed behind her. The sun was still warm in the late afternoon, and she could smell the daffodils in the front garden as she made her way down the path and through the gate onto the lane. It was only a short walk home, and it was only a small town, but she waved at, and greeted several people along the way. People she had known all her life. What would it be like in a big city where she wouldn't know anyone? Her mind drifted to Leeds; she had rarely been to Leeds or any big city. But she knew that's where her future lay and the hospital which could fulfil all her dreams of training to be a nurse. She shook her head as if to clear it of all such nonsense, and as she came into view of the cottage, she saw Dr Swanson's horse and buggy outside.

The horse taking advantage of the lush grass on the bank. Her heart skipped a beat, and she began to run, fearing someone in the household had taken ill. She entered the front door all of a fluster.

"Mam, I saw Dr Swanson's….." she began as she came to an abrupt halt. Dr Swanson was sitting at the kitchen table, taking tea with her parents. "I", she started again. "I don't understand. Is someone poorly?"

"No love, come on in and sit down," said Alice pouring another cup of tea from the old brown pot for Tilly.

"What's going on?" she asked hesitantly, looking from one to the other.

"Dr Swanson thinks you have the makings of a fine nurse," said her father and Tilly found that she could barely breathe.

"Is that what you want? To be a nurse?" he asked.

She could hear her brothers larking about outside and the crackling of the fire in the grate, yet Tilly felt as though she were somehow detached from reality. Was she dreaming? She began to worry that she would wake up at any moment and none of this would be real.

"Not like you to be at a loss for words, lass," said William as her mother put a hand on her arm

"Did you hear what Dad said, Tilly?" enquired Mum, and Tilly turned to face her tears welling up in her large blue eyes.

"Oh, Mum, Dad, more than anything else in the world!" she said as she looked for one to the other. Alice patted her arm and handed her a soft white handkerchief. Dr Swanson stood up,

"Well then…" he began, but Tilly butted in.

"But how? how can I?" her face was a picture of worry as she wiped her eyes and blew her nose, pushing her chair back from the table to stand before the doctor. He was smiling and shaking hands with her father and then Mam too.

"I'll be in touch, William," he said, and he looked over to Tilly and winked. She accompanied him to the door and outside to the buggy.

"I'm a fool to myself and, no mistake, doing myself out of the best nurses I've ever had - excluding Mrs Swanson, of course! I'll make some enquiries. I have a colleague who works at the Leeds General Infirmary. I'm assuming that is where you would wish to go, Matilda?" Tilly felt she was on cloud nine!

"Yes, please, doctor that is exactly where I would like to go" he nodded and replaced his hat.

"Not to worry now, Tilly," he said as he took his leave "there's more than one way to skin a cat!" and he heaved himself up into the buggy and took the reins, much to the consternation of the horse who had just settled in nicely to his task of rest and nutrition. They trundled off down the road leaving Tilly more than a little mystified by his enigmatic comment.

"Bloody Hell!" said Philip, her eldest brother, laughing and dodging her mock punches.

"Poor patients! But then it does get us off the hook when we're ill! It wasn't so much the forced feeding, but I'm sure the bandage was meant to go round the head and not over the mouth," he teased.

"Language please, Philip!" and though she sounded stern, Phil could hear the underlying amusement in his mother's voice. Tilly had just been offered a place to begin her nurse training at Leeds General Infirmary starting in September. She had questioned her parents repeatedly about the cost of it all, but it seemed Mam had a small nest egg from her family, and this was how they chose to spend it. Tilly felt guilt even through the elation, it seemed she was benefitting over the boys, but her parents had reassured her that was not the case, and though they had chosen not to enlighten her further, she had accepted their generosity with gratitude. Besides, she told herself she would be earning money and, therefore, able to contribute more so they could all benefit from her good fortune.

Her eighteenth birthday had come and gone. Dr and Mrs Swanson had given her a beautiful little fob watch and a fine pair of scissors engraved with her name. The boys had clubbed together to buy her a pair of strong brown sensible ward shoes, and her parents had provided her with a new leather suitcase. Tilly felt enormously blessed and excited at the thought of her new life.

A NEW BEGINNING

It grieved Alice enormously that neither her parents nor her sister would be at her wedding. They had chosen to holiday in Scotland instead and the note declining the invitation had arrived only yesterday. Formal and brief, as impersonal a note as Alice had ever received in her life. Alice looked up into the mirror above the dresser in the bedroom she had shared with Milly and Gladys, Williams' sisters since she had fled to the cottage only a month ago. She wore a fashionable hat courtesy of her own sister, and despite everything, she caught herself smiling. It was her wedding day, and she was determined not to be sad but to enjoy every minute of it. She had no doubt she was marrying the right man. His family had been so welcoming and kind when she had arrived on their doorstep, suitcase in hand, wet from the rain, cold, unhappy, and distressed. Fanny had opened her arms to the young woman, had instantly taken stock of her situation and invited her in.

"Oh, my dear girl, come in, come in", and she had guided Alice by the arm gently towards the warmth of the fire, shooing her interested brood out of the room "off you go and give Miss Wharton some privacy if you please," said Fanny Dobson closing the door behind them. She then had a second thought and re-opened the door.

"Arthur?" she called "Go and find our William. He's down at the allotment with Dad."

The door closed for a second time, and she turned back into the room.

"Give me that wet coat Miss Alice," she said kindly "you'll catch your death!" and she helped Alice out of the soaked coat and eased her wet shoes off frozen feet. She sat her in the chair closest to the fire and swept her own shawl from around her shoulders to place over Alice's'. Alice did as she was told almost automatically. Not a word had been spoken though tears ran silently down her cheeks, mingling with the raindrops dripping from her hat. Fanny rapidly removed the hat, pushing the hat pins, beautiful mother-of-pearl hat pins, she noted, securely through the fabric of the crown, placing it carefully on the table.

"Now then, lass, a nice cup of tea, I think", and she busied herself filling the kettle at the old sink. She then hung it on a hook at the side of the fire. She swung the mechanism over the heat, and very soon, whistling could be heard. She handed Alice a steaming hot cup of sweet tea. She had no idea if Alice took sugar, but that was what was needed at times like these. Alice sat quietly with her head bowed in a hunched up position, arms across her chest, hugging the shawl to her. She accepted the tea and placed both hands around the mug for warmth. She looked up briefly at Fanny,

"Thank you", she whispered, and the tears continued to flow down her usually pretty face. She resumed the position, but her shivering was not so violent, and

Fanny wrapped a blanket over her lap and around her legs. She then sat down in the chair opposite to wait. It wasn't difficult to figure out, and Fanny's mind was working overtime trying to organise the sleeping arrangements in the household to incorporate one more.

The fire crackled, and the mantle clock ticked softly as Alice and Fanny drank their tea in companionable silence. Gradually the shivering ceased together, and Alice laid her head against the back of the wing-backed chair and closed her eyes. Sniffing and an occasional sob broke through, but slowly Alice began to settle. Fanny placed a pocket handkerchief in her lap, patted her on the shoulder and gently told her to take her time. There was no rush, stay there, keep warm, and she would be back instantly.

Mildred and Gladys were beside themselves with excitement as Fanny gave instructions to set up the pull-out bed in their room for Miss Wharton. She handed them clean linen, blankets and a pillow re-directed from Gladys's bed. From the bedroom window, Fanny caught sight of her eldest son heading rapidly home with young Arthur in hot pursuit. Instructing the girls to get on with their task and to stay upstairs, she closed the bedroom door behind her and made her way downstairs, arriving in the small hallway as William bowled through the door.

"Calm down, Will. She's alright" her tone was soothing and gentle. She helped him out of his jacket and closed the door behind him as he entered the kitchen barring Arthurs' path.

"I don't think so, me lad", she said, turning him full circle and back out of the front door.

"Away with you. Go and see if Dad needs any help at the allotment."

"Aw, Mam! I've just been to the allotment. Can't I stay? Will might need my help" peering round the door, hoping for a glimpse, he ventured more in hope than certainty as his unusually exciting day had come rather abruptly to a halt.

"No, you can't, get yourself back down there and give your father a hand", came his mother's rather predictable response. A dejected Arthur then set off hunched over, hands deep in pockets, back towards the allotment where he just knew Dad would have him turning over the soil in place of his older brother. Will Dobson owed him big time, and that was a fact!

William thought his heart might leap right out of his chest, so he took a slow, deep breath as the kitchen door closed softly behind him. All of a sudden, he felt large, awkward and nervous as he twisted his cap in his hands. Alice glanced around the side of the wing-backed chair and smiled hesitantly at him. Within seconds he had enveloped her within his arms as he knelt before her kissing her hair and holding her close. Time seemed to stand still, and slowly he felt her tension relax, and she sank into him. He never wanted to let her go. The feelings of love were overpowering.

His mind was racing. What had happened? Was she here to stay? He hardly dared hope… yet how would he support her should he ask her to marry him this minute? Somehow that didn't seem wholly appropriate or the right time right now. As all these thoughts jumbled in his head, suddenly, all thoughts deserted him as Alice cupped his face gently in both her hands and kissed him softly on the lips. His senses reeled as the depth of the kiss turned suddenly to raw passion. She edged forward in the chair towards him, and his embrace tightened. She was showering his face with kisses, and they both began to laugh, delighted in each other. Happiness and relief. He pulled her onto the floor at the side of him, sitting with their backs against the solid chair facing the fire. He eased his arm around her shoulders, and she snuggled again into his embrace as close as she could get. For the first time in days, she felt loved, safe, and at home. She loved that Will hadn't asked anything of her, just accepting her need for him. He knew she would tell him what had happened to bring her to this when she was good and ready.

2016

I sit beside his bedside as he sleeps. The shaking has stopped completely. The dreadful shaking that has blighted his life for eight years has stopped. And he sleeps following surgery. Around us, people talk, and the nurses go about their business. The ward is at the top of the hospital, with panoramic views over the city and beyond how medicine has advanced in the last century. Procedures are now possible that would have been undreamed of a hundred years ago. Understanding psychological needs as well as physical and medical, the recognition and treatment of Post-Traumatic stress disorder may have saved hundreds of lives after the war had it been acknowledged. The thought of those poor men suffering, sometimes for the rest of their lives, affects me profoundly. Some of them were shot as deserters and only relatively recently pardoned by a different generation. There would always have been compassion and kindness from the majority of doctors and nurses, but that hasn't changed. Involving the patient in their own care and decision-making has changed for the better. Medical conditions are better understood now and so complex that the approach has to be multidisciplinary and comprehensive.

Yet we don't have to deal with the sheer volumes of badly injured men on the same scale, with no recourse to proper anaesthesia, asepsis, disinfectant or antibiotics. What the medical services achieved on the Western Front and elsewhere during the Great War was remarkable. Staff shortages, lack of sleep, dealing with their own grief at times and constant bombardment in the forward advanced clearing stations. We cannot comprehend now how they coped with the influx of hundreds of casualties and how they managed to save so many. Nursing has changed too. No longer handmaidens to the doctors, their own profession where independence is encouraged and nurse practitioners are becoming accepted and promoted. Injuries and illnesses are different, and God forbid modern nurses won't have to cope with the carnage their sisters had to face. The horror and wastefulness of another time, a lost generation stranded in a foreign country without the comfort of their loved ones, equates at least in part to the modern-day phenomenon of the elderly often dying lonely and alone, uncomforted by their families who often live great distances away insular and expecting the State to step in. My mind wanders as I sit patiently, waiting for him to wake up. I wonder how I know this. Have I read it or experienced it? How could I possibly have experienced it? These things happened a hundred years ago. Yet I can still feel the apron and smell the cleanliness. It must be my imagination, an echo perhaps? I decide to go in search of a cup of tea and maybe something to eat.

THE WARDS

Matilda Dobson had settled comfortably in the nurses' home. She had her own room with its own washbasin. The bathroom was down the hallway and shared with the seven other nurse probationers in her corridor. The baths were deep, and she felt totally indulgent as she soaked in hot water easing the aches in her muscles after a long shift on the wards. How she loved it, and she thanked her lucky stars on a daily basis that her dream had come true. The work was physically demanding but interesting. She loved caring for the patients, and she revelled in being kept busy.

After her initial twelve weeks of probationer training, the staff on the ward had been kind and welcoming, even Sister Fairbairn! They recognised Tilly as a hard worker, interested and curious and consequently took her under the collective wing involving her in small but interesting tasks, which interrupted the monotony of her daily tasks. Tilly didn't mind the mundane. She knew it was a means to an end. She was in awe of her senior colleagues, and her interest and enthusiasm endeared her to them. Her first two weeks of being stuck in the sluice cleaning out bedpans and other such unsavoury tasks were intermingled with taking temperatures, making beds and witnessing enemas, catheterisations, and wound dressings. She loved the banter between the patients and the staff. It reminded her of home. The men on the ward were a rare lot, working class, no-nonsense Yorkshiremen on the whole. When they were ill, they were ill and needed and wanted all the care the nurses could give. But once they were on the mend, they simply didn't want to be fussed over and would be up and about the ward helping each other and the nurses, sometimes to the distraction of the ward Sister.

"Joseph Wainwright, get back to bed! You'll burst those stitches, and then where will you be? Dr Thornton will not have it, and neither will I!" she would remonstrate.

"Oh, come on, love, I'm just not used to lying in bed like, I might burst me stitches, but at least I won't die of boredom!"

The men on the ward laughed, and the banter went on. Many of them had daughters and sisters, and they could see just how hard the nurses worked. It simply went against the grain not to give a hand as soon as they could. The hospital had been built in the 1840s funded by public donations. It was acknowledged as forward-thinking and attracted the best medical men and nursing staff from Yorkshire and beyond. The design was in keeping with hospitals of the era, large and cavernous with long "Nightingale" wards, named after the inspirational Florence. Beds ranged down both sides, thirty-two in all, with a nurses station in the middle and Sisters desk in full view of all and missing nothing. The bathrooms and sluice were at the bottom end of the ward, with the kitchen, linen room, and stores at the top end next to Sisters' office. The windows were long and positioned high above the beds. Light flooded in, but it was impossible to see outside. This mattered little to Tilly, who found her days were eaten up far too quickly.

Patients had to be washed and turned, beds changed, bottles and bedpans emptied, dressings completed (sometimes twice a day), meals served, patients were helped to eat and drink, and then it started all over again. Visitors were allowed in for limited periods of time, and then the nurses would be occupied by other tasks such as bandage rolling or sorting out the linen and cleaning the trolleys. Woe betides the unlucky visitor who dared to sit on a bed! The whole ward was cleaned and tidied to the very exacting preferences of each individual ward Sister. Cleanliness being next to Godliness in everyone's book.

The ward hierarchy was clearly defined. Sister at the top, then the trained "Staff" nurses, their years of experience counting towards their seniority, and then the Student nurses whose seniority was defined by their length of training thus far. First-year students like Tilly were at the very bottom of the Nursing pecking order. There were some male orderlies on the male wards and occasionally ward maids whose primary task was to clean, sweep, and polish.

Sister dispensed meals from the trolley, which was brought up from the hospital kitchens at each meal time by the porters. The warmth of the meals depended on how long they had been waiting to be collected and delivered to the wards. Meals were simple, nutritious fare, and considered to be part of the recovery process.

Good nutrition could be the difference between a good or poor recovery. Medication was in its infancy, and antibiotics had yet to be discovered. Infection was treated very seriously, and hand washing and wound cleanliness depended on the cleanliness of the ward and the vigilance of the sister and nurses. Ward Sisters prided themselves on low infection rates, cleanliness, sterile dressings, and good nutritional intake were foremost in the war against infection.

Above the level of Ward Sister was the all-important Matron. She had responsibility for all of the nurses and the care given in all the wards. She would report to the Medical Director and the Hospital Board. All of the ward Sisters and the Night Sisters, as well as the Matron herself, were unmarried. It simply was inconceivable that a woman could have a career once she married.

Her responsibilities would then be to her husband and children. Tilly found she would occasionally have cause to reflect on this subject, it seemed unfair that a man could have a career and family but a woman could not. She never dwelt long on it as her days were so full and interesting. If ever the situation arose, she would deal with it then. Ward work was interspersed with time in the classroom. Practical sessions from the Sister tutors and occasionally from the doctors. Tilly soaked it all up like a sponge. She was eager to learn and to share what she was learning.

Very soon after her arrival at the hospital and during the settling-in period, Tilly met the girl in the next room to her. They found they had an affinity and enjoyed each other's company. She liked Jane immediately, and they gravitated towards each other during their time off duty. The conversation was easy, laughter came readily, and they found despite the surface having little in common, they shared a sense of humour. Difficult shifts could be debriefed and scenarios shared, and Tilly found she liked her new friend more and more. They began to arrange to spend almost all of their off-duty time together, sometimes studying over the textbooks, sometimes taking a walk into town away from the hospital, visits to the theatre or cinema, or just going to a local café for afternoon tea and a chat. Tilly had only really known the company of her brothers, so Janes' gentle, feminine companionship was a delight. Jane's parents lived in the city, so occasionally, Tilly was invited home for tea or Sunday Lunch. Jane's sister Deborah was older and engaged to be married, but they all made Tilly very welcome, and she enjoyed her newfound friendships. Even the family dog, Magnus, a gorgeous little West Highland Terrier, made her welcome. Jane's Mum would always see them off on the bus, well-supplied with sandwiches and cake. These they would eat later, sitting in one of their rooms snuggled up in their dressing gowns, putting the world to rights. One day soon, she would reciprocate and take Jane home to meet her family.

MARRIAGE

William and Alice Dobson walked hand in hand along the Front in Scarborough. Neither could believe they could possibly be so happy. The wedding had been all they could have dreamed of despite the disappointment of Alice's family's absence. Alice thought her heart would burst with happiness. She had an affinity with the sea from being a little girl. The sound of the waves and the noise of seagulls made her feel safe, comforted, and at home. She knew her way around the seaside town as if she had lived there all her life.

She and Nan had looked forward to the family's summer holiday every year, and despite Adelaide's preference for Harrogate, they had usually managed to persuade their father to return to Scarborough. Nan's gift of a three-day honeymoon at The Grand Hotel had not only been unexpected but thoughtful, knowing her sister as she did. They had been overwhelmed, and the time had passed only too quickly. William was so proud of his beautiful wife; he tucked her arm through his as they strode along the promenade, each contemplating a return to reality the following day.

Will had now been a fireman on the engines for the past six months, and he was regarded as a grafter. The drivers liked working with him since he was reliable, and he knew what he was about. He caused them no anguish in the completion of his job. They all knew of his ambition to drive and supported him in his quest.

They would keep an eye out for him. In fact, it had been one of the drivers he worked with regularly who knew he was to be married who had suggested he speak to "the gaffer" about a little cottage in a row of railwaymen's houses which had recently become vacant. Will had been excited beyond belief when he had been offered tenancy. He and his parents had worked out that he could just afford it if he and Alice were careful over the next few years until he got his promotion to engine driver. Once the honeymoon was over, they headed back home to make preparations to move into their new cottage.

NEW BEGINNINGS

After three years of studying and hard physical work, all that stood between Tilly and the rest of her life was the result that today would bring. She woke early feeling nauseous and apprehensive and also excited. She pulled the covers up to her chin, relishing the warmth and comfort of the single rackety bed, enjoying the few moments before she would rise and meet the day.

Now she and Jane and the rest of their class stood outside the Sister Tutors' office in the school of nursing to await their fate. Apprehension was building, and the chatter had stopped. She clutched Jane's hand briefly as they looked at each other with wide, fearful eyes as they awaited their turn. "Nurse Dobson" came to the call, and Tilly looked pleadingly at Jane as she made her way forward.

The relief was intoxicating! She had passed. She felt euphoric, and her joy was also enhanced by Janes' success. They laughed as they linked arms and made their way down to the sewing room, clutching their authorisation slips for a Staff Nurse's belt and cap. They would be allocated wards tomorrow morning, but for now, the rest of the day was theirs to enjoy. Tilly raced down to the Post Office to send a telegram to her parents.

"I passed" was all it said. Each word had to be paid for, and Tilly was careful with money. She had saved a small amount for a celebration tea at home with her family and Jane on their next day off together. Today they had plans to celebrate with Janes' family, who had arranged a luncheon at a hotel in town. Tilly just couldn't stop smiling. Although she felt like the luckiest girl in the world, she knew she had worked hard and felt an enormous sense of achievement. Now she had her fingers crossed that she would be allocated Ward 4, Sister Riley's domain, male surgical.

Joy Riley was old school. Petite of build but large in personality. She ran a tight ship, didn't suffer fools gladly, and called a spade a spade. Small though she was, she thought nothing of putting recalcitrant doctors in their place. Her nurses loved her. She could be brusque, but she was never unfair. At times it seemed she had eyes in the back of her head. The patients were paramount. Tilly had felt the heat of her questioning only once during her placement, but it had made an impression on her.

"Nurse Dobson!" Sister Riley had called loudly, "Why did you only use two towels when you bathed Mr Friske? On what did you sit him whilst exiting the bath?"

Tilly had no idea how she knew this as the bathroom was at the far end of the ward, and Sister had not left her desk.

"I sat him on his used pyjamas, Sister, as we are short of towels", replied Tilly, somewhat flustered. "Humph, using your initiative, I suppose!" replied the Sister. "Carry on, Nurse. I will speak to the laundry."

The Ward day always began with prayers. Before the handover, the night shift and the day shift knelt down together at the table in the middle of the ward. It only took a couple of minutes, and the patients waited in respectful silence while Sister Riley thanked God for his blessings upon us, His help for the day ahead, and entreaties for whichever patient or nurse would benefit most from His particular attention to whichever misdemeanour was most in her thoughts at that time.

She was often quite unintentionally funny.

"We thank you, Lord, for your attention to Mr Boyce's flatulence and pray that prunes be withheld from the menu for the rest of the week. Amen"

Once prayers were over, there was often a rush to the sluice amidst much straining not to giggle or look at each other until they were out of earshot to be rid of their mirth in peace. It was a happy ward. Tilly's delight when her allocation was posted on the noticeboard was tangible.

So, life settled down to a pattern of work. Tilly continued to learn on the job and was keen to enhance her learning by reading about the subject. To this end, she was a frequent attendee at the hospital library on her days off when she wasn't able to go home. Jane's shifts sometimes clashed with hers, but they would meet up whenever they could, and Tilly found her days busy and interesting. Other than trips home or days out with Jane occasionally, Tilly really didn't have a social life. She hadn't noticed and didn't miss it, so it came as a bit of a shock to suddenly be asked out by a very good-looking Police Surgeon who had followed a patient up to the ward when he had been admitted following a riding accident.

To be honest, she had been so occupied obtaining all that he would need for splintering a fractured shaft of the femur. She hadn't even noticed him. The boy was blind drunk and had mercifully not even noticed his leg being manipulated into the splint, so it was sometime after he had been made comfortable that she became aware of being observed.

"Is there something I can do for you, doctor?" she asked as he leaned casually against the wall smiling at her. The surgeon who had fixed the leg had already left to complete his notes. And the student nurse Tilly had been mentoring was on her way down the ward with a pile of dirty linen to dispose of.

"Come out to tea with me?" he asked.

"I don't even know you!" Tilly replied, shocked at his familiarity

"Good opportunity to change that", he continued, "My name is Henry Lascelles. I have a day off tomorrow. I'm a jolly nice bloke, and I would like to take you out for tea…… please", and he half-bowed

"I can't, I'm sorry. My name is Matilda Dobson, I don't have a day off tomorrow, and I don't go out with men I don't know!...... Thank you"

She gathered the remnants of the dressing feeling flustered and uncertain, and started to make her way to the door. Henry Lascelles scooted to land in front of her.

"Well, Matilda Dobson, not only am I a very nice bloke, but I'm also a resourceful one, so I will find out when your next day off is, and I will ask you again. Until then, look after my patient, please, he is the cause of a fracas and witness to an assault, and once he's sober, I will be back to see you both!"

With this, he took her hand, kissed it lightly, bowed to her and left the ward.

Much to her surprise, Tilly found she was looking forward to the return of Henry Lascelles and arrived for work with a spring in her step. The boy with the fractured femur had sobered up and was not only in a great deal of pain but suffering from a stonking hangover. His mood was foul.

Consequently, the nurses were trying to avoid him, and he was making a nuisance of himself, throwing his breakfast tray onto the floor, and shouting obscenities. Sister Riley was not on duty.

"Right," thought Tilly, "first big test. I am not having this!" The boy's name was Sidney Brown.

Staff Nurse Dobson steadied her nerves, drew herself up to her full height and approached his bed.

"Good Morning Mr Brown. What seems to be the problem?"

"The PROBLEM, Nurse Fancy Pants, is I need looking after, and none of these fecking nurses is doing her job right. I need a piss and something for pain, and then I'm going home."

By now, the whole ward was alerted and listening intently. Tilly moved closer to the bed, leaned on the traction slightly, enough to make him wince and quietly said into his very close face.

"I will find you a bottle in which to piss, Sidney, and I will obtain enough pain relief to keep you comfortable. I will feed you, wash you, and do everything I can to aid your recovery. You will be with us for a minimum of six weeks, and if you want to be looked after properly then I suggest you show some respect. These "fecking nurses" are your salvation and the difference between a pleasant experience and a hellish one. Now, if you will excuse me, I have patients to look after."

With that, she let go of the traction, causing a fresh modicum of discomfort to Mr Brown and walked briskly away. You could have heard a pin drop. No one other than Sidney was ever sure of what had been said. But Mr Sidney Brown certainly heard, and his stay on Ward 4, along with his attitude, took a turn for the better.

The rest of the men on the ward developed a soft spot for "Nurse FP", a nickname never explained but used with respect and fondness.

The Courtship

Henry Lascells was right, he did turn out to be a very nice bloke. Once his involvement with Sidney Brown came to an end, he continued to appear at the ward doors at the end of the shift, and his persistence paid off. His masterstroke was to recruit Sister Riley to his cause. He was charming and, as it turned out, funny too. He told hair-raising stories and, other than his initial boast he was actually self-deprecating.

Tilly found that she enjoyed his company. He took her to places she had never dreamed of. They punted on the river, played tennis, and ate at fine restaurants, and visited the theatre and music halls. She introduced him to her family, and he even managed to impress them. The only concern she had was not having met any of his family. He played it down, told her very little about them, and never offered to take her to his home. At first, it seemed unimportant, but once she knew she was starting to fall for him, she began to worry that it was because they wouldn't consider her good enough for him. They socialised together with her friends, never his, and he evaded questions about his family.

She didn't insist at first, as he was just a friend, but then it started to hurt. No one seemed to know anything about him. He worked for the Police, had trained at a hospital in Sheffield, and said his family lived in York. That was all she knew. He was charming and enormously good fun, and before Tilly realised how deeply she was in love with him, it was too late. "Oh, glory be, that wasn't meant to happen," she thought as she sat up in her bed with her arms around her knees and her head full of the Civic Ball the night before when she had partnered Henry and had the best night of her life.

He looked so very handsome in his white tie and tails, and she had felt like a Princess. Mum had adapted an old gown of hers made from the most exquisite mauve organza, nipped in at the waist, and beaded over the bodice with little seed pearls which sparkled in the candlelight as Henry held her in his arms and danced her around the floor. She had felt as though she was floating on air. They were engulfed in a sort of isolation even in the midst of hundreds of other people, aware of the presence of others but apart from them.

Henry had led her out onto the balcony for some fresh air, and he stood behind her, holding her close. His head alongside hers, whispering into her ear, and making her laugh at his impressions of some of the more pompous guests.

"Do you actually know anyone here?" she asked, turning to face him with her back now to the balcony rail,

"I don't believe I do," he replied jokingly, "Apart from the Police Commissioner, of course, and I'm trying my best to avoid him for fear of his lady wife has me in her sights for one of her lumpy daughters!" they laughed easily together even with Tilly protesting.

"Oh, don't be unkind!" Momentarily Henry became serious and gathered Tilly into his arms, burying his face in her hair.

"I do love you, Tilly," he said, "Whatever happens," and Tilly's heart soared.

THE CHILDREN

The Dobson household was a happy one. The children started to arrive, and William and Alice felt blessed. Their home became a focal point for the whole Dobson family. It was full of love and humour, and whatever little they had, they shared it. Alice's little vegetable garden provided them with fresh produce, and she included the children who tended it as soon as they could walk. They could handle a trowel, use the watering can, pull weeds, and dig up potatoes. She never minded how dirty they became as long as they were learning and having fun in the meantime.

Alice's own skills developed over time, and she found great satisfaction in cooking, cleaning, growing, sewing, knitting, and bringing up her steadily growing family. Will adored her. He was definitely the man of the house and the breadwinner, but he deferred to Alice on all domestic matters.

Alice's only regret was her separation from her own family. Her parents had never reconciled to her marriage and continued to ignore invitations sent out with love and hope each time a baby was born and baptised. Her parents had stopped attending the local church, where Alice and Will were married and still attended regularly. Through Nan, they knew her parents travelled the extra mile to the next town. That hurt, but at least they still had Nan. She had made a break for freedom shortly after Alice's marriage.

Her mother's shock at Nan's acceptance at Cambridge was somewhat tempered by her pride in her social circle that a daughter of hers would be attending such a prestigious University.

Of course, it was frivolous, and what good could come of it? But Adelaide harboured hopes that Nancy would meet a suitable and clever husband as a result.

Alice, on the other hand, was proud and delighted for her sister, and during Nan's time away, they kept up a regular and lively correspondence. Nan unfailingly sent the children cards and gifts as their birthdays came around, and she became a great favourite.

Nancy would arrive on the doorstep unexpectedly laden with gifts and treats. She was an unusual Aunt, very "hands-on" with Alice's lively brood, and would often, absentmindedly, pick at leftover food on the children's plates whilst chattering constantly. She told wonderful stories, and she would grab them and tickle them until they had to beg her to stop.

Aunt Nan would readily play hide and seek, and often when they were little, she would hang them upside down by their ankles when she caught them. They loved it, and they loved her, vying with each other to sit on her lap or ride on her back, using her as a pony.

When Matilda was born, Nancy was touched and delighted when Alice and Will asked her to be the child's Godmother. Both Alice and Nan were profoundly moved during the Baptism as Nan held her niece and God-daughter in her arms, only surrendering her briefly to the Vicar over the font. Alice asked Nan, over the Christening tea, if she wouldn't like children herself. She was rather nervous about broaching such a personal subject with her sister,

"Lord, No!" laughed Nan, "the responsibility is too great! The delight of being an Aunt is that you can give them back when you've had enough!"

She slid her arm around Alice's waist, and they made their way out into the garden. Not for the first time, Alice wished her parents could be there. They were missing out on not knowing their grandchildren. She sighed and shook herself. Well, it was their loss. No point crying over spilled milk. She was very blessed. Alice would continue making an effort, and if nothing came of it, at least she had tried. Nan moved off to speak to Will, and Alice glanced across the garden to his parents, William Senior, and Fanny. Comfortably seated in the two old garden chairs fending off three small boys whilst Fanny had the baby on her lap, rocking her gently as she slept.

It was a beautiful and warm summer's day. Will was proudly chatting with his brothers as they shared a glass of ale. Fanny's fruit cake was the centerpiece of the feast, and the small children were itching to start on the tempting food. Nan indicated this to Alice and laughed as she made her way across to Fanny.

"Right, Mrs D, I do believe it's my turn," and she stooped down to take hold of the baby.

"Careful now, Miss Nancy, you sit yourself down here," said Fanny as she rose to put the kettle on. Many a time, Nan had asked Wills' parents to drop the "Miss," but they just didn't seem able to do so.

"Get Will to pass me a glass of small ale, would you, Mrs D? To be honest, it's a bit warm for tea."

NANCY

If Fanny was surprised, she didn't show it. Miss Nancy was a rare one, and if a glass of ale was what she wanted, then that is what she would get. Fanny admired Nancy greatly. She didn't know of anyone who went to a University, let alone Cambridge, and she instinctively felt it was wrong that she couldn't be awarded a degree simply because she was a woman.

Nancy had never mentioned it, but Fanny had heard Will and Alice discussing it, and she felt the injustice. Miss Nancy Wharton had gone on to find herself a job as an academic researcher at the Fitzwilliam Museum in Cambridge. She rented a small house nearby with a fellow lady academic and had started to make a life for herself independent of her parents. Adelaide had realised she had no option but to accept the situation, or she would lose both of her daughters. Walter was very proud of Nancy's achievements and insisted on a small allowance despite Nan's protestations that her salary would suffice. Adelaide insisted on her accepting the allowance. No salary would keep her daughter in the manner to which she was accustomed. Consequently, Nan put the allowance aside to provide lovely gifts, including clothing, for her sister and her family. Alice and Will would never have accepted offers of financial help, but gifts could not be so easily refused, and Nan wanted them to have nice things too.

Nan resided with her parents when in Yorkshire, the primary reason for which were her horses rather than their company. Walter had agreed to stable and upkeep two of Nan's horses, and she made the most of the exercise and company of her horses during her visits home.

The subject of Alice was forbidden after a particularly blistering exchange of words one evening following the announcement of Alice's first pregnancy.

Adelaide had retired to bed for three days. Walter had been forced to intervene, and the subject of Alice was banned. Nan had tried to appeal to her father's better nature, but she realised that however much he may wish to make amends, he would never oppose his wife.

Over the years since the estrangement, she respected his wishes, especially since he quietly condoned her contact with her sister. Visits home were never easy, but she continued with them out of a sense of filial duty. Adelaide persisted in her matchmaking activities, which Nan found both humiliating and irritating. Adelaide was equally embarrassed and irritated by Nancy's employment.

Riding out on her beautiful Hunter continued to delight Nan, and she never tired of the scenery around her.

"Yorkshire really is God's own County," she thought as she sat admiring the rolling hills and pretty wolds. The greenery around her was astounding. This was no doubt due to the amount of rainfall, but even on drizzly days, the mists and low clouds had a mystical quality she found captivating. Cambridge had its own beauty in the flatness of the fenland and big skies, but her Yorkshire homeland was something else.

Nan loved her life in Cambridge. She found her work at the museum both fascinating and fulfilling. The independence it gave her was thrilling. Meeting Meryl was a bonus. Their shared interests brought them together both intellectually and personally. Nan felt her life had never been better. The Whartons accepted Meryl as Nancy's friend and "roommate."

Meryl was a free spirit. She was unconventional, funny, and irreverent! She was a raconteur, and though Adelaide intrinsically disapproved, she couldn't help but like her and, fortunately, would never make the deeper connection. Meryl was continuously amused by the family dynamics and especially Adelaide's matrimonial aspirations for Nancy! Her mothers' persistence in the face of blatant refusal became a source of constant amusement between them.

Meryl was liked and accepted equally by the Dobsons. Alice suspected a deeper relationship but would never be as intrusive or impolite as to verbalise it. Ever the peacemaker and respectful of her sister's right to privacy, Alice kept her council. She knew Will would never even suspect such a relationship, but she often wondered how he would react and how accepting he would be if ever confronted with the truth. Live and let live, thought Alice. It may be illegal, but how on earth could it ever be proved?

The children accepted Meryl as an honorary "Aunt." She had a natural gift for teaching and would often suggest outings during their visits to the Dobsons' home. They might visit York Minster, a shopping trip to Leeds or visit any of the numerous country houses in the area. Or just simply have a nature ramble around the town and its environs. Aunt Meryl knew a lot about bugs and insects. She could name every plant and flower and was knowledgeable about all sorts of different subjects. The children absorbed her teaching like little sponges without even realising they were being taught.

Presents from Aunt Meryl were inevitably books, and they devoured them all; novels, story books, factual books, picture books, poetry, and even Shakespeare. Letters were written and encouraged, handwriting practiced, and grammar, punctuation, sentences, and paragraphing came naturally – or so it seemed to the children.

Aunt Meryl used interesting words they had to look up and tell her the meaning of, and the competition was then on to find and use the most interesting words in response. The child who had used the most interesting words since the last visit was suitably rewarded. This usually resulted in afternoon tea at a place of the winning child's choice.

History was Aunt Nans' domain, and this often took the form of learning through the plays of William Shakespeare. Nan also had an infectious talent for teaching through storytelling, and she instilled in them a love of the iambic pentameter through her abridged versions of The Bard's plays which they would perform for their parents and grandparents.

All of the Dobson children were bright and inquisitive, and their Aunts' gift for naturalistic teaching had installed in them a love of learning. Enquiring minds like theirs put their local teachers under some pressure as they were well ahead of their peers. This didn't always endear them to less gifted children, and more than once, the older boys came home with injuries and black eyes. They generally shrugged it off, as their opponents usually came off worse! Philip was the oldest, tall like his father, and rarely taken on by the school thugs. He kept an eye out for Arthur and Jack, but they could hold their own, thanks to Dad. Whilst fighting was not condoned, and the boys were warned never to throw the first punch, self-defence was accepted, and Dad made sure they had the skills. The town was not large, and everyone knew everyone else. Fights were rarely serious, and parents were generally sensible enough to bang heads together when necessary.

Alice made sure they remained grounded. She knew the value of a good education but realistically realised that her boys would need jobs. Their "class" prohibited them from further education even if they had been able to afford it. Their boys would not be accepted amongst the sons of the middle and upper classes. It wasn't fair, but that was the way of it. Plenty of working-class men had the intelligence but not the means to pursue such an unobtainable dream. She had heard Will, with his father and brothers, debating the issues of the day and knew for a fact that he devoured all reading matter, including the children's books, after they had gone to bed. Like many men of his generation, he was a frequent attendee at the library, expanding his knowledge in the little spare time he had. Nevertheless, the children continued to do their chores, run errands, clean boots, help about the house, wash up the dishes, make their own beds, and even help with the cooking. Unusually for the day, Alice wanted to make sure all of her children had the ability to feed themselves and not rely on a future partner. If nothing else, she would ensure they could all put a Sunday roast on the table: Yorkshire puddings and all.

THE RAILWAY

Will's promotion to engine driver eased their financial state considerably. Mostly he worked on the local line, but occasionally he would be drafted onto the main line – York to London or North to Edinburgh. Although those were very long days, sometimes involving a night away from home, the trains were generally larger and more powerful. Will found it exhilarating!

Driving a steam train was noisy and dirty work, but standing on the footplate in control of the powerful engine, with his cap on tight to his head, was thrilling. His firemen varied, they weren't always crewed together, but teamwork was essential. He understood the back-breaking work of shovelling coal into the burning furnace for hours on end.

Conversation was difficult, so they communicated by a form of hand signals and gestures. Will carried an extra smaller shovel when crewed with a mate, and they would fry bacon and eggs on it during the journey. Just the job with a big hunk of bread on cold mornings.

Yes, William Dobson considered himself a very lucky man.

HENRY

Henry Lascelles was in a quandary. He knew what he ought to do, but the actuality of it was becoming increasingly difficult. Matilda Dobson had become for him a reason to get up in the morning and to begin to think he might have some sort of a future. Selfishly he had never intended for it to be more than a brief and pleasant interlude in his otherwise dull and monotonous life. She was bright, beautiful, quick-witted, and full of fun. She had no idea he was not the person she thought she knew.

Henry put his head in his hands and let out a huge sigh. His office was located in Police Headquarters. He was constantly aware of the noise and bustle of the Station around him. The walls of his office were lined with books, the desk made of oak, large and old, and comfortingly familiar. He sat behind it, slumped in the old leather chair with his elbows on the desk cradling his head.

"Oh God!, Oh God! Oh, God!"

He knew he had only himself to blame. What had he been thinking? How could he ever make this right without breaking the heart of the one person in the world he would do anything to avoid hurting?

"You stupid, stupid bugger!"

Henry Roland Giles Lascelles had been born into the Yorkshire gentry. The eldest of four boys and two girls, he had been the apple of his father's eye. Educated at Giggleswick School, he excelled both academically and physically.

Captain of the Rugby XV in the winter and the Cricket XI in the summer, there wasn't a sport he didn't excel at. He played the piano exceptionally well and acted in and often directed the school productions. His acceptance to study medicine upon completion of his studies surprised no one who knew him. His acceptance of a place at Sheffield did. His parents couldn't understand him turning down a place at Oxford. What was the boy thinking? But Henry Lascelles was ever his own man. He liked Sheffield, he liked being in Yorkshire, and that was that!

Life was pretty good. He made friends easily, and his studies kept him interested but not so taxing as to interfere with his social life. His family allowance provided him with comfortable lodgings and the means to expand his "all-around education" by frequenting the local hostelries, music halls, and theatres. He could tell a fine story, drink with the best of them, and he was rarely short of female company.

Henry's tutors found him to be diligent, questioning, resourceful, challenging, and a pleasure to teach. His friends considered his humour and light-hearted approach to life by far his outstanding attribute. His generosity kept them all in beer, and his help with revision kept their heads above water at exam times.

Once he started his ward allocations, Henry also became a great favourite with the nurses. His natural charm brought out the best in them. Even some of the old-school "battle axes" developed a soft spot for young Lascelles.

"My goodness Sister Rose, but you're looking most attractive today! Have you done your hair differently?" asked in all innocence, and the nurses swore it was the only time they had ever seen the revered sister so flustered!

Henry was genuinely interested in the ward work and dynamics, the patients, and the nurses, and they responded in kind by including him in the chores. If he showed a willingness to learn, they would show him. It was all of interest to Henry, he appreciated how hard the nurses worked, and as their tasks were different from those of the medical staff, he felt he would be a better Doctor if he understood how it all linked together. This approach was somewhat at odds with most of his medical colleagues. Most of whom considered nurses to be their handmaidens and always at their beck and call.

There were a few Consultants who thought as he did, and he would particularly enjoy their ward rounds, especially in the company of the Senior Sister. She, of course, often knew more than the doctors on some subjects and considerably more than the medical students. It was a brave medical student who would be flippant or disregard the Ward Sister. Digging a hole for themselves was a common enough occurrence, usually rescued by whichever nurse or sister was accompanying the ward round, and usually before they had completely toppled over into the abyss.

Not always, however.

One particularly cocky medical student had, for some reason, known only to himself, thought it politic to wax lyrical on the subject of wound debridement and dressings during one such ward round attended by the vastly experienced and knowledgeable Sister Rose.

The Consultant had allowed the unfortunate student to proceed beyond the point of no return, digging his hole and poised on the precipice. At this point, the decision had to be made...... to pull him back or give him a gentle shove?

Sister Rose kept her counsel, and eyebrows raised as the venerable Consultant gave the gentle shove. "How very interesting, Mr Wallis, as this ward has the lowest infection rate and highest wound healing rate in the whole hospital, I suggest that you reconsider your data. You might want to consult with Sister Rose, who is acknowledged as something of an authority on wound healing."

With this, he and the team moved on, leaving poor Wallis well and truly put in his place. Ever after referred to as "wounds Wallis" the poor boy never quite lived it down.

Henry, on the other hand, kept quiet and absorbed it all. His time on the wards became almost the best part of his training. He had a gift for speaking easily to patients and loved the methodical process of interrogation and examination in the quest for a diagnosis. It was like a puzzle, putting the pieces together. It was all a matter of asking the right questions, which seemed to come easily to him. He liked the patients and wanted to be able to help them, and they responded to his easy professional manner by giving him the information he was asking for, and often more besides thereby aiding him in his diagnosis. The nurses found him easy to like and responded to his open and funny manner. They, too, would point him in the right direction, rescuing him during ward rounds with a well-placed, and beautifully timed hint.

"Mr Lascelles, a sign or symptom of tuberculosis?....... start us off," the Consultant would begin.

Henry froze his mind on another topic completely but Jolted back to the ward round, he was floundering. He knew the answer, but being put on the spot in front of twenty others……

"Still coughing, Bill?" he heard one of the nurses talking to the patient in the bed behind him, and the lightbulb went on.

"Haemoptysis, Sir"

"Indeed; Mr Rogers talk us through the investigations….." the Consultant proceeded.

Henry turned briefly, a smile of gratitude on his face. Bill - the patient- actually had a broken leg, but he was beaming at Henry and holding up both thumbs. Nurse Morgan smiled and winked; God bless her!

Once into his final year of study, Henry knew he wanted to be a surgeon. Technically the challenge was stimulating. He watched with interest and awe as abdomens were opened, legs amputated, and heads drilled. Anaesthesia was in its infancy, yet crude though it was, it had provided the difference between life-saving butchery and humane surgical improvement of life. Henry was fascinated and spent much of his spare time in the operating theatre watching the surgeons perform operations of all kinds. Observing their different techniques and following up on the recovery of the patients. Sheffield was at the center of the steel industry, and industrial injuries were commonplace in the days before health and safety. He saw beyond just the gruesome sights. He wanted to be able to alleviate suffering, repair injuries surgically, and improve not only the chances of survival of the injured but their quality of life. Surgery became his passion.

Henry studied hard to pass the final exams, but that was just a means to an end. He sailed through his House Officer posts within the next year with his focus firmly on the end result. His social life dwindled as his career gained ground. His friends, on the whole, had moved on, and away. His family saw less and less of him as he opted to stay on in his holidays assisting in the operating theatre. When it came to applying for Surgical Registrar posts, Henry wanted only one, to be on the Professorial Surgical team at The Hallamshire Hospital in Sheffield. His success was never in doubt. Henry's commitment and intelligence, as well as his dedication and loyalty, ensured his appointment. The Professor of Surgery himself had never seen such a rapid rise in a protégée. What's more? He liked the man.

Henry was both surprised and delighted to receive an invitation to the Prof's Christmas party at the end of his first year of residency. He suddenly realised how isolated he had become. His university friends had moved on and drifted away. He returned to his lodgings only to sleep and change his clothes. He ate at the hospital, studied in the hospital library, and slept in the "on-call" room whenever the demands of the job would allow.

Henry remained a great favourite on the wards and tried to accept offers of tea and cake with the nursing staff whenever he could, but his need to be operating became all-consuming. The invitation had stopped him in his tracks. It had never been his intention to cut himself off from family and friends, and he suddenly realised how much he missed the company of others. In the weeks leading up to the Prof's party, he began to look forward to it. He sent home for his dinner suit, had it cleaned, and even found time to buy himself a new pair of dress shoes.

Mrs Laughton, his landlady, was delighted to be asked for a bath of hot water to be drawn for him. She felt it was the very least she could do. Dr Lascelles asked for so little. She cleaned his rooms and washed his clothes, for which she was paid handsomely, but she always felt she could do more for him.

Henry climbed out of the cab, paid the driver, and stood in front of a very fine house in the suburb of Fulwood. He adjusted his collar, brushed himself down, and experienced an unfamiliar feeling of awkwardness. He smiled and shook his head, took a deep breath, and made his way up to the front door.

The house was Victorian in style, lights blazed from every window, and sounds of music and chatter emanated from within. It was a very welcoming façade. The butler opened the door immediately in response to his knock, relieved him of his hat and coat, and directed him toward the drawing room.

His hostess noticed him immediately and approached him with open arms and a huge smile. Mrs Johnson was an elegant and accomplished lady, she chaired several charitable committees, was an active member of the local Parish Church, and was a School Governor. Her social circle was wide and varied.

"Henry! How lovely. I'm so pleased you decided to come. You must be frozen, come on in and stand by the fire until you thaw out!" she kissed him on each cheek and, on the way to the fire, paused him at the punch bowl.

"You will have one, won't you? It's my own special recipe."

Henry gratefully accepted, and the combination of the alcohol and the warmth of the fire soon took its effect. They chatted briefly about the change in the weather, the very cold snap predicted was yet to arrive. His family was enquired after and her hope that her husband wasn't working him too hard. Henry started to settle, take in the luxurious surroundings, relax, and enjoy himself.

Mrs Johnson excused herself as more guests arrived. Henry was content to absorb the atmosphere and conviviality of the start of the evening. He recognised some of the other guests, some of them doctors from The Hallamshire, but most were merely acquaintances with whom he was on nodding terms. The ladies, he assumed, would be their wives.

He took in the beautifully furnished and decorated room. Despite its grandeur, it was also somehow comfortable, and he found himself wondering how that had been achieved. The wall lights were electrically lit, making the central chandelier sparkle. The mirror above the mantelpiece and the pictures on the walls were swathed in garlands of greenery, mostly holly and mistletoe, and ribbons depicting the reds, greens, and gold of the season. The fire at his back was wonderfully warming.

Henry had been to this house only twice before, both times for a dinner invitation and both were fairly informal. He had been included in the Prof's birthday celebrations the previous summer and then to a luncheon party only six weeks ago. The Prof and Mrs Johnson were a sociable couple. Their home was a haven for their four children, many friends and relatives who, if not in actual residence, were always welcome. It reminded him of his own family home, and he felt guilty to have been so absorbed in his work that he had neglected his own family. His mother regularly wrote despite his poor response, and occasionally he would receive notes from his siblings. But he was ashamed now to have been so incommunicative. He would put that right.

Henry glanced up to see the Prof bearing down on him and removing the glass of punch from his hand.

"She's not got you drinking that filth, has she? What you need is a proper drink" the punch glass was discarded onto a side table as the Prof steered Henry by his elbow through the guests to his study. The door closed softly behind them with a push of the Prof's foot. There he proceeded to pour Henry a glass of the finest Scotch malt whisky with a dash of water and handed him the tumbler. "That'll put hairs on your chest," he pronounced as he clinked his own tumbler with Henrys.

They both took a sip, rolled it around the palette, enjoying the smoky, smooth, rich flavour, and nodded at each other in approval. The Prof indicated the chair for Henry to sit at the other side of another glowing fire as he plopped down into his own. He let out a huge sigh and closed his eyes briefly, comfortable in the quiet companionship the two men enjoyed.

"I don't expect this will last long," said the older man with a conspiratorial smile, and he was right. The door opened moments later without a knock, and a very beautiful young lady put her head around the door jamb.

“Oh, there you are, Daddy. You’re to come at once, Mama is not best pleased to find you missing. You’re to escort Lady Frances into dinner.”

“Come in Charlotte, there’s someone I’d like you to meet.”

Charlotte Johnson was tall and elegant like her mother and absolutely stunning. She had dark, almost black hair, which was swept up into a fashionable chignon with just a few curly tendrils escaping, which softened the look around her perfect head. Her complexion was fashionably and naturally pale, but it was her large deep brown eyes that dominated her face. Her evening gown was simple but beautifully cut dark blue velvet hugging her slim figure and nipping in at the waist. The neckline of the dress was low and skimmed her shoulders, and the only jewelry she wore was a simple pair of diamond stud earrings.

Henry’s breath caught in his throat as he stood up. She approached him with her hand held out, smiling, and looked him straight in the eye. The Prof continued

“Henry Lascelles, this is my eldest daughter Charlotte.”

Henry accepted her hand, gently drew it up to his lips, and kissed it lightly.

“I’m delighted to make your acquaintance Miss Johnson” he could barely hear his own voice.

“Oh, Charlotte, please! You must be Papa’s brilliant protégée? How do you do, Henry Lascelles?”

With that, she hooked her arm through his and directed him towards the door whilst speaking to her father.

“Come on now, Daddy, we don’t want to keep Lady Frances waiting, do we?” and out they swept. Henry was mesmerised. The dinner passed in a blur of conversation, wit, and laughter, and Charlotte Johnson sparkled. Oddly for him, who was so used to being the life and soul of the party, he was content to sit back and listen and watch her. She had it all, beauty, grace, intelligence, and confidence. Why had he never met her before? She positively lit up the room, and he was only too aware that all of the young men present were hanging onto her every word. The end of the evening arrived unexpectedly and much too soon. He felt strangely nervous and unsure how to approach the subject of seeing her again. Should he ask her father? Was it too soon? What if he made a mess of it? Thoughts and scenarios raced through his head as he accepted his hat and coat. He needed to decide soon, or he would lose the opportunity. As he opened his mouth to speak, Charlotte said

“Come for Christmas dinner Henry, mother would love it, wouldn’t you mother? And don’t tell me you’re working, as it simply won’t do!”

“Actually, I am, as it happens, working, but I really would like to see you again….. If I may?” he looked from Charlotte to her mother and back again more apprehensively than he could ever recall feeling. Celia Johnson laughed

"I'd be careful, Henry, if I were you! You might be biting off more than you can chew," she said as she moved off, leaving them together in order to bid the other guests "Goodnight."

Charlotte looked quizzically at him.

"You volunteered, didn't you? Well, it can't be helped, and you really will miss out on a sumptuous Christmas Dinner……. and where are you going to take me to make up for my disappointment?"

Now it was Henry's turn to laugh as she again tucked her arm through his as he made his way to the front door.

"I'll have to think of something now, won't I?" he smiled at her, gallantly kissed her hand, and bade her goodnight. As he settled himself down onto the cab seat, he felt as warm and as happy as he had felt in a very long time. If Miss Charlotte Johnson was disappointed that he wasn't able to join her for Christmas Dinner, then he was content.

Matthew and Celia Johnson closed the door on the last of their guests and made their way into the drawing-room arm in arm. The party had been a success, but then Celia's parties usually were.

She had the knack of a natural hostess, choosing the right people to bring together for the right occasion. Matthew was inordinately proud of her, though for a Yorkshireman to admit as much was an unlikely scenario. He handed her a small glass of port as he poured a whiskey for himself, and they sat down together on the comfortable sofa in front of the fire.

They had been happily married for twenty years. There was little they didn't know about each other and nothing they couldn't discuss between them. Matthew could be brusque, but he was honest, open, and straight to the point. Celia loved that about him. There was no hidden agenda.

Her husband was brilliant at what he did. He worked hard, and was sometimes at the hospital more than he was at home, but his wife understood. Being married to a surgeon wasn't without its challenges. Celia had the responsibility of the house and raising their children. Their lives were busy and full, never without interest, and Matthew knew he would be lost without her. As he settled into the sofa, he eased an arm around his wife, and she leaned into him. They could hear their children in the billiards room quietly chatting as they clinked billiards balls, as competitive as ever.

"Charlotte was on form tonight," commented Celia.

"She took quite a shine to Henry Lascelles."

The clock on the mantelpiece ticked softly as a moment of silence ensued.

"Hmmm," noted Matthew after some contemplation

"Is she well, Celia?" he asked, continuing to stare ahead at the fire

"For the moment, she is," replied his wife, "and it's so lovely to have her home. We need to treat her normally and give her lots of love: family life will help, and the Doctors think she needs more mental stimulation. She's a bright girl, and her frustrations could be that she's just not active enough. Feeling useful will benefit her. She needs a project."

Matthew ingested this information without comment as he swilled the whiskey around the base of the crystal glass. Their eldest daughter had become a source of anguish, bright and beautiful as she undoubtedly was. Charlotte suffered from mood swings, and her "nerves" had recently necessitated a stay away from home in the care of a branch of medicine with which Matthew was largely unfamiliar. Psychiatry was in its infancy, but the family doctor had persuaded them to allow Charlotte to be treated away from home once her behaviour had begun to impact the whole family.

Matthew, in particular, had struggled with the concept. He had found it hard to admit that she needed care they were not able to give. For all he was able to help others, he was totally out of his depth when it came to his own daughter. His delight in having her home and "cured" was tempered only by the opinion of the psychiatrist that the condition may recur. Seeing her now as she was, he conveniently parked that piece of information and convinced himself that whatever had caused the breakdown had passed, and Charlotte was once again restored to the bosom of her family. He did, however, ponder on his wife's closing statement. With a little more apprehension, looked at her, and commented.

"As long as she doesn't make Henry Lascelles her new project!"

CHARLOTTE

Christmas came and went, and Henry's work continued apace. He was operating on more complex cases now and beginning to lecture about surgery to the medical students. He found he enjoyed lecturing and interacting with the students' inquisitive minds.

As New Year approached, he considered asking Charlotte to the Hospital Ball. She had never been far from his thoughts when his workload and study permitted him any free time. In fact, he felt guilty that he hadn't made more of an effort to see her, given how much he thought about her. Out of propriety and courtesy, Henry caught the Prof as they were finishing a case in theatre and asked if he might see him on a personal matter.

"Of course, of course, Henry," replied the older man

"Come to my office when you've cleaned up" he dried his arms to the elbow, rolled down his sleeves, snatched his coat from the door, and exited the room.

Henry stood apprehensively in front of the wide old desk in the Profs' office, feeling like a schoolboy in front of the headmaster. He clasped his hands behind his back. The Prof was seated before him looking up over the rim of his reading glasses.

"To the Ball, eh?" he said. "I didn't realise they still had them," though he knew perfectly well that they did.

"Have you asked her?" he enquired, sitting back and folding his arms.

"No, Sir, I thought it best to ask you first," replied Henry.

The Prof maintained his gaze, enjoying the younger man's discomfort

"Well, it's very good of you, Henry, but I don't want to go to the Hospital Ball! You'd better ask Charlotte!"

He had a wicked glint in his eye as Henry realised he was being teased, he let out a huge sigh of relief. As the Prof guffawed, and the tension dissipated. They spent the next hour debriefing the afternoon's cases over a brandy. Henry returned to his lodgings very mellow, though he'd had the foresight to scribble a note to Charlotte, which her father had agreed to courier.

"It will be alright, Matthew," said Celia later that night.

"It's just what she needs at the present time, and who knows.... It could just be the making of her" Matthew wasn't so sure. Something deep within him was beginning to make him feel uncomfortable. He couldn't pinpoint exactly what it was, and he certainly couldn't verbalise it to himself, let alone anyone else. Therefore, like most men, he dismissed it, ignoring what he didn't want to know. In the years ahead, he would have cause to reflect on that decision. He should have listened to his instincts.

It was a whirlwind romance. Charlotte Johnson dazzled at the ball, and Henry was the envy of every man in the room. Holding her in his arms, Henry couldn't dance with her enough. She moved exquisitely, throwing her head back and laughing in the delight of the moment. Her vivacity was intoxicating.

He began to think about her constantly. She entered his thoughts day and night, he wrote her letters, and she responded in kind sometimes twice a day. His concentration was suffering, and his colleagues noticed more absentmindedness. This was very out of character. It took a real effort now to concentrate on his work and his studies as the final exams loomed. He knew if he failed them, he would be letting himself, the Prof, and many other people down. He wanted to accept every invitation to the house, but with great determination, he knew he had to prioritise.

Charlotte encouragingly said she understood and gave him some space. Her father praised her restraint. He supported and helped Henry in every way he could, believing the distance between them now would either make or break the relationship. Happy though he was to see his daughter delight in Henry's company, he maintained his unspoken reservations.

Henry Lascelles had a bright future ahead of him, of that Matthew was certain.

"Let him be, for now, Charlotte," he advised.

"Write to him if you must but do allow him to study. His future depends on it."

Henry did focus, he studied hard as the final exams approached, and he took every opportunity to operate and observe operations. His surgical technique, high level of success, and low rate of infection were impressive. The Prof couldn't help but take quiet pride in his protégée's achievements. He himself quizzed Henry relentlessly and pushed him hard, knowing he was capable of it. When Henry presented himself for the fellowship exams, he knew he was ready both practically and theoretically.

The Prof kept him busy in the weeks following the exams. Keeping occupied would limit the amount of time he had for "dwelling upon" how he might have done.

What the Prof hadn't realised was how quietly confident Henry was. Not given to false modesty, Henry knew he had done as well as he possibly could have. He was content and waited patiently with an expectation of success. Henry returned to his lodgings following a succession of busy shifts on the first Saturday evening he could recall having off duty in weeks. He was exhausted but happy and looked forward to a long lie the following day, all the more anticipated because of its rarity. Mrs Laughton fussed about him like a mother when as she seated him for a meal of steak and kidney pie followed by jam roly-poly and custard.

Henry ate like a Lord and complimented his landlady on her culinary skills. Once he had digested his meal, he took the luxury of a soak in a hot bath. He then sat contentedly, wrapped in his dressing- gown in front of the fire in his bedroom. A mug of tea warming in his hands.

The bed was comfortable, and he slept as soundly as he had done in months.

He was woken by the persistence of the doorbell. He glanced at his watch, quarter to ten on a Sunday morning. The doorbell rang again as he gathered his senses. Mrs Laughton would be at church, of course, but surely he wasn't the only occupant in the boarding house? By the constant ringing, he could only assume he was.

He sighed, pulled on his shirt and trousers, and made his way downstairs. Barefooted, he picked up pace as the persistence of the ringing intensified, and he flew down the last flight of stairs. He pulled open the heavy front door only to be almost bowled over by Charlotte Johnson as she fell into his arms, kicking the door closed behind her.

His astonishment mounted as she grabbed hold of his hand and pulled him towards the staircase. "Quickly, Henry, show me your rooms," she said as she started upstairs, pulling Henry behind her. He caught hold of her on the first landing.

"What? How? Charlotte?" was all he could manage, brains still scrambled from sleep. She turned and threw her arms around him, and before he could gather his senses further, she was kissing him. He felt caught in a whirlpool, tumbling downwards but afraid to stop in case it wasn't real.

Charlotte was then laughing and shushing him and pulling him upstairs. They almost fell into his rooms clinging to one another and at the same time trying to devoid each other of clothing, desperate in their sudden need of each other physically.

My God, but she is beautiful, he thought as his lips found the naked skin of her throat and breasts. She arched backward, opening herself to him, and they fell in a tumble across his unmade bed.

A thousand thoughts raced through his consciousness as she nibbled his ear, murmuring endearments whilst pulling at his remaining clothing. He was suddenly overwhelmed by love and lust in equal measure. Her response was equally desperate and a complete revelation to him. He was on fire and desperate for her.

"I want you, Henry, now! Yes! Yes! Please Do it now!" she begged to bury her face in his shoulder as he poised above her. He was lost, she spread her legs, and he felt her hands on his naked buttocks, and they were joined.

"Oh, Yes!" she cried and arched her back further, pulling him into her. He had never experienced anything so explosively exquisite. They were consumed and reached climax quickly. Such was their need. They held onto each other through all the little aftershocks, and Henry thought he had never felt such peace. Seconds later, the reality of what had just happened started to dawn on him, but he pushed the thought aside as he gathered her into his arms, kissing her hair.

“I love you, Henry,” she said softly, and then she sat up suddenly,

“That was amazing! And I would love to do it again, but if I am not outside the church at the end of the service, there will be hell to pay!”

Then she leaned across him, propped on one arm, and kissed him long and hard before leaving the bed and scooping up her discarded clothing, re-dressing, and adjusting her hair beneath the retrieved hat. She glanced back at him.

“You’ll have to help me, lazy bones if I am not to look completely wanton and ravished when I meet my parents!” Henry flew out of bed laughing, wrapped the sheet around his waist, and applied his mind to the task of female dressing. She was very soon almost back to how she had first appeared at his door and definitely fit to meet the parents.

He was very tempted to undo all his hard work and delay her departure further. She kissed him again, dropped her hand to give him a gentle squeeze, raised her eyebrows, laughed at his shocked reaction, and swept out of the room, leaving Henry confused, baffled, delighted, surprised, and satiated.

Reality soon set in, and he was determined to speak to the Prof, not only to formally ask permission to court her, but if the time was right, he would ask for her hand in marriage.

He loved her. He convinced himself he did. There was no doubt he had ravished her, and any honourable Gentleman would do the decent thing. He couldn't bear the thought of the Prof finding out what had happened. For regardless of provocation, he should have had more restraint and not been so weak to be bowled over by a beautiful woman, however insistent.

Henry had enormous respect for Charlotte's parents and a great fondness for the whole family. They would do very well together, he decided, and he did love her. She was wild and impulsive, but that was part of her charm. Life would definitely not be boring, and besides, he needed a wife, as all good surgeons did.

It was something of a shock, therefore, having rustled up courage to approach Prof Johnson, to be told in a very matter-of-fact manner that Charlotte had gone away.

"Gone away, Sir?"

"Where to?... Why? "Henry enquired, standing before the desk in the Prof's office, his spirits sinking.

"Her Mother thought it best, Europe probably."

He seemed ill at ease as he searched the desk drawers for whiskey glasses.

"Why?" repeated the Prof. "Who knows? Best not to meddle in the affairs of the fairer sex, eh? Will you join me in a tipple?" And he lifted a glass for Henry to see.

"No, thank you, Sir," replied Henry

"Did she leave me a letter or a note?" asked Henry, both bewildered and disappointed.

"Leave you a note?" asked the Prof

"Why would she do that?" and he proceeded to pour a slug of amber liquid into his glass.

"Now, about tomorrow's list…." The Prof continued.

Henry heard little, standing rooted to the spot, gazing ahead, and shortly he was glad to be dismissed. On his way out, he turned and asked.

"Can I write to her?"

"Best not," replied the Prof looking up briefly, a small sympathetic smile barely touching his lips.

Henry buried his hurt and confusion in his work. The results of his exams confirmed not only a pass but a distinction, and he now had the right to call himself "Mr" Lascelles.

Try as he might, he couldn't help but think about Charlotte occasionally and wondered if she had regretted what had happened between them. He really couldn't think of any other explanation for her disappearance. He tried not to dwell on it. His old Granny had a saying.

"If it's for you, it'll not pass you by," and Henry had a feeling she could be right.

THE FAMILY

The Johnsons continued to invite him to the house, but he rarely went. Celia welcomed him as she always had but deflected any questions relating to Charlotte. Henry found he missed her more there. He wondered if they knew, yet they showed no signs that they did. It puzzled him, but as the months passed by, he began to think of her less. He had re-established contact with his own family and made an effort to visit them more during his time off. His sister, Mary, had recently become engaged to be married to the local landowners' son. A chinless wonder in Henry's opinion, but his money obviously made up for his lacking of personality and knowing his sister as he did, he thought they would probably suit each other very well. He would have a trophy wife, and she would be rich. Perfect.

Henry discovered a kindred spirit in his brother Rupert much to his delight. Four years younger than Henry, he was barely out of the schoolroom when Henry started his medical studies. Now he was a successful Banker and gifted cricketer – when his employment would allow.

They had much in common and settled easily into familiar conversation. They shared a sense of humour, and Rupert could be quite cutting about his sister's fiancée in the snug bar of their local hostelry. The landlord was delighted to welcome Henry back, telling him how his profits had plummeted in the years since he'd left. Rupert had no doubt their sister would have

"Poor Hugo" completely under her thumb by the time they returned from honeymoon.

Their Mother, Emily Lascelles, was equally delighted to have Henry back in the family fold. She was immensely proud of him and had begun racking her brains in the search for a suitable wife.

"Really, Mother, please don't," Henry pleaded. "I will have a lady of my own choosing."

"But you don't meet anybody!" Emily complained.

"Perhaps one of Hugo's sisters? Keep it in the family?"

He knew she was joking as he pulled a face of exasperation, and Rupert chimed in.

"Lord save us from the frumpy sisters of our soon to be brother-in-law!"

It was good to be home. Henry had lost sight of how comforting familiarity could be. Their easy laughter prompted the appearance of their father out of his study, and as dinner was about to be announced, they drifted towards the dining room together.

Thunderous feet clattered down the staircase as the younger siblings responded to the dinner gong, starving as usual. The twins, John and Elizabeth, were arguing, and Edgar, the baby of the family trying to keep up. Emily looked happily around the table at her offspring, content to have the family united again. She counted her blessings and, with grace, thanking God for each and every one of them. She glanced at her husband at the far end of the table and smiled. He could always read her thoughts. As he held her gaze, he winked.

Mary's wedding came and went with the spring. She and Hugo honeymooned in Italy on a mini–Grand Tour. Henry had never been much of a traveller, but he was interested enough to start reading about Rome in particular, which did appeal to him. Somehow, he never could quite make the next step of organisation. He rarely used all his entitled leave, he preferred to work, but it did occur to him that if ever he found the right companion to travel with, Rome was definitely the destination he would choose. Henry rarely daydreamed, but as he sat gently tipped back in the old leather chair in front of the equally old and battered desk in his shared office, that is exactly what he was doing when there was a knock at the door. He settled the chair back onto its four square feet and said,

"Come in."

REALITY

The door swung slowly open, and framed in the doorway stood a figure that made his heart skip a beat.

"Hello, Henry," she said, smiling gently as she moved into the room and closed the door behind her. Henry stood up and moved around to her side of the desk, but he hesitated. She was just as beautiful as he remembered but seemed more subdued somehow, and he was unsure of how to proceed. His mouth was dry. Where had she been? Why hadn't she contacted him? Had she come to the conclusion that she wasn't for him? But then, why come now? This all happened in moments, and so far, he hadn't said a word. She stood before him, holding her reticule before her, and she looked up at him. What he saw bored into his very soul. She was as nervous as he was. Her eyes were wide and filled with tears.

"I'm so sorry," she said, not averting his gaze and allowing the tears to fall.

She took the tiniest of steps toward him. That was all he needed, he opened his arms, and she moved into his embrace to be engulfed by him. Kissing the top of her hat – which instantly struck him as odd and funny – he eased it off her head and dropped it to the floor. Now he was kissing her face. Explanations could wait. She held him tightly around the waist, and the tears flowed.

"I'm sorry, Henry, I'm so sorry," she kept saying over and over.

"My darling girl, don't be sorry. You're here, and whatever it is, we'll sort it out together. I love you!" He guided her towards the visitors' chair. It surprised him to hear the words voiced so naturally. He had put such thoughts from his mind, but now she was here, and he had declared himself so frankly, he felt at peace. The questions could wait.

"No, Henry," she said as she resisted his invitation to sit

"I prefer to stand. I need to talk to you" then she smiled at him shyly

"Do you mean it, really? Do you love me?" she seemed unsure, anxious even, but the beautiful smile was definitely there as she took out her handkerchief and wiped her eyes.

Henry perched on the end of the desk in front of her. He took hold of her hand and looked up into her face.

"You know I do. Can't you tell?"

She moved towards him, and as the gentle swell of her belly touched him, he knew. His eyes dropped to check visually, then his head snapped up to meet her gaze, questioning her silently.

"I didn't know it could happen like that. Really I didn't. I don't know what to do, Henry."

She looked so young and frightened. What it must have taken for her to come to him like this, he couldn't imagine, and his heart swelled at her bravery.

Henry stood up in front of her, took her face gently between his hands, and kissed her.

"We'll marry, of course," he said, then hesitated.

"You do want to marry me, don't you, Charlotte?" Her response was to throw her arms around him, making him topple backward into the visitors' chair, pulling her onto his lap and laughing.

The next hour was spent just basking in each other's company. She smiled as she settled into his embrace but was uncharacteristically quiet, allowing him to chatter on about his work and his reuniting with his family. Every now and then, the enormity of her pregnancy would hit him. He was going to be a father!

Charlotte settled in the chair as Henry got up. Her eyes followed him around the room as he stoked up the little fire and put the kettle on to boil, his paperwork forgotten for the day. A sudden thought occurred to him.

"Does your father know?" he asked her, now starting to feel a little apprehensive.

"No," she smiled, "not yet, but mother knows, but not about you, of course!" and she slowly started to open up a little. She was quieter than he had ever known her to be, but she spoke steadily to try to fill him in about what had happened after she left him that Sunday morning.

She had been so ecstatically happy she said that she had wanted to tell the world what had happened. She knew she couldn't but had found it difficult to behave normally for the rest of the day. She couldn't sleep, she said, and had wandered the house and gardens until her mother had found her curled up on a bench in the summer house, cold and exhausted. Naturally, she had taken a chill and developed a cough. Her memory of the next few days was scant. She supposed she had been ill, and her mother had taken her down to the south coast to stay with relatives.

She thought she must have been very ill because she remembered so little of that time, and once she was better, mother had brought her home.

She had been sick over the past months, actually vomiting, she said and assuming she still wasn't well, Celia had asked the family doctor to visit. Strangely her father had not been involved, and it was only when the doctor had given his diagnosis that Charlotte realised why.

She was terrified as she listened to the doctor and her mother discussing her and what was to be done, almost as if she wasn't there. Impossible, adoption, abroad were the words that flitted through her detached consciousness, and she realised plans were being made without consulting her.

"Can't be allowed to happen" and "Could make her worse" were murmured as if she didn't even exist. Charlotte could take no more. She left the room, gathered her hat and coat, and left the house. She didn't believe her departure had even been noted.

Charlotte had walked briskly to the nearest park, sat down on a bench, and given herself time to think. A baby. Henry's baby. Memories of that day flooded back to her, and she started to feel excited again. Then fear crept in. It had been four months ago. Had he moved on? Would he want to help her? Instinctively she knew he would. She had to see him. She made her way back to the house and straight into her father's study.

"Daddy, I want to see Henry Lascelles," ever to the point. Matthew looked up,

"Do you now? The poor man has just got over moping about you. Don't go stoking that fire again, Missy. That's my advice."

She smiled and raised an eyebrow.

"He was moping about me?" Matthew laughed. He couldn't help it.

She was infuriating and captivating, sometimes at the same time.

"Where will he be, Daddy?" she pleaded.

"Will you leave him alone, Charlotte? He will be catching up on reports in his office. I expect unless an emergency has come in, in which case he'll be in the theatre. I'm going to the hospital tomorrow. If you still want to see him come with me in the morning," but she was already on the turn.

"Can't wait until tomorrow! I'll get a cab," and she was off, passing her mother in the hallway at speed.

"Charlotte! Please," cried Celia, but Charlotte was already on her way through the front door.

"Invite him for dinner!" shouted Matthew as her footsteps clipped each step on her way out.

It had all been such a rush, and then inexplicably, she found herself standing outside his office. Only at that point did reality hit her, and she found herself shaking. She walked away from the door and sat down on a bench in the corridor. She lost track of time. Her thoughts were everywhere and nowhere. Did she love him? Did she want to marry him? What if he didn't ask her? What if he didn't even want to know? She took a deep breath, stood up, straightened her coat and hat, and picked up her reticule.

"Well, Charlotte Johnson, there's only one way to find out," and as she stood in front of his door and knocked, she found she was fighting back the tears welling up in her eyes.

THE DIAGNOSIS

"It's no good, Celia. You cannot conceal it from him! He has to know" Matthew was pacing up and down the carpet in his study.

"What if it makes a difference?" pleaded his wife. "What if he won't take her on?"

"He'll take her on, alright! She's expecting his child! He'll take her on if I have to frog march him to the altar, but he has to know."

Celia was seated in the comfortable old chair by the fire.

"That won't be necessary," she responded.

"Sit down, dear and be calm, he's asked her to marry him, and she's accepted, so that's one difficulty out of the way."

It had been a trying day. Her suspicions about Charlotte's "condition" had been confirmed by Doctor Roberts. Charlotte had fled by the time Celia had noticed she had left the room. Once she had located her, Charlotte had fled again. None of Charlotte's belongings had been taken, which was reassuring. So Celia had gathered herself up to confront her husband with the momentous news when Matthew had confounded her with an announcement of his own.

"Charlotte has gone to find Henry Lascelles."

It didn't take Celia long to put two and two together, so she swallowed the words she had so carefully constructed and said,

"Oh, has she, darling? Did she say how long she would be?"

"I told her to invite him for dinner! I do hope she doesn't keep stringing him along. He's a decent chap. Under different circumstances, they might have made a go of it…."

Matthew lit his pipe, pondering over the whole little ceremony of packing down the tobacco after having tapped the empty bowl, showing it the match and all the sucking in to get it to draw. Celia found it all rather tedious but didn't comment as he obviously so enjoyed it. As he settled down opposite her, Celia decided to seize the moment.

"Darling, Charlotte is expecting"

"Expecting what?" asked Matthew, barely interested, but when the pause became prolonged, he looked up and met Celia's steady gaze.

"A baby"

A realisation hit him.

"What?!" he shouted, almost choking on the pipe smoke. "Whose is it? I'll kill him!"

"NO, you won't kill him, Matthew. You will calm down, and we will make a plan for our beloved daughter."

Once again pacing the rug before the fire, Matthew fumed, but he hadn't made the connection. Celia sighed

"I think he might be coming for dinner."

DOMESTICITY

Henry was not looking forward to the next few hours. He and Charlotte had returned to his lodgings in order that he might dress for dinner, and now he gripped her hand tightly as they entered the Johnson house. Matthew and Celia Johnson stood together in the hall as they entered

"Good evening, Sir, Mrs Johnson," started Henry feeling extremely uncomfortable.

Charlotte gripped his arm encouragingly as Matthew spoke.

"Go upstairs and dress for dinner, please, Charlotte, then join us in the study. Celia, please ask Mrs Buckley to delay dinner and then join us. Henry, after you," and he indicated the direction of his study. Henry heard the heavy door close firmly, and as he turned around, the Prof stood before him looking kinder than Henry had any right to expect.

"I love her, Sir, and we will marry."

"Yes, yes, very good, good…." started Matthew

"Sit down, Henry"

"If you don't mind, Sir, I'd rather stand."

Matthew grunted and poured them both a whisky.

"I'm afraid there's a bit more to it than just marriage," began Matthew.

“Sir?” queried Henry

“Oh, for God’s sake, sit down, Henry. This might take a while.”

Henry sat, beyond puzzled.

“It’s called Manic Depression. Charlotte has a condition known as Manic depression” his expression exuded sympathy.

Henry felt as though he had been punched in the chest

“What is that?” he asked. Dim recollections of his basic psychiatric training stirred in his brain

“Mood swings, only more so,” continued Matthew floundering himself in having to share something so personal and about which he himself wasn’t entirely sure.

“Not sure how it occurs or what causes it. She can be very up, and she can be very down. Sometimes warranting hospital admission.”

He looked down at his whisky glass, incredibly sad.

“That’s where she’s been since you last saw her. In the hospital.”

“Is there a cure?” asked Henry, and Matthew shook his head.

“It’s the depression following the manic phase that’s the worst. She can’t be reasoned with, and we can’t manage her behaviour at home any longer. We have the other children to think about.

In between bouts of depression, she can be relatively normal, even brilliant, as you witnessed last Christmas. But she is always going to have it. We don't know if it will stabilise or worsen with the years ahead, and we have been told that pregnancy could exacerbate the situation."

Henry sat opposite the Prof, stunned. The fire crackled in the grate, and he stared into it in silence. His thoughts and dreams crashed and exploded in his head. Matthew watched him, giving him time to process the devastating information. Celia returned quietly to the study and took over the chair her husband had just vacated.

"Does Charlotte know?" asked Henry, still staring into the fire.

"She knows," replied Celia, "what she doesn't know is that pregnancy and childbirth may exacerbate a deterioration."

"Or it might not?" said Henry, clutching at straws.

"I suggest you speak to her psychiatrist before you commit yourself any further," suggested Matthew. All thoughts of killing the perpetrator evaporated.

"He's a good chap, knows his stuff. I'll write the appropriate letter. Take Charlotte with you. She has a right to know what will affect her future."

The silence was broken by the opening of the study door and the entry of the subject of the discussion. Charlotte was beaming and looking beautiful and happy as she advanced toward them.

"Why so glum? I do hope you haven't been beastly to my future husband?"

Henry finished his whisky, smiled at her, and stood. He circled his arm around her small waist. He felt protective of her, he loved her, and she was expecting his child.

He would meet with the psychiatrist, he needed to know more, and he would do his own research. There had to be a way to help her, and if there was, he would find it. On a surge of positivity, he squeezed her to him,

"Where and when would you like to be married, my darling?" he asked her, and the tension in the room dissipated. Celia's relief was palpable as she hastened dinner, and the conversation took a very different and lighter direction.

The psychiatrist turned out to be a very knowledgeable man, and Henry warmed to him immediately. He had known Charlotte since her early teens when he had been approached by Prof. Johnson in strict confidence about his troubled daughter.

The office of Dr Benjamin Greenstreet was not in a hospital but in a very smart area in the city of Leeds. Matthew had been as good as his word and provided both an introduction and a letter of authority for the eminent doctor to speak to Henry frankly, disclosing certain confidences he would not otherwise have been able to share. Besides, as Charlotte accompanied Henry, she happily consented to her medical history being shared with her future husband.

It had made sense for the Johnsons to seek help for Charlotte out of the environs of Sheffield. It was less likely Charlotte would be recognised and subjected to speculation. Her privacy reasoned, Matthew, was paramount, but in the judgemental society in which they lived and the stigma attached to any form of mental illness, Matthew had to acknowledge it was more than Charlotte's privacy that was at stake.

Henry read all the literature available, which was recommended by Dr Greenstreet and more. Knowledge about manic depression was scanty at best and, outside of the specialty, poorly understood. There was no known "cure," no certainty about the future, and no guarantees.

Whatever the difficulties and uncertainties ahead, Henry was determined to be positive. To be the rock Charlotte needed in her life, and to provide her and their child with love, stability, and safety. Charlotte was glowing and caught up in the excitement of the wedding preparations. He adored her. They would face this together……and who knew? The doctors could be wrong.

They were married within the month, amidst little pomp and ceremony, just family and close friends.

Charlotte was radiant, and his heart swelled as he stood at the altar making his vows. Her beautiful dress masked the gentle contours of her belly, and he thought she had never looked lovelier.

The pregnancy induced a glow about her, which enhanced all her natural beauty. Some questions were asked, of course, but Henry explained it away as a whirlwind romance, love at first sight, so why wait? His mother was sceptical but kept her thoughts to herself. He was certainly marrying into a good family, and Emily Lascelles readily warmed to Charlotte, though there was something she couldn't quite put her finger on. The families blended well. The day had dawned bright and sunny with not a cloud in the sky. Optimism was in the air, and the future looked bright.

After a honeymoon in Italy, the newlyweds settled down in a small house Henry had purchased in a middle-class area of Sheffield. He hired a cook and a cleaning woman to come in daily until Charlotte found her feet, and they settled down to domestic life.

Charlotte was enchanted with the house and determined to be a good wife. Henry tried to get home from work as soon as he could, and he encouraged Charlotte to visit her family home and invite her mother and sister to visit her. Initially, all seemed well. Charlotte had made the acquaintance of the neighbours, one of whom had been particularly kind to the young doctor's wife and had taken Charlotte under her wing.

Mrs Newton was an older lady and a very good cook, a "salt of the earth" Yorkshire woman, and Henry felt very blessed that she lived next door. Charlotte would sit in her kitchen chatting and watching her work, and almost without realising it, Mrs Newton had her peeling vegetables, preparing meat, and making pastry. It became her new obsession. She would accompany Mrs Newton to the marketplace, where she learned what to buy, from whom, and at what price. She soon started trying out her new skills at home, much to Henry's delight and amusement. The hired cook soon became superfluous to need.

DISASTER

Sadly, it wasn't to last. By the eighth month of her pregnancy, Charlotte became more and more withdrawn. She stopped visiting Mrs Newton and refused to answer the door to her or even to her own mother, closing the curtains and pretending she wasn't at home. Initially, Henry was unaware as Charlotte was often in bed by the time he got home, pleading tiredness due to the pregnancy. He began to notice that the house was less well-kept and increasingly untidy.

Charlotte told him the cleaning woman had let her down – again – but it turned out that it was Charlotte who kept sending her away. Henry's own occupation with his work had distracted him from Charlotte's increasing level of depression until he returned home one night to find her manic, wild-eyed, and destructively throwing objects at the walls. She seemed not to recognise him and began screaming at him to "get out!" this was followed rapidly by a hurled vase which shattered against the mantelpiece.

Henry's level of shock rooted him to the spot in front of this vision of his own wife, almost unrecognisable and behaving as though possessed. She was throwing herself about the room, and he feared not only for her safety but for that of the baby. The noise of the latch lifting on the back door brought him back to reality, and his relief at seeing Mrs Newton's head peering gingerly around the door was obvious.

"What can I do, Henry?" she asked.

"Mr Newton is just behind me. What do you need us to do?"

Charlotte was screaming and shouting, and flailing out as Henry approached her in an attempt to calm her down.

"Send Mr Newton for Dr Jaggers, and please use the telephone on the hall table to contact Charlottes' parents. Can you do that?" he asked, his panic rising.

The telephone had only recently been installed so the hospital could contact him at home.

Never had he been so pleased he had accepted the offer.

"The number is in the book at the side," he shouted after her.

Dr Jaggers was their General Practitioner, nearing retirement and vastly experienced. Henry couldn't help but wonder if he had ever encountered in his long and distinguished career anything like this before.

"Charlotte, it's me, Henry, your husband," he pleaded with her as he tried to approach her, his hands out in front of him. "I'm not going to hurt you."

Charlottes' hair had escaped its fastenings, and she took up a defensive stance to repel him. He stopped short of touching her.

"What's happened darling?" he gently asked, concern all over his demeanour

"Come and sit down, love. We'll have a cup of tea and talk about it?"

Mrs Newton stuck her head round the door a second time to tell him the Doctor and Charlotte's parents were on their way and that she would put the kettle on.

"You will have a cup of tea now won't you love?" she asked Charlotte, but there was no response.

Henry then realised how cold the room was. The fire had not been lit, Charlotte must be frozen, but he dared not light it and introduce yet another danger.

"Come and sit down with me. You'll need warming up," he said encouragingly, sitting down and patting the sofa next to him.

Charlotte looked straight at him as though he were a stranger, with cold, unfeeling eyes.

"Get this out of me," she said in a low hard voice, pointing at her pregnant abdomen. Her stance remained defensive, and the wild, manic look in her eyes chilled him to the bone.

"Get it out now, or I'll kill myself and it."

Prof and Mrs Johnson were in the front room with Charlotte. Mrs Newton had made tea and sandwiches, and she squeezed Henry's forearm as she prepared to return to her own house.

"I'm just next door, Henry. Let me know if there is anything else I can help you with?" with that, she headed out, closing the back door softly behind her.

Henry was standing at the door to the living room with Dr Jaggers as Matthew entered the hall and closed the door behind him. The elderly GP was remarkably calm and frank.

“I’ll have to induce her, Henry,” he said. “If she’ll let me.”

“But the baby will be premature,” pleaded Henry. “Isn’t there another way?”

“Look, this is a case of puerperal psychosis if ever I saw one” Dr Jaggers looked weary and full of concern “to be honest with you, this is as bad a case as I have ever seen. She needs to be admitted to Menston, but first, we need to do what she wants and get that baby out. If we don’t, it’s as good as dead anyway. Let me talk to her and Matthew if you would call Dr Greenstreet. He needs to see her as soon as she is delivered and out of that particular danger.”

Menston: High Royds Hospital at Menston in Leeds. A large gothic Victorian Institution for the insane.

“Oh, dear God,” thought Henry, “This can’t be happening.”

Dr Jaggers induced Charlottes’ labour that very night, and he arranged for two midwives to attend her throughout the confinement. He himself remained at the house in case of complications but mostly slept in the armchair by the now-lit fire. The Johnsons had returned home once Charlotte had been sedated and had settled at the end of a telephone call should they be needed. Mrs Newton had made arrangements for warm blankets and plenty of hot water.

Henry lit the fire in the bedroom hearth, fireguard in place because despite the potential danger, they needed the room to be warm and comfortable not only for Charlotte's comfort but, most importantly, for the premature infant. Mrs Newton had also emptied and cleaned the bottom drawer in the range to make up a warm makeshift cot for the baby. She couldn't persuade Henry to eat anything, but she continued to ply him with cups of hot sweet tea. He would have a mouthful and then abandon it. Neither could he settle. He was up and down the stairs wanting to be with Charlotte but fearing her reaction to him. The two midwives had the situation well in hand. Sisters Rogerson and Young had seen most things in their careers, and their calmness and experience instilled in Henry a confidence he desperately needed. Unusual as the situation was, the midwives went quietly about their work professionally and with great kindness. Their support of Charlotte impressed Henry, and he slowly began to relax, knowing they were in safe hands.

Once the sedation had taken effect, Dr Jaggers had broken Charlottes' waters to induce the labour, and she had established quickly, as young women often do, especially when difficulties arise. Nature's way, some would say.

The midwives kept vigil during the night, unusually for the day they had encouraged Henry's presence. In the calm of the warm bedroom with Charlotte now settled and the reassuring presence of the midwives, Henry had fallen asleep, his head and arms on the bed at Charlotte's side, from sheer exhaustion.

The next thing he was aware of was a gentle shaking of his shoulder and groaning sounds emanating from the bed. Sister Rogerson had her finger to her lips to quieten him as he gained full consciousness. The other midwife was talking quietly to Charlotte, who was now making grunting noises. The light was starting to filter into the room, and, as he adjusted his eyes, he realised his baby was about to be born. Sister Rogerson was stoking up the fire, and then she called softly down to Mrs Newton to bring up the hot water. There was no panic, no raised voices. All remained calm and ordered as he heard the sister gently say

"Come on now, Charlotte. You can do it. Give a big push."

Charlotte seemed to be completely in her own world and yet responding to her body's need to expel the little person inside of her. Henry realised that she was pushing involuntarily with only soft encouragement from the midwife. Before long Sister Young looked up and encouraged Henry to glance down beneath the sheets to see the crowning of his baby's head, he was amazed and in awe, as very gently the head was born. The midwife supported it patiently, waiting for it to rotate in line with the shoulders. With the next contraction, Charlotte gave a huge push, and the baby glided gently out. Sister Young wiped its face and talked to it as the first signs of life appeared. Limbs began to move, and a snuffling sound made way for a lusty cry. Henry realised he had been holding his breath as the baby had been a blue colour, but, with the first cry, the colour changed immediately to pink. The sister looked up at him.

"It's perfectly alright, Mr Lascelles. Give him a minute. He's just fine" it was then Henry realised he had a son!

Once the umbilical cord was cut and secured, she handed the baby to her colleague to check him over, dry, and wrap him warmly.

Charlotte had seemed to acknowledge the piercing cry of the newborn as she turned her head to the side, away from the baby. Sister delivered the placenta and cleared it away. It would be burnt in the fire in the kitchen. Charlotte was made clean and comfortable. The midwife was doing her work all the while talking to her as though she was listening and all was well. Charlotte was persuaded to have something to eat and drink, but then she slept. She wanted nothing to do with the baby.

Henry held his son in his arms, feeling immensely sad that Charlotte could not share such precious moments with him, and yet he was also swamped with love for the child. He would protect him and see to it that he would want for nothing.

The next few days passed in a hive of activity. Charlotte remained in bed, sedated for the most part.

She showed no interest in the baby and did not want it near her. Her breasts were bound to discourage lactation, and a wet nurse was found. The Midwives remained, with colleague relief, to support and monitor Charlotte through the early post-natal period. Dr Jaggers and The Prof were in consultation with Dr Greenstreet, who visited the house to assess Charlotte. He didn't want her sedated any more than was absolutely necessary, but as the sedation was withdrawn, her mental state deteriorated, and she again became wild and disruptive. She almost seemed like a different person from the beautiful, vibrant girl Henry had married. The baby was cared for mainly by the wet nurse, and Mrs Newton, the bottom drawer in the kitchen range, kept him warm and comfortable. Despite being born a month early, he was a good weight and took readily to feeds. Henry spent as much time with him as he could. Holding this perfect little being in his arms was what kept him grounded in those dreadful few days. Celia and Matthew were attentive and supportive, but nothing could relieve Henry of the feeling of failure he felt. Sitting with the baby in his arms by the range in the kitchen, he felt he had failed Charlotte as a husband and his newborn son as a father, needing others to help him care for his innocent child. The house was full of people, and Henry had little time to think, let alone grieve for a love he felt he had lost.

The Prof had arranged some leave for Henry, but decisions had to be made. Between Matthew and Dr Greenstreet, the decision to move Charlotte to Menston was taken completely out of Henry's hands.

In addition, the baby would go to Johnson's house, and a Nanny would be hired. Henry would return to work, and he would live at the Johnsons, and the little house would be closed up.

Henry was too physically and emotionally exhausted to argue.

Once Charlotte was settled in the mental hospital, the situation didn't improve. Henry was heartbroken when the hopes he had of recovery were dashed. The treatment currently available and advised was brutal. Electroconvulsive therapy (ECT) or lobotomy is when an instrument is passed into the frontal lobe of the head and agitated to induce behavioural and personality change.

Henry couldn't bear the thought of either. Although he knew Charlotte had had some ECT in the past, he wouldn't consent to it anymore, and he frankly forbade any talk of a lobotomy.

Henry visited as often as his work would allow, but she didn't respond to him other than with aggression. Charlotte became agitated, and he found the staff discouraging his visits. He felt helpless that it was his fault somehow. If only she hadn't become pregnant, perhaps things might have been different. But then he wouldn't have the beautiful little child as a consequence of their love, and he couldn't be regretful of that. Henry had to accept that he couldn't help her. She was lost to him.

The baby was named Peter Charles Matthew, after his Grandfathers.

The little boy very quickly became the hub of the Johnson household. In his despair, Henry had allowed the care of his child to be prioritised by others and had initially been glad of it, but by the time he was ready and able to resume his fatherly responsibilities, others had stepped into the breach. He reasoned with himself that Peter was happy and cared for. He was grateful for it, and he didn't feel he had the right to insist or to remove the child from the only security he had ever known.

Henry returned to work and buried himself in his own form of security. Operating, he kept up a punishing schedule. He slept in his office, ate, and bathed in the doctors' mess, only returning to the Johnsons infrequently to see Peter. There was little comfort or peace in his life at this time. Charlottes' family was very kind, but increasingly he felt like a lodger rather than part of the family. Something had to change.

Then Matthew threw him a lifeline. His friend, the Police Commissioner, was looking for a Police Surgeon in Leeds.

WAR MONGERING

Tilly was disturbed by all the talk she heard, both at the hospital and at home, from her brothers. She read the newspapers with increasing dread. Her brothers were beside themselves with excitement. But she didn't think it would be fun. Would it be a great adventure? Would it all be over by Christmas?

Tilly became increasingly irritated by all the bravado and martial rhetoric she was hearing. Dad thought it wouldn't come to that, or at least that's what he told her and Mum. The boys, it seemed, were itching for a fight. Philip had married his childhood sweetheart, Ellen, four years earlier, and they had two young children; Billy, who was three, and the baby, Rose, who was now one.

Tilly had thought Philip had more sense. Arthur worked as a farm hand locally and had recently married the farmer's daughter. They had a tied cottage on the farm, which Violet had soon had in tip-top shape. Tilly liked Violet enormously and had been honoured to be her bridesmaid at the wedding. Now she saw fear in the eyes of both of her sisters-in-law. Mum kept quiet, but Tilly knew she was just as fearful. Of the younger boys, Jack was now twenty-one, and Richard was just fourteen. Jack was apprenticed to the local builder, and Richard was still at school. Rich was the clever one, and Mum and Dad had almost burst with pride when he had gained a place at the Grammar School.

He was especially good with figures, and Tilly knew her parents had high hopes he would become an accountant once he matriculated. His initiative, ability, and talent with mental arithmetic had gained him a job in the newsagents. Delivering papers before school and totalling up the takings after school. Rich was canny with his money. Tilly knew he kept it in a tin under his bed.

Tilly hoped he had ambitions beyond accountancy. University even, but it was unheard of in their community, and the cost could be prohibitive. Tilly had been saving from her wages. She knew she had been lucky to achieve her dream. Maybe she could help Richard with his if the opportunity ever presented itself. She would talk to him. That might prove difficult, at first. She had to track him down and then extract information from him. Rich played his cards very close to his chest. Her youngest brother was not one to say much, but he took it all in.

The chatter around the family tea table that Saturday was all about war, and Tilly had had enough,

"You have no idea what you're talking about, Phil," she all but shouted.

"You wouldn't be so keen to go off and get injured if you saw what I see on a daily basis. Pain and fear, and disfigurement mostly. Do you want that, Phil?"

"Oh, don't be so soft, our Tilly. I don't plan on getting injured! I just think someone needs to teach these Huns a lesson, eh lads?"

"Oh, for goodness sake, Phil, you have a wife and children now. Grow up!"

She pushed back from the table and headed out to the backyard for some fresh air. Her Dad joined her, both of them leaning casually against the kitchen wall

"Don't take on so much love. It may not come to that"

"Really, Dad? I think that we both know that it will, especially if all the young men in this country are as stupidly fired up about it as that lot in there!" she replied, pointing a finger back towards the kitchen. William sighed.

"It's something new, love, they're excited, and it's something monumental in their young lives."

"Aren't you scared for them, Dad?" she pleaded.

"Of course I am, Tilly," he replied, "war is brutal. We both know that, but if it comes to it, it won't be of our making, and we can't allow our allies to be intimidated. Or where will it stop?"

Tilly found refuge in her father's arms. He kissed the top of her head and patted her back as he had done many times before when she had been in need of comfort as a child. The silence between them was without awkwardness. They were like spirits. She knew he was right, but it didn't make it any easier.

"How's young Henry anyway?" Will asked quite out of the blue

"You haven't mentioned him lately. Is everything alright?" and that was it. Tilly's tears flowed. Will held her close through the sobbing. When she began sniffing, he dug his handkerchief out of his pocket and handed it to her. It was large and red with white spots on it, and it smelled of him. She blew her nose and wiped her eyes. Some minutes passed, and it seemed as if time stood still.

"He's married, Dad. His wife is suffering from a mental illness, and he has a little boy who is cared for by his Grandparents."

There, she had said it. The moon was still in the sky, she continued to breathe in and out as she always had done, and the world had not come to an end. Will kept her in his embrace and again kissed the top of her head.

"I'm sorry to hear that, love," he said gently, and his heart broke for her. Several more minutes passed, he took a cigarette out of his pocket, lit it, and had a smoke with one arm still around her shoulders. No words were said. When he had finished, he dropped the tab on the floor, crushed it with his heel, stooped to pick it up, and flicked it over the back wall winking at her as he did it.

"Mum will kill me if she finds tab ends in our backyard," he said, smiling, and he turned back towards the kitchen, guiding Tilly gently with him.

War was declared on 4th August 1914. Tilly could hear the cheering and jubilation from the ward. At the end of her shift, she made her way back to the Nurses' residences via the hospital chapel. Tilly hadn't ever had great faith, but now suddenly, she felt the need for a higher being and comfort in His presence. She entered the small chapel reverently and took a seat at the back. The quiet stillness of the place, in the midst of the busy hospital, felt like a refuge. The tall stained-glass windows above the altar and the dark wood of the pews felt comforting, and she was aware of a sense of peace as she knelt to ask for God's protection for her family, for her brothers, and for Henry Lascelles, especially for Henry Lascelles. It had been six months since he had told her the truth, and she was still devastated. Tilly had done the only thing she could do and cut off all contact with him. She knew she had no choice, and to be fair to Henry, he had supported her decision by not contacting her further, which had made it marginally easier to try to get on with her life. She had to admit he had been a gentleman, but on reflection, it hadn't been easy at all, and it was only after she had severed all contact that she had realised how very much she loved him.

"Please, God, keep him safe," she prayed.

ISOLATION

After his split from Tilly, Henry again buried himself in work. He had no social life, and any time he did have, he spent in Sheffield with Peter at the Johnsons' house. The family discouraged him from visiting Charlotte, she barely acknowledged them anymore, and she had to be kept in a locked ward for her own safety and that of others. Henry felt guilty but allowed himself to be persuaded it was for the best.

Henry paid the fees for her care and sent regular hampers for her, which contained toiletries as well as foodstuffs he knew she liked and which might tempt her to eat. Occasionally he would write to her, but he never heard back. Her parents would update him on her condition and liaise with Dr Greenstreet, but he felt isolated and increasingly side-lined. Henry believed her parents had her well-being at heart, so he didn't contest it, and he didn't talk about it.

His own family also had contact with Peter, and he knew the child was wonderfully cared for and loved, just not by him. That rankled, and at times, he felt like going and just walking out with him..... But to what? To the care of a Nanny whilst his absent father worked all hours, exhausting himself deliberately, so he didn't have to dwell on his own disastrous domestic situation? No, Peter was the one good thing to come out of the relationship. He was better off where he was, even if it broke Henry's heart every time he had to leave him.

Tilly met Jane in town for afternoon tea at Rhymer and Schorers department store. She hadn't seen her friend for several weeks, but it made no difference to their close relationship. They just carried on where they had last left off. Jane was working in one of the Medical Wards, and when their time off coincided, they enjoyed a day out together in town or at the park with a picnic. Their friendship endured and blossomed. Jane had supported Tilly through the break-up of her relationship with Henry. She was a good listener, and she gave sound advice. Now she had sought Tilly out and had instigated this meeting. Jane seemed unusually excited, and Tilly was intrigued. They sat together in the elegant tea room of the department store, having divested themselves of their hats and coats. There seemed to be a new enhanced atmosphere in town today, thought Tilly. Placards displaying stark headlines. Men in uniform were much more prominent than ever before. There was definitely a build-up to something. Tilly felt uncomfortable about it, but she was determined not to spoil her afternoon out with Jane. They would talk about other things. The waitress took their order and disappeared towards the kitchen, all bustling in her black and white outfit with the frilly white cap.

Tilly was surprised when Jane leaned across the table and took her hand firmly.

"I've joined up, Tilly," she said, beaming. "Come with me. They are going to need good Nurses."

Tilly was speechless. She gazed at Jane in disbelief, wide-eyed and trying to take it in. Jane chattered on about "doing her bit," but Tilly was only half listening trying to regulate her thoughts about this as Jane was more animated than Tilly had ever known her to be.

"What do you mean, Jane?" was all she could manage.

"I've joined the Army, Tilly. Queen Alexandra's Imperial Military Nursing Service. I've handed in my notice at work, and I have to report to Aldershot by the end of next month. I need to do something to help Tilly, and it could be such a big adventure. Do come with me? It would be a shame to miss out, and besides, they say it will all be over by Christmas anyway."

Tilly was horrified. First, her three brothers had practically raced to the recruiting office to sign up, and now Jane! Dear sweet, kind, and sensible Jane!

The rest of the afternoon gave Tilly much room for thought. As they drank their tea, she listened to Jane enthuse about her new venture, but joining up herself never occurred to Tilly. She simply couldn't put her parents through it. Outwardly they were stoical, but Tilly knew how devastated they had been when their three eldest boys had practically fallen over each other to sign on the dotted line. Thank goodness Richard was still too young. He had, of course, felt very left out, but it would be a comfort to Mum to still have him at home.

Tilly made an effort to return home as often as she could to support her parents at such a difficult time. They began to knit socks and gloves and jumpers as they chatted to pass the time and be of use. Together with Ellen and Violet, they joked that they had a proper little cottage industry going. Philip, Arthur, and Jack had all joined the Leeds Pals division of the West Yorkshire Regiment together with many other local lads from the towns and villages. Lads they had been to school with, worked with, got drunk with, and even fought with! The camaraderie was huge, and all over the country, "Pals" battalions were being formed, encouraged by the recruiters. "Fight for your Pals," the posters said, and it hit a patriotic note. Uniforms were worn with pride, and they couldn't wait to get off and onto basic training. It would all be such a big adventure!

William advised calm at home, support, and practical help. He dissuaded Tilly's forthright views.

Alice and the sisters-in-law were uncharacteristically quiet, keeping busy with household tasks, housework, laundry, cooking, childcare, and the cottage industry of knitting and sewing. Aunt Nan and Meryl still visited whenever they were up in Yorkshire. The Wharton Grandparents were failing physically, and live-in nurses had to be engaged. Alice had offered her care but had been rejected. As old and infirm as she was, Adelaide still refused to be reconciled with her eldest daughter and would not even consider her offer of help.

Nan could willingly have murdered her there, and then she told Alice. But as sad as it made her, Alice was resigned, and not for a minute did she regret her decision to marry Will. They had a wonderful life together, had five healthy, wonderful children, and now are even grandparents themselves. No, Alice had no regrets, and she wouldn't dwell on what was not to be.

CHANGE COMES

Tilly had now been a Staff Nurse on Ward 4 for three years. She loved the work, which was varied and interesting, and not a day went by when she didn't thank the powers that be, and her parents, that she had a job she loved and control over her own life. Her personality and professionalism had won over her colleagues early on. She was respected and trusted by both the medical and nursing staff. Her organisational skills made her a favourite with the doctors who were anything but organised, and they recognised a good manager as well as a good Nurse. Always prepared for the ward rounds, she was willing to challenge decisions and even make suggestions, not something the doctors were used to, and some of them even found they liked it! Nurse Dobson was an asset.

Tilly had begun to feel that she needed more of a challenge and had started to think of what she might like to do next to expand her experience and learn new skills. Sister Riley had sensed this, she would be sad to see her move on. But the girl was going places, and she was not one to stand in her way.

Tilly quietly began to consider her options. She had always loved looking after the surgical patients in particular and had recently been approached by one of the consultant surgeons. An eminent medical man whom she had come to know professionally during her time on the ward. He was a crusty, old-fashioned gentleman, didn't suffer fools gladly, was very direct and could be rude, and thought little of upsetting the nurses if all was not exactly to his liking.

He was also arrogant, but he was very skilled at his job. He and Tilly had clashed for the first time during her first few months on Ward 4.

He had been behaving abominably during a large ward round. Showing off to the medical students at the expense of the nurses. On this particular occasion, he had forgotten that he had borrowed a set of patient notes the previous day and failed to return them. Tilly had assumed he would bring them with him and judging by the large stack of notes carried by his Registrar. Her assumption appeared to be correct. At the appropriate bedside, the elderly surgeon was spouting forth about the patient's diagnosis and treatment, holding out his hand to Tilly, expecting said notes to be placed there.

Tilly looked expectantly at the Registrar, who fumbled the whole pile to the floor in his anxiety.

The surgeon took one look and exploded, mostly at Tilly for not having produced the notes when requested. The whole ward fell silent, the nurses vanished, and the medical students physically shook. Tilly herself was shaken but refused to be treated in such an unjust and disrespectful manner. As all the nurses had by now disappeared to various bathrooms, Tilly suddenly terminated the ward round half way through. A barrage of verbal abuse erupted from the surgeon in a very ungentlemanly manner, and there was not a nurse to be seen who could take over.

Tilly turned on her heel, returned the notes trolley to the desk, and marched swiftly off the ward. She found refuge in the linen cupboard, and as she closed the door firmly behind her. Then she took several deep breaths. She heard the surgeon still shouting as he led the whole team away from the ward and down the stairs. Tilly doubted that would be an end to it, but she straightened her apron and cap, opened the linen room door, and returned to the ward to a round of applause.

The nurses were especially supportive of her and admired her stance, many of them had been treated in a similar manner, and it had been accepted. Tilly was determined then and there that it was not acceptable behaviour anymore. Not on her watch, things would have to change. She would speak to Sister Riley tomorrow.

Halfway through the drug round, Matron James appeared at the ward door. Tilly locked up the drug trolley, handed the keys to her junior colleague, and made her way toward the ward doors.

"Good Morning, Matron," she said

"Please come into the office," and Tilly held the door open for the older lady to pass.

Once in Sister's office with the door closed, she faced Matron James standing up straight with her hands clasped before her.

"I take it you know what this is about, Nurse Dobson?" Matron asked pleasantly enough

"Yes, Matron," replied Tilly, and Matron James sat down in the chair

"Let's have it then," she said, and Tilly divulged the facts of the incident, uncluttered by any visible emotion though inside she was seething.

Matron listened carefully. A veteran nurse much respected in the hospital, Matron James had pretty much seen it all. She was not unsympathetic and in no way condoning the behaviour of her medical colleague. If anything, she admired the feisty nurse and could see a time when the likes of Nurse Dobson would become more common. However, that time was not quite now.

"I will speak to Mr Lund about the notes, and you will apologise for abandoning the ward round and inconveniencing such a busy man," she said, and she stood up.

"I don't expect to hear that there has been any repeat of this scenario," she said as she reached the door. With her hand on the latch, she glanced back at Tilly, smiled, and winked. Then she was gone.

Tilly's fury dissipated immediately. That brief facial expression had transmitted understanding, empathy, and support all within moments. In her current fragile state, that meant a lot to Tilly.

She did apologise when the surgeon returned to resume the ward round. The missing notes had miraculously reappeared, and despite no outward sign of contrition, she had no further problems with Mr Lund. He was pleasant and businesslike and would even, on occasion, defer to Tilly's superior knowledge of nursing matters. Something he had only ever been known to do with Sister Riley.

Now she had been asked to join him and Sister Riley in her office quite out of the blue.

"Mr Lund thinks you have the makings of a theatre Sister Nurse Dobson" began Sister Riley almost before the door had been closed behind Tilly

"I don't want to lose you, but I have to admit, he's probably right."

Tilly was amazed and excited. She looked from one to the other, unsure of what to say.

"Cat got your tongue, nurse?" asked the Sister.

"Oh, no, Sister, I'm sorry, it's just so unexpected. I had only recently been thinking of a change, and now I really don't know what to say," replied Tilly.

"Well now, are you in favour of the idea?" asked the surgeon.

"The thing is, we need a new nurse on the team. Someone who is not going to be intimidated by the likes of me, someone who won't go all girly and faint at the first sight of blood, someone with a bit of backbone. Someone like you, Nurse Dobson. Do you want the job? If you don't say so now, there's plenty of others who would jump at the chance……" and he continued on until Tilly found herself smiling at him.

"Thank you, Mr Lund," she interrupted. "I would like the job very much, with Sister Riley's blessing, of course."

"Blessing be damned!" he continued "report to Sister Wright in theatres first thing Monday morning. Joy, arrange it, will you?" he held out his hand to Tilly, and she took it. He had a firm shake, and with that, he swept out of the room and down the stairs before she truly realised what had just happened.

Tilly was sorry to leave Ward 4, they gave her a grand send-off that weekend, and she realised the time was right. She needed to move on. She had learned an enormous amount from Joy Riley, skills she would transfer to whatever specialty she worked in.

Part of a good Ward Sister is to develop her staff and prepare them for the challenges ahead.

Tilly knew she was ready, and it was primarily due to Sister Riley's guidance, nurturing, and encouraging example. She would be forever grateful.

Tilly left the ward at the end of her final shift a little sad but mainly excited and floating on air. Her first instinct had been to share the news with Henry, but then reality checked in, and she knew that was no longer possible. She didn't even know where he was or if he even thought of her anymore.

Jane wrote regularly at first, and Tilly devoured her letters. She talked of the training camp at Aldershot, her fellow nurses, and the new uniform with which she had been issued. It all sounded very exciting, if rather military! Which made Tilly smile. Jane admitted to being a little homesick, but she was looking forward to beginning to nurse on the wards and hoped that one day soon, she would be posted overseas where she could really be of some use. For now, there was plenty of work in the home hospitals, and Jane would be kept very busy.

Tilly wrote back full of her own news about her new job. She found she liked theatre nursing, although some of the sisters were more than a little intimidating! Initially, she had found herself cleaning, restocking, and autoclaving. Tasks she had been more than proficient at when she worked at Dr Swanson's surgery, and she felt that if she never rolled another bandage, it would be too soon. But her dedication and hard work paid off, and her willingness to help, and especially her lack of moaning got her noticed. She began to be asked to "Scrub up" to assist the theatre sisters as they started to teach her about the instruments and the art of assisting in operations.

Tilly was a quick learner and soon began to identify the different instruments and recognise which were used for which operation and which were particular favourites of individual surgeons.

Her first operation as a primary scrub nurse was for an appendicectomy performed by a fairly junior doctor. She noticed his hands were shaking. His senior colleague also scrubbed up and stood slightly behind him, chatting with the anaesthetist. As nervous as she was herself, Tilly felt for the young doctor, and she caught his eye over the mask.

It's my first, too," she whispered as she handed him the scalpel.

"You'll be fine. We'll make a good team!" His eyes smiled back at her, and he was fine. The operation went well, and as they cleaned and dressed the wound, the young doctor thanked her very briefly, but it was enough. Tilly knew what it was like to be nervous and under pressure, and if she had helped him in any way, then she was glad of it. Tilly prospered in the surgical atmosphere in the theatre and noted that she was often as not allocated to Mr Lund's list. He had a reputation for throwing instruments and having violent outbursts amongst the theatre staff, so they were happy to allow Tilly to scrub for the old curmudgeon. Tilly's professional and efficient manner somehow calmed the old man. If he chose to believe that it was entirely down to him that this asset had been added to the team, then they weren't about to contradict him.

WAR AND REUNION

News came from home that her brothers were to be called up as part of the British Expeditionary force. They were jubilant! Tilly travelled home to support her parents, but she was scared and irritated at the same time. She tried to remain composed as she helped prepare them for deployment. Keeping Mum's spirits up was paramount. She was sad for Ellen and Vi, and she shared their anxieties. But mostly she felt for Mum, three sons off to war at the same time.

To live with the constant worry, uncertainty, and fear would be hard to bear. Tilly was determined to remain positive and as supportive as it was possible to be. She knew her Dad was just as worried, but in his usual male and Yorkshire way, he just didn't show it. William was the backbone of the family, very proud of his sons, and despite his fears, he recognised their need to go and the necessity to stand up for what was right. As a family, they all made the effort to travel to Malton to a photographic studio to have a photographic portrait taken. A memento, Tilly supposed, in case the worst happened.

They all made an effort to look cheerful, all but Mum, who looked as though she was about to be shot.

They said their goodbyes at Malton Station, but Tilly travelled with them to Leeds Railway Station to see them off with the rest of the "Pals" and the West Yorkshires. Tilly hugged each of her brothers, in turn silently praying for their protection and safe return. They hugged her back but distractedly, talking and beaming excitedly and looking around at the crowded station full of soldiers in uniform. They joshed each other and shouted greeting to other "Pals," then remembering to task her with looking after all at home and not to fret too much. They each promised to write, but she doubted it.

"Keep your heads down and don't do anything stupid," she advised amidst their laughter and larking about. All too soon, the train pulled in, and kit bags were retrieved and thrown onto the train.

"Stay out of trouble!" she shouted above the cacophony of noise and steam whistles as the train started to pull away.

"And come home safely," but her words were lost in the wind and the rain.

Tilly stood alone amidst a crowd of people on the station platform as the train disappeared into the distance, with tears streaming down her face. Slowly the bustle on the platform dissipated, and she pulled her handkerchief out of her pocket. Drying her eyes and blowing her nose. She took a deep breath. Life goes on. She would return to the hospital and write a letter home so Mum and Dad would know she had seen her brothers off safely. She would also go home on her next days off, something to look forward to.

By now, the platform had all but emptied, so she turned towards the stairwell to leave when a figure caught her eye. Standing quite still and looking at her was Henry Lascelles. Tilly caught her breath and found she was rooted to the spot. As handsome as ever and dressed in a dark overcoat and hat, Henry moved slowly toward her.

"Hello, Tilly," he said, smiling

"What are you doing here?" she asked

"The same as you I expect, my brother has just boarded the same train. He's been commissioned in the West Yorkshire Regiment."

Tilly stood stock still though she wanted nothing more than to be enveloped in his arms, and again the pain in her chest was palpable.

"Will you join me for a cup of tea, Tilly?" he asked pleasantly. Tilly smiled and nodded. They walked closely together without touching towards the station café. She felt an almost undeniable need to touch him, the power of which was almost overwhelming. As he opened the café door for her to pass through and put his hand gently on her back to guide her and she felt it almost burn through her clothing. Henry ordered two teas and a teacake each, and as they sat opposite each other waiting to be served, they drank each other in.

Henry reached across the table for her hand, and she gave it gloved as it was

"I hear you're the new star of the LGI's theatres," he said, and Tilly laughed.

"I don't know about that! More the scourge of a certain eminent surgeon!"

The teas arrived, and once the waitress had left, they fell quite naturally into conversation.

They spoke of her job, their families, the war, their brothers joining up, Jane having joined the QAIMNS, about Peter and even of Charlotte. Charlotte, it seemed, would never recover. The pregnancy had pushed her over the precipice into insanity. Puerperal psychosis, they called it, and Henry was being pressured to consent to her undergoing lobotomy, supposedly in an attempt to alter the progression. He didn't think he could do it. It was brutal, and there was no guarantee it wouldn't make her worse. Her parents felt it was worth the risk, but Henry had his doubts. Tilly felt his pain. She thought her heart would break for him. They had always been able to converse. It seemed so natural, even now, that he should confide in her in this way, even on so personal a matter.

"I'm so sorry, Henry," she said. "I wish there was something I could do to help you."

"Oh but you do my love, just to be able to confide in you helps so much. There are so few people I can speak to quite so frankly, and for that, I'm grateful."

He had called her "my love," and Tilly thought her heart might burst right out of her chest.

They moved on to more light-hearted subjects, and more tea was ordered and drunk.

Before they realised it, the little café was deserted but for them, and the waitress hovered, wanting to close up. Henry paid the bill, left a hefty tip, and followed Tilly out of the café back onto the platform. He tucked her arm through his, and they set off for the short walk back to the hospital.

Tilly didn't want it ever to end. As they passed the Civic Building with the hospital in sight, Henry guided her towards a bench, and they sat down together.

"There's something I need to tell you, Tilly," he said, and Tilly experienced an instant feeling of foreboding. He still had hold of her hand and half facing her, he began.

"I have also joined up. The Royal Army Medical Corps."

Tilly felt sick

"I have to report to Millbank in London next week."

Tilly felt as though the earth beneath her feet was shifting. They sat side by side in silence, still holding hands, and Tilly put her head on his shoulder. The streets were strangely quiet, and drizzle had just begun to fall.

"I can't bear it," she said so quietly he barely heard it.

"Yes, you can bear it!" he replied as he gently squeezed her hands

"You are strong, and whatever happens, you will be alright. You have your profession and your health, and you have your family. People rely on you. I rely on you."

"That's not fair," she said as she raised her head and looked up at him.

"I know it's not fair, but then life is not fair. I want to tell you how I feel about you and how things would be if circumstances were different, but I can't. We have to deal with the cards we are dealt, Tilly. One day you will meet someone else, and I hope he will give you everything you deserve. I have to let you go, and you have to let me. Help me do this, Tilly, please, help me to be strong?"

She knew he was right, as she had known it was right the last time they had parted. Today's meeting was not planned. If he had been standing at the other end of the platform, they might never have seen each other. They could so easily have been ships that pass in the night. She couldn't regret meeting him. She loved him with all her heart even though she was not at liberty to tell him so.

Somehow, she sensed that he knew.

"Will I see you before you leave for London?" she asked

"I don't think that is a very good idea. The train is leaving very early in the morning anyway. Don't come, Tilly. It might just be the undoing of me."

They stood up to leave, and she clasped him to her holding him around his waist with her cheek on his chest. It lasted only moments, but it spoke volumes.

"Kiss me goodbye? And then, Henry, I will do as you ask."

With that, he held her gently by the shoulders, and their mouths met. It was thrilling and so desperately sad at the same time. She kissed him back with all the love and tenderness she could not vocalise. This kiss will have to last me a lifetime she thought, so she didn't waste a second.

He walked her to the Nurses Home but didn't prolong it. He was conscious that they might be recognised, and he didn't want to compromise her in any way. He kissed her fingers briefly.

"Be happy, my love," he whispered, and then he was gone. Tilly returned to her room, collapsed on her bed, and cried and cried.

Tilly was kept busy in the operating theatre, But every spare minute she had, she thought about Henry. It was disturbing just how often he encroached on her thoughts. As the week went on, she found she was increasingly anxious. What if she never saw him again? What if he was killed? She found it difficult to settle, so at the earliest opportunity, she made her way down to the Railway Station to enquire about early trains to London. Apart from the milk train in the very early hours, the first scheduled departure was at six in the morning, but what day? He hadn't said.

Tilly hatched a plan with the help of the hospital switchboard operator. Nelly Morris was her name, and she had a soft spot for Tilly. Nelly's brother Tim had been a patient on Ward 4, and during his fairly prolonged stay, Tilly had allowed Nelly to visit him either before she went on duty or afterward. This had saved Nelly a great deal of time, and she had never forgotten Tilly's kindness. Nelly had the telephone number of the Police Surgeon's office, and she was only too glad to help when Tilly asked her. Nelly connected the number, and Tilly spoke to the duty officer. The surgeon was out of the office at present. Did she want to leave a message?

"Oh, perhaps you can help, Officer," Tilly began. "I am Mr Lascelles's sister, and I have stupidly mislaid his letter telling me of the time and day he is leaving, and I have a parcel to pass onto him from our mother. He will be so cross with me when he finds out, please can you tell me? Do you know?"

Tilly hoped she was convincing though she felt guilty at having to tell lies to a police officer!

"Hold the line Miss, and I'll see what I can do," came the reply, and several long minutes passed before the officer returned with the details she wanted

"Six O'clock tomorrow morning, Miss, and do give Mr Lascelles our Best Wishes. He's a fine gentleman, and he will be much missed around here. "

"Thank you so much, Officer. I certainly will, and thank you."

Tilly's shift the following morning began at seven thirty, so she was up early and down to the station well before time, waiting on the platform for the London-bound train. The station was already busy, and porters were moving goods and luggage around on trolleys and barrows. There were also a number of men in uniform, official looking with checklists. Tilly supposed they were dealing with the administration of troop movements. It was very cold, and she was so pleased she had put on her warmest overcoat. She huddled into it now and waited. She was nervous. He had told her not to come, and she was breaking her word. How would he react? She just knew that she had to come. She had to see him.

The platform started to fill up, and she was terrified she would miss him. The train pulled in, and a porter began unloading a luggage trolley into the guards- van in front of her. She saw her opportunity and took the initiative, asking if she could climb up onto it to get a better view. The porter smiled, shook his head, and helped her up. She scanned the platform, and there he was, just coming up the stairs from under the tunnel, suitcase in hand, talking to a young man at his side.

"Henry!" she shouted, waving madly and trying to get down from the luggage trolley. He heard her immediately, handed his suitcase to his companion, and headed quickly towards her, weaving and jostling with the crowds on the platform. She fell into his arms, and he was laughing and kissing her face.

"I'm sorry. I know I said I wouldn't, but I had to come!" she said, but she knew she was forgiven.

Henry twirled her around and hugged her tightly. By now, his young companion had caught up with them.

"John, this is Miss Matilda Dobson, Tilly, this is my brother John" he explained. John smiled at her and held out his hand.

"How do you do, Miss Dobson?" and they shook hands.

"I am well, thank you, and I am pleased to meet you," she said. "Please call me Tilly."

Her arm was still around Henry, savouring every minute she had with him.

"There's no need to wait, Johnny," said Henry.

"You get off home, and thanks for coming."

"I can see that!" laughed John as he hugged Henry briefly, handed over the suitcase, and shook his hand "stay safe, won't you?" and he bade farewell to them both, making his way towards the exit.

It no longer seemed a concern if they were seen. Henry and Tilly hugged each other tightly, kissing and both speaking at once in an effort to say what had to be said before it was too late. All too soon, a whistle was blown, and the soldiers began to embark on the train. Henry left it as long as he dared before boarding, throwing his suitcase in, and returning to lean out of the window. Tilly held on to him for as long as she could, looking up at him.

"I love you! I love you!" she cried as the train began to pull away

"Oh, God, Tilly! I love you too! Write to me. I'll send you my address," Henry shouted, but he was moving away quickly now and waving wildly.

"I will!" Tilly mouthed to him, and she ran alongside the train to the end of the platform blowing kisses until she could see him no longer.

She was elated and heartbroken, and fearful all at the same time. Immediately she felt she had done the right thing and wiped tears from her eyes. She set off at a brisk pace back to the hospital for the start of her shift with a new spring in her step.

Henry was as good as his word, and a letter arrived within days enclosing his address. Tilly wrote extensively to him, pouring out all she had never felt able to before. The words flowed off the pages. It was as if she were speaking to him, and it gave her a deep sense of peace. His letters were equally long and full of his experiences. He told her about Millbank and starting Officer Training, his fellow Officers, Life in the mess, and how he had to adapt to the Army's way of doing things. He wrote lightly and with humour, he made it sound fun, and he told her of the camaraderie as it developed. The talks and lectures and how he was learning all manner of things that would be useful to him in the field. He expected to be deployed to a field hospital following basic training anytime in the next few weeks. Tilly worried about him, she hated the thought of him being "In the field" and in danger, but she kept the tone of her letters light and chatty. She was sharing incidents she thought would amuse him and regaling stories about her colleagues she thought would make him laugh.

Tilly kept the rekindling of the relationship strictly to herself. She couldn't bear the disapproval or criticism she might expect from her parents. Deep down, she felt guilty, but she buried it.

She would deal with that another day.

2016

The shaking has returned, at times worse than it was before, more violent. His disappointment is sad to witness, and I fear depression may set in. It's difficult being so far away, and I'm sure he doesn't tell me the whole story. We meet up in Sheffield, he gets the train, and I drive the hundred or so miles north. I collect him from the station, and we go together to his appointments. Mostly we see the Parkinson's' Specialist Nurse, and she tries again to adjust the electrodes. Initially, there seems to be an improvement, but it just doesn't last. He has had no success with the patient-controlled device. A CT scan is performed, and we wait to see the Neurosurgeon. However little it may be, at least there is hope. One hundred years ago, patients with neurological conditions would have had practically no hope. Our understanding has increased, and blessedly compassion has also increased.

My mind flitters backward to dwell on battle-injured soldiers for whom there was no help. "Battle Shock," or Post-traumatic Stress Disorder (PTSD) as we now know it, was not initially recognised, and once it was, it was not understood. Some interpreted the effects as cowardice, and as a result, a great injustice was perpetrated when some of these damaged young men, some only boys, were shot. The grief experienced by their families is difficult to comprehend. To offer up your child "For the King and the Country" only to have him shot by his own side is difficult to comprehend. The death of a father, son, brother, or husband in battle would be a grief beyond understanding, but to lose that person to a firing squad of his own comrades is a whole different level of grief. Those families must never have recovered. Only when posthumous pardons were eventually granted by the British Government could any kind of healing begin, much too late, of course, for those immediately affected.

DECISION

Tilly woke in the night in a hot sweat. She felt as if she was suffocating. It took only moments to realise where she was, so she sat up quickly and swung her legs over the side of the bed. Her heartbeat began to return to normal as she regulated her breathing. She reached for her shawl as it was cold in the early hours of the morning. Then it occurred to her.

"What on earth are you doing, Tilly Dobson? Four of the men you love most in the world are about to be sent out to France, and you are of no use to them at all sitting here! You have skills that will be needed in France. You can be useful out there, so swallow your pride, accept that it is happening, and volunteer!"

Once she had made the decision, she couldn't wait to get on with it! How she was going to get through the rest of the night, she had no idea! As soon as she could, she rose early, washed and dressed, made her bed, tidied her room, and, after breakfast, made her way along the corridor to Matron's Office.

Explaining her decision to her parents was easier than she expected. She knew her Father would support her, but she hadn't expected her mother's reaction to being so understanding. Alice had been expecting it. She had braced herself for the day Tilly would come and say she wanted to be of service and needed to join the ranks of the Nurses volunteering. Now the day had arrived, and Alice felt remarkably calm and proud of her daughter,

"If I were twenty years younger with your knowledge and nursing skills, I would be doing the exact same thing," she said as she hugged Tilly to her.

"It doesn't mean I like it, though!" and she smiled briefly. Despite her outward appearance of support and joviality inside, she was crying. Tilly must never know. Her focus must be on her job and not worrying about her parents at home.

Tilly once again had a cause to thank the good Lord above for the blessing of her family as they rallied around her in the weeks leading up to her departure. Gathering together what she believed she would need in her quest to work at a field hospital in France. Her precious fob watch and engraved scissors, so kindly given to her by the Swansons, a small torch, Dad had found in the shed, sturdy shoes and boots, linens, woolens, hats, and gloves. The cottage industry had been working overtime. She was given writing paper and pencils by Aunt Nan and a box Brownie camera to record some visual memories of her experience. Nan also gave her access to her very own savings account. Tilly was amazed to learn that Aunt Nan had set up savings accounts for all of her nephews and niece to be accessed on their twenty-fifth birthdays. Tilly was still only twenty-four but was ever-practical. Nan had made the exception. She would not have her niece travelling to foreign parts without the security of accessible finances. For once in her life, Tilly was speechless as she hugged Nan and Meryl with the knowledge that such generosity gave her a degree of freedom and independence she had only ever dreamed of.

Leaving the security of Leeds General Infirmary after six years was more of a wrench than Tilly had expected. The staff held a tea party for her at the end of her last working day. They had clubbed together to buy her a very beautiful silver belt buckle to adorn her first sister's belt. She knew she would treasure it forever.

Following the outbreak of war in August 1914, The British Red Cross formed the Joint War Committee with The Order of St John. The two organisations worked together to pool resources and fundraising activities. The committee provided the organisation of nursing staff in the United Kingdom and abroad in support of the Military forces. Qualified nurses were licensed professionals who had spent three years in training, in a hospital with a recognised school of nursing. Voluntary nurses – known as VADs (Voluntary Aid Detachment), were untrained nurses who willingly gave their time to help care for the wounded. Even later on in the war, VADs were not generally trusted with the work of their trained colleagues, except in emergencies and when no other option was available. Neither were they initially welcomed nor treated well by the trained nurses, though this did change as their experience and abilities became recognised. As the war progressed, VADs became very skilled and increasingly relied upon as the number of badly wounded men mounted. When the

Joint War Committee took control of the VADs and the trained nurses, the two departments came under the direct control of Dame Sarah Swift. Dame Sarah had been Matron of Guys Hospital in London.

From the outset of the war, trained nurses were sent abroad at short notice under the banner of the Red Cross. Initially, Tilly had intended to join her friend Jane and had applied to the QAIMNS, but she had been rejected for being too young. At twenty- four Tilly was underage as they only accepted single women from the age of twenty- five. After her initial disappointment and having decided she couldn't wait until her next birthday, Tilly began to realise that being part of the Red Cross organisation would actually suit her better. Still strict, of course, The Red Cross was less regimented and militaristic. Being able to dispense with the military training Tilly was pleased to be able to concentrate her efforts on actual nursing. Over two thousand women offered their services in 1914 alone.

The selection was before a Selection Board, once the application had been submitted. References were sought after the interviewing process. Tilly found there were a number of rules to be adhered to when applying for a full-time nursing position. Naturally, she had to produce her Certificate of three years of training and a recommendation from her last Matron. Accepted candidates would be subject to vaccination against diseases such as typhoid.

Candidates were required to sign an agreement to serve in a home hospital for a period of six months at a salary of one guinea a week. Insurance, outdoor uniform, travelling expenses from London, and board and lodging were provided. Laundry costs were 2 shillings and sixpence a week, and lodgings at a suitable hostel were provided between engagements. Indoor uniforms had to be provided by the nurse herself. A permit was obtained from the War Office for the cloth to be purchased, and an application was made to the Controller of Woollen and textile fabrics in Bradford, Yorkshire.

The annual holiday allowance was two weeks per year, exclusive of days spent travelling and sick leave.

Tilly's experience as a surgical and theatre nurse, together with excellent references, made her acceptance to the ranks of the British Red Cross assured. She expected to be posted to a home hospital, to begin with, and began to collect the items specified once the comprehensive list arrived in the post.

One calico or canvas bag – six feet four inches by three feet – to be filled with straw at camp

One pillow or pillow bag

Two blankets

One mackintosh rug

One enamel wash basin and a piece of soap

Two towels, one large enough for bathing

One duster

One knife, fork, and spoon

One enamel cup and saucer

Two enamel plates

Two tea cloths

One brush for boots

A bicycle lamp or a candle lantern

The requirement for a duster caused Tilly some amusement, and she was further amused by the suggestion that she may wish to bring with her "small luxury items," such as a deckchair!

The items were duly sourced and collected in preparation for her departure. Her Father had provided a large tin trunk on which he had painted her name in bold capitals. Tilly decided that she could probably dispense with the deckchair! She also decided against taking her silver belt buckle. Her fear of losing it outweighs the pride she would have felt in wearing it.

Christmas of 1914 was spent with her family. Her brothers were also granted a few days' embarkations leave as they were expected to be mobilised overseas in the early weeks of the New Year. It was an anxious time, but everyone was determined to put their concerns aside and enjoy the time they had together.

Christmas morning was spent opening presents after attending morning service. Alice prepared Christmas dinner to be eaten later in the afternoon. A special treat of roast goose with all the trimmings followed by Christmas pudding and brandy sauce. Nan and Meryl joined them during the course of the afternoon together with their Dobson grandparents. The house was stuffed to the gunnels, emergency chairs had to be purloined, and the tables were set together, beautifully decorated by Ellen and Violet. The children were beside themselves with excitement as fifteen people prepared to sit down to dinner. The noise level escalated until suddenly, there was an enormous crashing sound coming from the kitchen. The noise ceased instantly, no one moved for a split second, and then a loud stream of profanity emanated from the kitchen,

"Damn, and blast the flaming, sodding thing!"

In all their lives, they had never heard their mother swear, and the whole family looked towards the kitchen wide-eyed and shocked. Then, as one, they looked at William. The whole incident could only have been a minute or two, but it seemed longer. William sat quite still, his face fixed. The kitchen door then burst open, and Alice stood in the opening, wiping her hands on her apron, hot and flustered and completely out of character, shouted.

"I could be dead in there for all the help I'm getting!"

William took the pipe out of his mouth and calmly looked at her.

"Nay lass," he said perfectly deadpan, "We knew you weren't dead!" and the house erupted into laughter. Alice was ushered out of the kitchen, seated, and handed a glass of sherry. The girls completed the assembling of the vegetables into dishes, gravy stirred, and large fluffy Yorkshire puddings lifted out of the oven. William rose as the goose arrived on the meat platter before him, steaming hot and smelling like heaven. Grace was said, and once the bird was carved, they all settled down to address themselves to a very fine home-cooked Christmas dinner. The banter around the table soon resumed, and the love of the family, the warmth, and comfort of all being together would long remain in the memories of all present.

Later that night, after everyone had gone home or up to bed, Tilly sat before the dying embers of the fire, lit a candle, wrapped her warm shawl around her shoulders, and wrote to Henry. He, too, had been granted leave to visit his infant son over the festive period. She knew he was in Sheffield and had planned to take Peter to Leeds to visit his own parents. Like Tilly, he was expecting a posting any time soon, and she had no expectation of meeting up with him. Tilly wrote in her usual cheery style, telling him about her own Christmas, amusing stories of the brothers' antics, and her own preparations for joining the Red Cross in the New Year. There were times when she questioned her wisdom in maintaining contact with him. Her case was hopeless. She knew it, and how could she ever move on? But she loved him, and they were both the victims of circumstance. It wasn't his fault any more than hers, and who knew what would happen to any of them in such uncertain times? Her letters gave him hope, he said and cheered him up. He couldn't imagine not having them to look forward to any more than she could, and that was good enough for now.

FRANCE 1916

Winter had truly set in at the Base hospital, and keeping the men warm and comfortable became a daily more difficult task. Fuel wasn't short but sometimes difficult to access, and they burned whatever they could find in the wards' pot-bellied stoves. Blankets were piled onto the beds, and trying to block out draughts at the windows and doors was a priority. The men were stabilised and moved on as quickly as it was possible to process them through the system. Many had started their journey at the very beginning when they had been scooped off the battlefield straight into the Regimental Aid Post (RAP). Those who could get there under their own steam or carried and helped by others did so, but many relied on the services of the stretcher-bearers. At the RAP, the wounded would quickly be assessed by the sole Medical Officer, patched up, and sent either back to his unit or labelled and passed back down the line to the Advanced Dressing Station (ADS). The RAP had no holding capacity other than a couple of stretcher cots for very short-term attention. In battle, the casualties were transported directly to the ADS. However, necessity dictated the use of Collecting Posts (CPs) and Relay Posts (RPs) to avoid congestion. Teams of Stretcher Bearers from the Royal Army Medical Corps (RAMC) were strung out over miles of ground impassable by motor or horse transport, and they shuttled the wounded between posts passing them on back "down the line" to the next team. A "carry" could be anything up to four miles over the muddy and shell-pocked ground, either in trenches or above ground. Equipment at these posts was the same basic issue as at the RAPs. Anti-tetanus serum, assorted bandages, dressings, sulphur and boric ointments, cotton wool, blankets, and hampers containing such medical comforts as Brandy, cocoa, Bovril, and biscuits.

In a textbook situation, the ADS would be sited about four hundred yards behind the RAPs. It would be in tents where necessary but preferably in school buildings or large houses, the main dressing stations sited roughly a mile further back still. In the Great War, this was seldom the norm.

The Field Ambulance (FA) was the most forward of the RAMC units and the first line of documentation. There was one FA attached to every Brigade. In action, two of these were forward, and one held in the rear. When the Division was out of the line, the FAs were allocated special tasks such as Scabies Centres. For other ailments there was a Divisional Rest Centre (DRS) or a bath unit. If the latter, they were usually sited in a brewery where up to fifty men could be bathed at one time in the large vats. Local women would be employed to launder and repair clothing.

The Casualty Clearing Stations (CCS) were to facilitate the movements of casualties from the battlefield back to the Base Hospitals. These were large units holding a minimum of fifty beds and one hundred and fifty stretchers in order that they could treat a maximum of two hundred sick and wounded at any one time. The CCS were usually situated about twenty kilometres behind the front lines, roughly mid-way between the front line and the base area, and ideally about five hundred yards from a main railway line or waterway system. Transportation to a CCS would have been via motorised or horse-drawn ambulances. Here the wounded could receive the life-saving surgery they needed and encounter Nurses for the first time, but treatment was still only limited. CCS would usually be grouped in twos or threes and would work in a relay. One would be closed to incoming wounded whilst treating the casualties and readying them for evacuation by train, barge, or ambulance to one of the Base Hospitals further back in the line towards the coast. Another CCS would be empty and ready to receive new casualties from the next encounter with the enemy. A third CCS would be treating the sick but ready to evacuate in order to receive battle casualties in an emergency. Motor Ambulance convoys attached to the CCS would collect the wounded from further down the line. Mobile X-Ray units served the British Expeditionary Forces during the Great War and would be sent to assist the CCS during the great battles.

The holding capacity was about four weeks in order for men to be returned to their units or to be transferred back to a Base Hospital. The seriousness of many wounds challenged the facilities of the CCS, and as a result, their positions are marked today by large Military Cemeteries. The General Hospitals were located in Base Areas such as Etaples, Boulogne, Rouen, Havre, Paris, and Le Plage. Ideally, they also needed to be located near railheads or waterways to facilitate the movement of casualties onto the Ports. Hotels, large houses, and Casinos were requisitioned, but other hospitals were constructed on open ground and consisted of hutted and tented accommodations. Many of the General Hospitals were voluntary hospitals supplied by the British Red Cross and St Johns combined organisation and also some by the titled Ladies of Great Britain.

The holding capacity of these hospitals was such that a patient could remain until fit to return to his unit or sent across the channel by Hospital ship for more specialised medical attention or discharge from the forces.

A new and odious type of warfare was first used on the 22nd of April 1915 at three o'clock in the afternoon. Chlorine gas was released by the German Forces in the Ypres sector. Nothing like it had ever been used before, and the effects were devastating. The men affected died slowly of asphyxiation, drowning in their own secretions despite every effort to help and comfort them. There was no defence, and by the end of the month, over twelve thousand Officers and men had been admitted to the field ambulances of the Twenty-Seventh Division alone. The immediate response remedy had been to urinate over a cloth or handkerchief and to hold it over the nose and mouth. Emergency masks were quickly made up using cloth and women's veiling to cover pads of horsehair and cotton waste soaked in hypo sulphate of soda. Ninety-eight thousand of these masks were sent to the front line. Buckets of a mixture of hypo sulphate, water, soda, and glycerine were placed in the trenches to renew the effectiveness of the pads. The medical services of the 1st and 2nd Armies, together with women of the locality, were employed in the construction of these masks. Two years later, a further horror was visited on the allied troops when Mustard Gas was released, causing a twelve-hour delayed effect which then began to rot the body from both within and without, thereby causing a prolonged and very painful death four to five weeks later. Lachrymatory gases cause blindness.

Chlorine gas had been a horrifying introduction to warfare nursing for Tilly, the gasses could be embedded in the men's clothing, and this posed a risk to the staff removing them. Several of the orderlies had been overcome in this way in the initial period. The drivers and stretcher-bearers had reported gas hanging around in potholes and sunken roads for weeks after the attack.

Tilly worried desperately about her brothers. She constantly asked if her patients had any news of The West Yorkshires, but no one did. Henry, she knew, was safe in England at this stage, yet to be posted abroad. Tilly's letters home left out the graphic detail of the injuries, and she concentrated more on the men's recovery and camaraderie and their morale-boosting initiatives. Her parents could do without any additional worry.

The first Christmas away from home approached. The Nurses made every effort to decorate the wards as best they could, saving treats sent by their families in order to gift a little something to their patients. Spare time was scarce, but they used it well. Quiet moments saw them making paper hats and bunting out of whatever was available to make the wards more festive. The Padre was keen to form a choir to sing Christmas Carols to the men on Christmas Eve. Tilly willingly volunteered along with doctors and fellow Nurses, orderlies, stretcher-bearers, and cooks. If anyone showed even a half-decent singing voice, they were immediately commandeered into the choir. Tilly found it was often the simple things that meant the most to the injured men. As they gathered together that Christmas Eve, each singer holding a lighted candle and the Nurses wrapped warmly in their winter capes singing old and much-loved Carols to the men. There was a tear in many an eye. The singing might have been less than perfect, but Tilly knew she would never forget that night, and the response of the men on the wards was rapturous. The comfort of familiarity, a kind word, a small gift, and a decent meal provided the patients with a welcome respite for a short while.

The turnover of patients was steady at first, and the routine of cleaning, preparing, making up beds, filling them with injured, nursing duties, and moving the men on became a familiar pattern. Tilly's hard work, compassion, and nursing skills did not go unnoticed. Word began to infiltrate the hospital via the wounded men. There was to be a "big push," and it became increasingly obvious that plans were being made in response. Extra supplies were requisitioned and the staff were deployed. Matron called Tilly to her office. After the usual formalities of greeting and polite enquiry about a family, she unusually asked Tilly to sit down.

"For someone who has been with us for only a short time, Nurse Dobson, you have impressed me." Tilly was about to open her mouth to thank Matron but thought better of it as Matron's hand came up to stop any dialogue.

"I like your no-nonsense manner and calmness under stress, and I would like you to consider a move to a Casualty Clearing Station nearer the Front."

Tilly now found she was unable to open her mouth to speak. All her secretions had dried up.

"I'm giving you the option Nurse because of your age and Red Cross appointment. My Army Nurses wouldn't have that luxury! I believe you would be an asset, and I'm sure I have no need to tell you that very soon, every Nurse will be needed. Some of us will be pushed to our limits, but I believe you have what it takes, Nurse Dobson. And I will be recommending you for a posting. Unless you decline, of course? I will need to know by tomorrow."

Tilly could barely contain herself. Casualty Clearing Stations were as near as Nurses got to the front line. Her apprehension was quickly overridden by excitement, and she suddenly found her tongue untied despite a dry mouth.

"I can let you know now, Matron. I would be honoured to go on your recommendation."

"Excellent!" replied the older woman, and she stood and held out her hand, which Tilly shook firmly. How she managed to return to her accommodation, she was never quite sure. Within forty eight hours, Tilly had packed up her trunk, dressed in her outdoor uniform, and presented herself at the train station. It was milling with troops in transit, and tellingly wounded soldiers waited patiently to be moved further back down the line, hoping for repatriation.

CAPTAIN LASCELLES

Henry Lascelles had been promoted to Captain in the RAMC by the time he received his posting papers in August of 1915. He had now been at the CCS for four months. Winter had set in, which had, as he discovered, its own challenges! The ground was iron hard and made digging graves especially challenging.

"Best not lose anymore, Sir," commented a corporal. "Can't get 'em in the ground!"

It was frustrating to be losing men at all, as most at this stage were dying of disease rather than injuries sustained in battle. Henry was sure this was just the beginning , and had he allowed it, the contemplation of what was to come would have kept him awake at night. The days were busy, and he found that he was revisiting some of the doctoring skills he hadn't used since his surgical career took off. He enjoyed the company of the men and was gratified to find he had lost none of his diagnostic ability. The pompousness of some of his Medical colleagues irritated him, and "Army Regulations" struck him as ridiculous on occasion, but generally, he felt of use, and the heavy workload prevented him from maudlin on his disastrous personal life. It was nighttime as he lay in his cot bed when he felt most alone and worried about what lay ahead, not for him necessarily but for those he loved. He read and re-read Tilly's letters, and despite having read them countless times before, she could still make him laugh. She had such an amusing turn of phrase and was quite irreverent about some of her senior Nursing colleagues. She often caused him to laugh out loud. Goodness, how he missed her, and he missed Peter too. His Mother and Celia Johnson wrote regularly and had even included a formal photograph of Peter posing proudly in a sailor suit, obviously taken at a local photographer's. A beautiful boy, now two years old and practically orphaned, thought Henry, even though both of his parents lived.

EN ROUTE

The morning of Tilly's departure for the Casualty Clearing Station arrived bright but cold, and she was glad of her robust outdoor uniform and sturdy leather button-up boots. She wore as much clothing as she could comfortably conceal beneath her uniform, and the rest of her belongings were packed neatly into her tin trunk. Each time she packed the trunk, she thought of her Dad and his meticulous lettering of her name across the top. The memory caused her a moment of homesickness, but it soon passed as Private Riley, one of the ward orderlies, arrived to carry her trunk down to the transport, ferrying her to the rail head.

"We'll miss you, Sister, no mistake," he said by way of conversation. "Been a ray of sunshine around these parts these past months you have," he continued as they reached the motorised ambulance.

"Good Luck Miss" they shook hands briefly, he saluted her, and he was gone.

Tilly was touched. She reflected on her time at the hospital as the ambulance bounced over the rough roads trying to avoid potholes. It had been hard at first. Leaving all that had been familiar to her and" bunking up" with other Nurses in a similar situation had actually been the breakthrough for her. Once they realised they were all in the same boat, so to speak, they soon found common ground. Nurses the world over are a similar breed. It was interesting to discover where each had come from, where they had trained, and what experiences they had each had. A sense of humour, sometimes ill-placed, had caused much laughter and broken the ice. On the whole, Tilly had to admit she had had a positive, even enjoyable time, and she would miss her colleagues. The work had been hard and challenging. Dealing with injury and disfigurement in such young men was heartbreaking. She couldn't help but think of her brothers when nursing the men, and she hoped avidly that if ever they were in a similar situation to her patients, the Nurse looking after them would care for them as she cared for her patients. Their needs were often complex, and it was all Tilly could do to keep on top of it. Not only the physical care and practicalities of wound dressing and cleanliness to avoid festering the wounds but the emotional needs of young men badly injured and dying. Some days Tilly felt completely and emotionally drained. She knew she was not alone in this, and in the rare periods of free time, they had, the Nurses naturally shared experiences and supported each other. Tilly knew she had a lot to learn, and she absorbed every different experience, quietly questioning the doctors and senior nursing staff. She watched older nurses with more experience minister to the men, and though there were many different ways to approach a similar problem. She would quietly squirrel away, for future reference, the qualities and practices she admired most. Not all the practice was good, this had been glaringly obvious even in her civilian days, but that also provided a learning experience, and subtle ways could be found to bring such practices to the attention of her superiors. Tilly knew corners sometimes had to be cut, but there was a way of doing it which didn't inconvenience or disadvantage the patient. Once she realised this, she knew she was learning. She was also learning to be resourceful and inventive in the times of greatest difficulty when the pressures of supplies failed and physical tiredness set in. Realising she did have the ability to cope was a huge morale boost for her, and the whole experience of military nursing made her feel useful and relevant.

The jolting of the ambulance suddenly ground to a halt, and the back doors were swung open for disembarkation. The driver held out a hand to her to help her down. Gladly she took it, and along with her fellow travellers they made their way to the station platform. It was milling with troops in transit, and many wounded soldiers waited patiently to be moved further down the line, undoubtedly praying for repatriation. Some were on stretchers, some were "walking wounded," bandaged and on crutches, and others had no visible signs of injury other than haunted looks on their faces. Tired, desperately tired, and sad, such as Tilly had never before witnessed. Nurses and orderlies were attending them as best they could as they waited patiently to be moved on. The care was, by necessity limited, to providing drinks, cigarettes, and a kind word. The men didn't seem to mind. They were only too happy to be out of the action and the horrors of battle. The respite was in short supply at the Front.

Tilly was constantly humbled by the bravery of the wounded. She had witnessed it in the hospital when horrifying wounds had been cleaned and dressed with very little in the form of pain relief. The men seemed to regard any demonstration of distress as a weakness and seemed determined not to succumb in front of the Nurses or their fellow patients, as there was only a limited amount of privacy. The gritting of teeth and bearing it tore at Tilly's soul. Some of the wounded were little more than boys, and she held their hands, mopped their brows, and gave whatever words of comfort she could during the torture. Even more heartbreaking was to see the dread on their faces the following day as the Sister, or sometimes the Doctor appeared again with the dressing trolley. Each man resigned and waited his turn. Very little pain relief was available, aspirin was hardly adequate, and morphine was used only in the worst cases. Occasionally the case warranted anaesthesia with chloroform, but this was not something that could be done daily. Tilly realised quite early on that some of the men were dying of shock, and Tilly, too, dreaded the wound dressings but only because of her compassion for her patients. She learned to be thorough but as quick as she could safely be to minimise the suffering. Once she had developed her own technique, she had to admit she found it interesting. Once she had overcome her natural distaste and assault on her olfactory senses, usually caused by gas gangrene, she found she was volunteering to dress the worst wounds herself as gently as was possible. During these times, she would strike up a conversation with the patient, asking them where they came from and telling her about their homes and families. Nothing like gas gangrene had ever been seen before the battles that opened the horrors of the war in Flanders and Northern France. Modern warfare ballistics carried fragments of clothing into the wounds .The heavily manured soil of the region produced an ideal environment for the soil-based bacteria to flourish, producing gas and causing the wounds to balloon up with gasses. The smell was indescribable, and the men died like flies as there was no defence. No antibiotics and no reliable disinfectants. The surgeons cut away as much of the infected tissue as they dared, amputating limbs in an effort to stop the spread, but it still spread like wildfire, and the men died from the toxic effects of the products of the bacteria. Getting the men to medical facilities as fast as possible became essential in trying to combat it.

This was easier said than done as the roads were at times impassable and the weather contributed heavily to deep mud, the transport was unreliable, and the teams of field ambulances ferrying the men backward down the line of evacuation were often impeded by the weather and the craters resulting from heavy bombardment. Shortage of staff and sheer exhaustion as the casualties mounted.

Quite naturally, Tilly began to do what she could to help the patients on the Station Platform as she waited with them for her train to arrive. She was conscious that she would be going in one direction as they were going in another, and for a moment, she experienced a fleeting feeling of apprehension. The nurse, already working on the platform, directed her to the canteens of water, and she began to help the men, who were unable to help themselves, to have a drink. She lit cigarettes and held hands, wishing them well, enquiring where they were bound for, and comforting those most in need. One of these was a young soldier with an abdominal wound heavily bandaged and lying very still on his stretcher. His face was deathly pale, but his eyes were alert and followed the activity going on around him. Tilly knelt by his side as she helped him to sip water. Not something recommended with an abdominal wound, but all could see it would make no difference, and allowing him to die of thirst would be a great unkindness.

"Would you like a cigarette?" she offered, smiling at him.

"No thanks, nurse, they're bad for you, me Mam says," he replied, and tears welled up in his blue eyes.

"Am I going to make it, nurse?" he asked, searching her face. "Will I make it back to me, Mam?"

Tilly swallowed hard and smiled at him. She held his hand and discreetly wiped his tears with her clean white handkerchief.

"Well, of course, you will," she said cheerfully. "What sort of talk is that?"

"Only she'll be ever so cross with me. She told me not to go. I'm not old enough, really, but I didn't want to miss out. I wish I'd heeded her now."

He lifted Tilly's hand to his face and openly wept. The train whistle blew just then, heralding the arrival of the ambulance train, giving Tilly just enough time to compose herself. "Come on now, love," she said to him, trying to rally his spirits.

"Here's your ticket home!" and she stayed with him until he was boarded. As she was about to leave him in the care of another, she had a thought.

"Don't worry about your Mum," she reassured him. "She'll be so relieved to have you home she won't even remember to be cross!" she smiled and waved as she stepped back down onto the platform acknowledging his smile and raising a hand in farewell.

Her own train arrived within the hour. Once she had attended to the loading of her trunk, Tilly found a seat by the window and settled down for the long slow journey. She hadn't even asked him his name, but she found herself praying for him and for his Mum, for she feared that, like many others, his Mum could be receiving a telegram that would bring an end to all hope. She prayed that her own Mum would never receive such a telegram, but she knew that the odds were high that she could. "Please, God, keep the boys safe."

The train trundled along as Tilly dozed, wrapped in her travelling cloak, and she woke suddenly with her cheek against the cold window. The clickety-clack of wheels on rails had lulled her to sleep. Falling asleep at the drop of a hat was a talent she had developed recently. Many Nurses could, she discovered, and to be perfectly honest, it was a Godsend. A necessity even, and she thought of the Stationary Hospital on the cliff tops where she had so recently been, what she had learned, and how she had adapted. She thought of the staff with whom she had worked, how she had come to like them and even love some of them. Leaving was hard but necessary, and she remembered fondly the huts in which they had nursed under difficult conditions. The Voluntary Aid Detachment (VAD) untrained nurses Tilly had come to know had become her friends. She had no time for the pettiness of some of her "Sister" colleagues taking umbrage at the men calling them "Nurse" or even "Sister." The men didn't differentiate, a Nurse was a Nurse, and they were glad of them all, whatever they were called.

It had been quite the issue when Tilly had first arrived at the Base hospital. But once the VADs had begun to prove their worth, most of the Nursing Sisters had become more tolerant. Tilly understood their chagrin. After all, they had undertaken a three-year training, passed difficult exams, and worked to consolidate that training and extend their knowledge. Many of the VADs had come straight out of the schoolroom or out of privileged drawing rooms, had a crash course in first aid, and were dispatched to hospitals. Initially, many were like startled rabbits caught in the headlights of one of the military trucks, but with guidance, encouragement, and kindness, they settled in and knuckled down to whatever tasks were asked of them. This in itself was amazing, as certainly the more" Upper class" girls might never even have made a cup of tea before, let alone emptied bedpans. They had scrubbed and cleaned, fetched and carried, made and changed beds, helped the men with menial tasks, and were always at the beck and call of the Ward Sister. They didn't complain, except to each other on occasion! And they worked the same long hours as all the rest of the nurses, taking their turn on night duty with everyone else. Tilly had taken to the VADs in her hut immediately, and they responded in kind by putting themselves out to help her. She was always "Sister" at work, but in off-duty time she was Tilly. The understanding was that none of the other Sisters, and especially not Matron, would ever know. Mostly the VADs were addressed by their surnames, even between each other but in private, Tilly used their first names, on the same understanding. They were of a similar age, and circumstances had brought them closer together. They needed each other for friendship, support, morale, and for hope.

When convoys of wounded came in, they were very busy, but the men who could be moved were cleaned up, wounds attended to, and moved on quickly via the hospital ships back to "Blighty" – a common euphemism for England. Most men hoped if they were to be injured, for a wound to be bad enough to give them a ticket to "Blighty" but not so severe as to kill them!

Some of the men were diseased rather than wounded, and some required isolation. But again as soon as they were well enough to travel, they moved on. There were times between battles when there was little to do. Once the huts had been scrubbed clean and restocked, beds made ready for the next intake, the nurses were granted time off. Usually a half day, occasionally a whole day off. Then they would delight in getting together for a walk to the nearest village, scrounge a ride into town and either shop or treat themselves to afternoon tea. Sometimes they stayed on the cliff tops, if the weather was fair, watching the little boats out from the nearest harbour, wondering what fish they would catch today. Some were happy to sunbathe in the sunshine, read or write letters home. Paddling on the seashore was a favourite pastime for Tilly, and she would chatter and gossip with her friends as young girls do. There was an enormous sense of freedom during those times. Tilly sometimes wondered if the straight-laced rules of society would be challenged once the war was over.

She didn't see how it couldn't be. After all, women were working in many previously male-dominated workplaces. Bus conductors and Policewomen. She had even heard of women working in munitions factories. Working women were becoming respectable, even valued. Times were changing.

During her time at the hilltop hospital, Tilly had made a special friend, a VAD nurse called Nell Rodgers. Helen (always known as Nell) was the eldest daughter of a family of four girls and a boy. Her parents were Publicans in Lancaster. Nell was a natural carer and, like Tilly, would have become a trained Nurse if circumstances had allowed. She had looked after her siblings for as long as she could remember while her parents worked. Her Maternal Grandmother, unusually, was a Midwife and ran a small Maternity home. Nell had seen a great deal more than many girls of her age, and she longed to be a Midwife, too, one day. With the support of Granny, Nell jumped at the chance to be a VAD. Her parents were not so keen but felt obliged to consent. After all, she had practically raised their other children, and she deserved a chance herself. Compared to life in the pub, being a VAD was easy, and Nell loved it. She didn't mind the menial tasks. Clearing up sick was nothing unusual for a Publicans' daughter, and the organisational skills she had developed in rounding up her siblings for school in a dressed and breakfasted manner would serve her well. Tilly liked her from the outset. Nell was cheerful, resourceful, funny, and enormously good company. They had the same ridiculous sense of humour, both being from “The North.”. Each teased the other about being from “the wrong side of the Pennines.” They naturally sought each other out and, whenever possible, spent time in each other’s company. When Nell was transferred to Tilly’s ward, they were both thrilled at the prospect of working together. It came as no surprise to anyone that this arrangement worked well, and they complemented each other. A third person was then added to the mix when a grumpy American orderly of the RAMC came to work with them. Neilan was his name, but that was literally all they knew about him. How an American came to be working with the RAMC was a puzzle to all, and Neilan was not about to enlighten them. Nell made it her number one priority to find out.

NEILAN

Neilan was not at all impressed to be posted to Ward 98. His work was faultless, but he had no time for pleasantries, declining all offers of social interaction. He simply didn't get the northern sense of humour which mattered not at all to Nell, who kept up a stream of conversational questioning and teased him relentlessly. Neilan ignored her mostly, but Tilly started to see beyond his cool manner. He was educated and thoughtful to the men and kind in moments when he didn't think anyone would notice. For the first few months, the work in the ward was relentless as battles raged, and it was all they could do to attend to the patients. The most serious cases were nursed more by Tilly with as much privacy as an open ward would allow. They did have some screens, but they were woefully inadequate. Neilan and Nell did the bulk of the back-breaking work of washing the men, changing linen, making beds, and keeping the area as clean as circumstances would allow. They also ensured the men were fed and watered, assisting them to eat if necessary. They helped Tilly with the dreaded dressing trolley and, by the end of the first week, had developed a respect for each other's roles, appreciated their organisational skills, and found they had the makings of a fine team. Each seemed to anticipate the others' needs, and consequently, the work became more organised, easier, and more enjoyable. Once the men were out of danger and feeling better, they would help with the chores of the day if they could. Soldiers don't like to be idle, and if they are bored, mischief is never far behind. They would start to fight with each other if not occupied, and a major occupation became discovering what Neilan was doing in the RAMC. Nell had allies. Neilan continued with his work, giving nothing away and ignoring the questioning and prying, rarely dignifying any question with a response. "None of your business" was as much as they would get.

"Oh, come on, Neilan!" Nell would say.

"We won't tell anybody if it's such a secret, will we, boys?" It kept the lads occupied in the time they waited to be moved on. Perhaps he was a fugitive? Wanted for robbing banks? Perhaps he had fled an unhappy marriage? Neilan went about his duties giving nothing away and protecting his privacy. It was all good fun. They were genuinely interested to know why this tall and handsome young man was nursing British troops in Northern France so far away from home. Occasionally Tilly thought she noticed a slight smile at the corner of Neilan's mouth as the questioning went on, and occasionally she felt duty-bound to defend him. On the whole, though she knew he could fend for himself and though she didn't encourage the banter, neither did she stop it. Nell was relentless, though, and one afternoon caused a rare comment by the tolerant Neilan.

"She's hassling me again, Sister!" he called out to Tilly. "And I'm sure that is against Army regulations."

Tilly shook her head at him.

"Then tell us the big secret!"

"Oh, not you too, Sister!" he cried in mock desperation. "How do I get a transfer out of this Ward?"

The laughter emanating from the men was a real morale boost. They really appreciated Neilan's more relaxed and easygoing manner, quite different from some of the RAMC orderlies they had encountered so far. Those men, though efficient on the whole, were not always gentle and somewhat lacking in compassion.

One night, Neilan managed to procure some beer for the men, and those who could partake were each issued a small medicine glass. Tilly was "specialling" a very sick boy at the end of the ward. Although she was aware of the beer in the ward - most of the men would be moved the following day - she was reluctant to spoil their treat. She could see no harm in it, so she turned a blind eye. Her trust that Neilan would not overstep the mark was justified. The men enjoyed a rare treat, and no harm was done.

Once the men had all settled down for the night, Neilan joined Tilly at the young boy's bedside. He put a cup of tea on the bedside table for her and touched the boy's hand gently. "Hang in there, buddy," he said softly, and he patted Tilly's shoulder as he turned to leave. Tilly caught his hand "Neilan?" she said "can I ask you something?" as she looked into his face. He rolled his eyes, expecting the same line of questioning he had been avoiding for months, but he stopped and waited.

"What is your first name," Tilly asked.

Neilan looked surprised but smiled down at her and shook his head as if not quite understanding the British, but after a moment of careful consideration, he answered, "Greg," he said, and with that, he turned and left.

All too soon for Tilly and Nell, Neilan received the posting he had been waiting for, and they learned a little more about their new friend's motives. Neilan had come over from America determined to join the Royal Flying Corps. He was already a pilot and had been devastated when he had been declined. His family owned land out in the mid-west of the United States, and flying had become his passion when at university. Once the war had been declared in Europe, he knew he wanted to be there. Despite his own country's neutrality, he found he personally condemned the bullying tactics of Germany against her smaller neighbours and sided with the British when they went to their allies' aid. He gave up his teaching post and headed east, boarding a ship bound for Liverpool. His family was abhorred, but Neilan had principles. Besides, he wanted to fly, and it would be an adventure. Being turned down had never occurred to him, but he was nothing if not persistent, and when the recruiting Officer had offered him the Royal Army Medical Corps by way of a stopgap, he had accepted. Becoming an orderly was not so different from caring for his disabled sister, and that he had been helping with his whole life. When she had died of tuberculosis during his first year of university, he had almost given up. But once he had talked things over with his father, he realised he could honour her memory by living his own life to the full and doing things she could only ever have dreamed of. His decision to travel to Europe at the outbreak of war had not been anticipated by his family. Deliberately putting himself in harm's way was not part of the plan they had envisaged for him. His departure had been traumatic, but he believed his mother would come to understand and support him. At least, he hoped so.

His time in the RAMC had been varied, to say the least. He had encountered bullying, pettiness, and downright ignorance, but he had also discovered camaraderie, sacrifice, resilience, and determination. The posting into Ward 98 had really been the icing on the cake, especially as it resulted in his objective. He realised he had come to enjoy the company of women, for a start, and as annoying as Nell was, she was also hard-working, reliable, and caring. The relationship between her and Tilly was special, and being accepted by them and included in their friendship meant a lot to him. He would miss them. He had been told at the outset that if his work in the RAMC proved exemplary, he would be considered favourably for transfer. It seemed that had now been ratified, and he knew it was more than likely Tilly's recommendation which had prompted Matron into providing a reference for the RAMC board. Now that his transfer to the Royal Flying Corps was ratified and common knowledge, he was flooded with congratulations and offers of handshakes from the men, not unexpectedly comments began to emerge

“Well, bugger me! I never expected to have ‘me bloody arse wiped by a bloody Officer! That makes a change!” commented Private Evans, causing a hoot of laughter. Neilan took it in good part and realised he would miss the banter, something he never expected he would! Tilly and Nell would miss him too. They were sorry to lose him not only because he was good at his job but because he had become a good friend. He was different, being American, and they loved that. He promised to write, but they took that with a pinch of salt. They would, however, both take an interest in his flying career for the rest of the war and beyond.

Neilan had sought Tilly out as he was packing up to leave. He caught up with her as she was leaving the ward and making her way to the mess tent.

“Hey! Sister – Tilly-- wait up,” he called to her, and she stopped and turned around as he ran towards her coming to an abrupt halt.

“Look, I just want to say thanks, and I think you should transfer to the RFC’s own Nursing Service” Tilly looked puzzled and shook her head as she hugged him briefly.

“But they don’t have their own Nursing Service, you idiot!”

Neilan laughed as he released her but kept his hands on her shoulders and looked closely into her face saying.

"Ah! They might not yet….. but they will! You mark my words Lady, and when they do, you get your papers in. We're going to need good Nurses like you!" as an afterthought, he added.

"Don't bring that gobby little shite with you, though. She'd be the cause of more broken hearts than Fritz!" and with that, he was gone leaving Tilly both laughing and crying at the same time.

THE CASUALTY CLEARING STATION

Tilly had felt the parting from "the gobby little shite" much more acutely. She found she really had made a friend for life in Nell. Their friendship had become more than Tilly had ever experienced with any of her other friends, a soulmate was a rare thing in a friend, and one she knew was exceptional. Not having to explain yourself to another or justify your actions, finding a friend who just accepts you as you are "warts and all." They had come to be able almost to communicate without speaking and in such a relatively short time.

Nell had practically begged Matron to be posted to the Casualty Clearing Station with Tilly but without success. She was needed where she was, Matron said.

"But I would be so much more use there with Sister Dobson!" pleaded Nell, but Matron was intractable.

"You will remain here, Miss Rodgers, and there will be no further discussion on the matter."

Nell had hugged Tilly tightly in farewell, words not really necessary and each feeling almost grieved at the parting.

"I will get that posting, Tilly, by fair means or foul! You just see if I don't!" she promised.

"You be careful, Nell - don't do anything foolish. Once the war is over, we can be wherever we like and do what we like! We can pull pints in your pub or go and work for your Granny! Maybe we'll even become Midwives?!" that caused them both to laugh, which helped to ease the parting. Nell stood and waved until the ambulance conveying Tilly to the Railway Station was out of sight.

Tilly had no idea how large the Casualty Clearing Station actually turned out to be. She was aware that its function was to facilitate the movement of casualties from the battlefields to the hospitals in the least amount of time. Treatment could only be life-saving and limited, but in times of stress, surgical teams could be brought forward as the number of personnel increased to deal with the volume of casualties expected. The earlier the intervention, the greater the chances of survival for the men.

Tilly's arrival interview with Matron was enlightening and, fortunately, during a relatively quiet spell. It appeared that the usual staff quota was seven Medical Officers (MOs), one Quartermaster, and seventy-seven other ranks. Tilly's mind wandered briefly. Why seventy-seven? There was also a dentist, a Pathologist, seven Nursing Sisters of Queen Alexandra's Imperial Military Nursing Service (QAIMNS) various other non-medical personnel attached to the CCS. Tilly was taking up one of the QAIMNS posts, since the previous Nurse having succumbed to "nerves" and was convalescing at one of the Nursing homes for the care of Sisters situated on the coast.

Each CCS carried its own marquees and wooden huts so as to create medical and surgical wards, kitchens, sanitation, a dispensary, operating theatres, medical and surgical stores, an incineration plant, ablutions, and a mortuary. Accommodation for the personnel had also to be provided. Sanitation was dug, and a water supply was assured.

Casualty Clearing Stations were usually located about twenty kilometres behind the lines, midway between the front and the base hospitals, and most were situated as close to transport systems as possible. CCS were as far forward as nursing staff were permitted to be. Tilly had heard tales of women nursing at the Front line in their own makeshift First Aid Posts, though not under the auspices of the British Army. How these women managed was a wonder and cause of admiration to Tilly, but she had to admit that this was probably as far forward as she was prepared to go.

Matron made Tilly most welcome, though she was the only Red Cross Nurse at the CCS. Her fellow Sisters were delighted to have her, especially in light of her theatre experience. This, Matron said, would be invaluable in the event of an influx of casualties from the forthcoming action when it was likely that the theatre teams would be working round the clock. The CCS, Tilly was informed, were generally grouped together in twos or threes and worked in a relay. This made sense as it gave the staff a chance to deal with the casualties they already had before the next big intake.

Tilly's accommodation was to be shared with two QAIMNS Sisters. It was somewhat cramped but better than a tent. After all, they were on active service. Her roommates seemed very pleasant, very Army, and sticklers for regulation. Nevertheless, Tilly had her own standards and was generally in agreement. She also liked order and precision, and anything for the benefit of the patients was alright with her.

Settling in was easier than she had anticipated. Sally Minchin and Sonia Reid were both just a little older than Tilly. They had met each other during training camp and, despite quite different backgrounds, found they got on well and were fortunate to have been posted together both to the Stationary home hospital and now to the CCS. Sally Minchin was Scottish, from Edinburgh, and had trained at the Infirmary, qualifying just a few years before Tilly. Sally had thick red hair and dark brown eyes with clear and peachy skin, which Tilly thought was just beautiful. Sonia came from London, her dad was a dock worker, and she escaped the family home as soon as she could. Her father was a drinker and violent, she said, so Sonia had decided the Army was for her. She signed up, and fell into the Nursing Branch somewhat by accident. Becoming a Nursing Sister was the pinnacle for Sonia, all the more special because of her background. It seemed her dedication, aptitude, hard work, managerial skills, and leadership potential had been recognised and channelled for the optimal benefit of the British Army. She was a bit rough and ready, was Sonia, but had a heart of gold, and her straight-talking appealed to Tilly, who rarely called a spade anything other than a spade! Tilly found she liked and admired them both and loved to hear their stories over a hot cup of cocoa or tea at the end of the day.

Sally was also a theatre Sister and happily showed Tilly around. She was also there for her as she found her feet in the new and strange environment. The surgery, said Sally, was basic and fast because they were literally saving as many lives as they possibly could. The finesse of surgery would have to be done back at the base hospitals if the men survived. It could be brutal, she warned, mostly amputations, and arresting haemorrhage. Treat the shock, patch them up, and move them on down the line.

Sonia explained her specialty to Tilly. Triage was a system of sorting out the most urgent cases and labelling them with information such as medications given and treatment received so far. This enabled medical teams at varying stages down the line to be able to process the movement and treatment faster than they could without the benefit of current information of treatment already given. The very worst cases, deemed too severely injured to survive, were held to one side, given morphine, and whatever comfort could be afforded. Men more likely to survive had to take precedence. It was a responsible and difficult position to place anyone in, but the doctors and senior nurses undertaking Triage had to keep in mind the bigger picture and banish images of young boys crying for their mothers with no hope of survival in order to salvage life wherever they could.

The men were triaged at every step of the medical line of evacuation from when they were first scooped off the battlefield to their arrival at the base hospitals and even the Home hospitals. The system was new, but it worked well. By the time some of the men reached the CCS, they had already been through the RAP and ADS. So one of Sonia's tasks was to re-evaluate them on arrival. Some men would be in a worse state than when initially seen. They may have been delayed hours, if not days, since the injury. They were triaged on their current condition and the level of care needed. Some of the men may have improved, especially if the shock had been addressed early on. Tilly was fascinated. It seemed so logical. Sonia also organised the care of the patients once they were sorted into the wards, and she supervised the orderlies who generally carried out what care the wounded received at this stage.

By the end of her first day, Tilly was apprehensive but optimistic. It would undoubtedly be a challenge, but she knew she had the skills. But, did she have the stamina? She promised herself she would do her very best to make her parents proud.

Sally had orientated her to the layout of the camp, the wards, the staff accommodation, and the theatre block. Theatres themselves were in block buildings, the equipment was basic but clean, and the room was relatively light and fairly airy. Two theatre tables stood alongside each other in this particular building. Sally informed her that some had three or more tables running alongside each other in times of battle. If they were lucky, Sally said, they would each have a surgeon, but there had been times when one surgeon had been servicing two tables just as fast as he was able. This caused Tilly to blanche slightly. Goodness, but she hoped she would be up to it! The theatre Sisters learned how to assist in the most economical fashion and to be quick about it. Or lives would be lost. One of the other doctors would act as an anaesthetist, but in reality, whoever was available could be called on to administer the anaesthetic. During the last "push," Sally informed her it had been the Padre.

The surgeon's name was Major Martin Kyle. He was a regular in the RAMC, with service in the Boer Wars and experience in the surgical treatment of wounds inflicted on the battlefields of the high Velt. The hot, dusty, and dry conditions couldn't have been more different from the cold, wet, and dirty battlefields he now found himself dealing with. Surgeons generally headed the surgical teams, which were sent down from the base hospitals to boost the operating capabilities when the need arose. They were becoming increasingly necessary during the aftermath of the fighting and more effective to have surgical teams at the CCS permanently, ready to receive and operate on the wounded at the earliest opportunity, which was proving to be life-saving.

Major Kyle was a charming gentleman, very old school in his attitude to lady nurses, but his opinion of their usefulness to the comfort and morale of the men and to the doctors generally had changed remarkably during the Boer War Campaign. He was not too proud to admit he had been wrong about the nurses once he had witnessed their dedication, commitment, and sheer hard work in the hot, dusty, and trying conditions. They never complained or made excuses, and their efficiency and morale-boosting qualities were an added bonus. The men liked being nursed by a woman, and why this came as a shock to him initially was hard to explain. Major Kyle was not a man whose opinions changed readily, but on the subject of the value of the QAIMNS and, indeed, the Red Cross Nursing Sisters, they found they had a champion.

Tilly liked him immediately. He looked gruff and irascible, but after her experience with Mr Lund, Tilly felt confident they would work well together. She was determined to be every bit as good as the military nurses, to be slick, efficient, precise, and she would speed up with practice.

Her first few days at the CCS passed pleasantly enough, and she was grateful to have the time to find her feet, meet the staff, and feel at ease in the different surroundings. The weather helped, it was a lovely spring, and she spent her off-duty time in the company of her newfound friends. At times she could close her eyes and almost believe she was on holiday. The noise of the guns soon put paid to that notion, and she knew it couldn't last. The noise of the heavy guns at the Front became almost unbearable at times, and she thought of the soldiers actually at the Front and how the noise must be affecting them. Their nerves must be shredded, and surely they would be deaf if ever the fighting stopped long enough to find out.

Initially, the work was easy enough. A few cases and stragglers were brought in, treated, and sent on their way, mostly back to their units. They treated a few septic fingers amongst the staff, but mostly the work involved cleaning, scrubbing, disinfecting, sterilising, stocking linen and bandages, and making beds. Extra supplies arrived and had to be checked and signed for in accordance with army rules and the Quartermaster's instructions. Tilly was well aware of what it was all for and was keen to keep her apprehension to herself. They didn't talk of impending battles even if they had known much in advance. The plan remained to be ready and prepared. While they waited, they enjoyed each other's company and took the opportunity to find out more about each other. Sally, she discovered, had run away from home to join the QAs in order to avoid matrimony with the local Parson! The Parson had declared himself smitten with her, and though her father had gone along with her wish to train to be a nurse, he assumed she would willingly trade in her career in order to marry. Sally was not of that opinion herself and couldn't imagine being married to a Vicar! Especially not that Vicar, whom she told them, reminded her of Uriah Heap, which caused them to fall about with laughter. Sonia was determined never to be at a man's beck and call. She would govern her own life, she said, and after her unfortunate experience in her own home, who could blame her?

Tilly's letters home were full of her new experiences and newfound friends. She played down the danger they faced as she couldn't add to the worry her parents faced on a daily basis. She described the camp as best she could without any reference to where they were in France. She didn't want her letters home to be scored out with ugly black censorship markings. Occasionally she would get a hastily constructed note from one of her brothers, but they were not letter writers. She mostly heard their news in letters from her parents or sisters-in-law. Tilly's letters to Henry continued. She sent them to the last address she had for him and hoped they would be forwarded on. His letters to her became increasingly scarce. She told herself it was because he was busy, but deep down, she wondered if there wasn't another reason.

The atmosphere in the camp was one of anticipation as June arrived. Matron was keen to empty any still occupied beds, and the whole of the staff became increasingly sick of checking equipment, restocking stores, and rolling bandages. Sunday, the 25th of June, turned out to be a gloriously sunny day. Once released from tedious and repetitive tasks, Tilly and Sonia took the opportunity to bask in the warm sunshine at the back of the huts. They decided it was really too warm for a stroll in the nearby woods. So they set up a couple of chairs, laid a blanket on the ground, and, armed with books and letter-writing equipment, settled in for a restful afternoon. Poor Sally was on night duty and banished to the isolation of the communal tent. Tilly laid back in the not-terribly-comfortable chair and reflected that perhaps she should have brought a deck chair after all!

In the days that were to follow, Tilly would recount those hours as the most peaceful of her time in France. Within days the peace was shattered by an almighty bombardment that went on day and night, putting everyone on edge. Newspapers began to report that it could be heard back in Kent! Strangely they received no more than the usual numbers of waifs and strays with illness and minor injuries. But everyone sensed that something monumental was about to happen. Surely this had to be the harbinger of the "big push," and they all privately dreaded the fallout of wounded as a result. No one vocalised their concerns. It was important to maintain morale, but secretly they all prayed they would be up to the task ahead.

Once it started to happen, the CCS, like many others, was totally overwhelmed with wounded and dying soldiers. The casualty rate on the first day grossly outnumbered anything the medical services had prepared for. The wounded arrived in convoys thick and fast. It was all Sonia and the Medical officers could do to keep up with the Triage. All personnel were drafted in to assist, and they systematically sorted the men according to the severity of the condition. These soldiers had come pretty much straight off the battlefield, and the horror and shock on their young faces told their own story. Far too many were beyond help on arrival. It had simply taken too long. They were gently put to one side under the care of one of the QA Sisters, whose task was truly heart-wrenching. All she could do was offer comfort, fluids, and morphine, and many were beyond that. As the casualties mounted, a whole tent was allocated for these men, and a doctor would have to certify death when he could be spared from caring for the living. The Padre was constantly in demand giving extreme unction and last rites, comforting the men, and helping the Sister provide terminal care.

Those badly injured men who could possibly be saved were hurried into the pre-operating area. Clothing was stripped off, cleansed as much as possible, and rushed into the theatre for anaesthesia. Chloroform was the anaesthetic used, supposedly administered by a doctor. But in the event of all the doctors being at full stretch, the reality was that anyone available, with any degree of knowledge, and sometimes without, was employed.

Both theatre tables were manned and fully operational for the first dreadful twenty-four hours after the wounded began to arrive. Major Kyle operated constantly, and Tilly was at his side as his "scrub Nurse." The team was completed by a theatre orderly and an anaesthetist. For the first time in her career, Tilly was fully aware of just how fast she needed to be in order to keep up with the surgeon to ensure the men survived to be moved on as quickly as was possible for the next case to be on the operating table. Any surgical cases that were judged suitable to survive the journey back to the base hospitals were sent on, so just the life-saving cases were performed at the CCS. As Tilly had expected, most were amputations, arrest of haemorrhage, removal of large pieces of shrapnel, and control of bleeding. They performed bore holes into the skull to relieve pressure, removed bullets, and pulled dangerous fractures into alignment. Hygiene was compromised. At times due to a shortage of water, the instruments had to be cleaned, and that was prioritised. There was also so little time for the niceties of nursing care. Saving lives overrode every other consideration. The second surgeon was another Major by the name of Doig, and he too operated flat out with another Sister, theatre orderly, and anaesthetist. The very first lull in the workload finally arrived, and Tilly realised they had been on their feet operating for ten hours. Visiting the ablutions was an absolute priority. Matron had ensured the teams had sandwiches and tea between cases, but there had been no opportunity to leave the theatre until now. Tilly was exhausted. On return to the theatre, she saw Major Kyle asleep on a chair in the scrub room, sandwich in hand. She didn't have the heart to wake him, so she laid a blanket over his lap and made her way quickly back to her sleeping quarters. She knew it wouldn't be long before they were needed again, and everyone had to take what rest they could when they could. The noise and bustle of the hospital couldn't keep her awake, and she fell onto her cot into a deep sleep without even undressing.

All night the convoys arrived and departed. Bringing in the wounded and transporting them away again, back down the line. The noise from the guns makes the whole scenario seem like a taste of hell. The wards were full, and the Sisters and orderlies constantly removed and bagged filthy clothing, a lot of it lice-infested, dressed wounds, washed what and who they could, made up fresh beds, sent badly wounded men to the operating theatres, and then accepting them back. Morphine was used for only the worst cases. There simply wasn't enough, yet the "Tommies" didn't complain. They were so relieved to be away from the Front they would pretty much put up with anything.

Tilly woke early, amazingly enough, given her level of exhaustion the night before. The noises of the CCF commencing its working day hastened her to wash and change her clothing and have breakfast before presenting herself in the operating theatres to relieve Sally. Her poor friend looked as done in as she had felt the night before.

"Oh, thank the Lord!" said Sally, and they hugged each other briefly before grouping together with the other theatre Nurses for a handover report. The night sounded to have been as hectic as the day, and today didn't look as though there would be any letup in the work. They were no longer "on the take," but they still had to nurse the wounded and replenish the supplies, moving the men on as fast as they could. Major Kyle was still operating. He had apparently snatched only a couple of hours of sleep in the night and, brushing off any attempt to persuade him otherwise, had resumed his work at the operating table. Tilly was allocated to join him.

"Well, good Morning, Sister!" he greeted her as she relieved the Sister at his table. "I trust you are well-rested?" despite his undoubted tiredness, he was still capable of some teasing. "I do hope you have had a decent breakfast, my dear. Croissants and hot chocolate, I hope?"

"Yes, indeed, Major," replied Tilly, warming to the subject, "I have asked the Maître D to save you some. Unfortunately, he tells me all the decent croissants have been devoured by the nursing staff, so he has saved you a very appetising dry biscuit and a tin of bully beef."

She took her place at the opposite side of the table and handed him a suture to close the wound.

"Well, that's good to hear, Sister, as bully beef is my particular favourite!"

She smiled at him, and the patient was soon cleaned up and transferred back onto a trolley for returning to the postoperative ward.

"Thank you, Sister," said the Major as he shed his gown and disappeared into the scrub room to wash his hands. Tilly was full of admiration for him and for his stamina, sincerely hoping that he would now be able to get some decent rest because, all too soon, he would be needed again.

Tilly set too to clean the theatre along with the rest of the theatre staff on duty. Sterilising instruments and repacking dressings for the next intake of wounded. They would need more supplies, and she would speak to the Quartermaster. Private Fawcett, the theatre orderly, offered to undertake that task, which was opportune as, at that precise moment, Matron sailed into the room requesting Tilly's presence on the morning ward round. Colonel Brownlow, the Commanding Officer of the CCS, was reviewing the post-operative patients and issued his instructions regarding further medical care or deciding if the patients were fit to be moved. He proceeded in a brisk and efficient manner yet managed to have a kind word for the men on his way. Tilly was amazed at the turnaround. The Casualty Clearing Station lived up to its name. Once the decision had been made regarding the men, the ambulances swung into action, and it was all hands on deck. By lunchtime, Tilly was quite dizzy but satisfied that they had achieved their objective and cleared out as many of the wounded as it was possible to do. The rest of the day and into the night, preparations were made for the next day's intake of wounded. Tilly was allotted two hours off duty during the evening. She made her way back to her quarters intending to write a letter home, but, in fact, she fell asleep on the bed, finding herself later being roused by Sonia. She brushed herself down and reset her headdress returning to theatres, but as all was still in order there, she was dispatched to relieve another Sister in the post-operative hut nursing the men too unstable to move. Sister Kelly was in charge, and between them, the work proceeded steadily and efficiently. One of the injured was a boy of nineteen who had had a below-knee amputation complicated by a haemorrhage. He had also been hit by shrapnel which had peppered his young body. The surgeon had picked out what he could during the course of the operation, but there hadn't been time to be too precise, and a significant amount would have to be removed at a later date. The soldier's name was Arthur Watts. "Call me Art Nurse. Everyone does," so Tilly did the same. He was a good-looking lad despite his pallor. He had lost a great deal of blood but was receiving a blood transfusion, an amazing new procedure that was a new tool in the doctors' arsenal and already saving lives. Patients dying of shock were now being given fluids earlier and blood as soon as possible. The effects were making a huge difference in survival rates. He was less breathless than he had been but still benefitted from sitting up, which Tilly was able to help him with. She plumped up the pillows behind his head. He winced due to some shrapnel embedded in his shoulder, but as his breathing eased, he looked carefully at Tilly and asked.

"Am I a sight, Sister?" Tilly looked back into his face and smiled.

"You are a bit, but I expect the girls at home will all be swooning over your scars soon enough!" she said and was pleased to see him smile.

The staff were horrified at the injuries they were seeing and the reports of the amount of dead. It was inconceivable, yet the work proceeded relentlessly. There was little time to truly digest and reflect on the horrors of what was the start of what would be known as the Battle of the Somme. Every other day they were "on take", and with very little sleep. Tilly and the rest of the theatre teams were fully employed either in theatre or with post-operative care. The very worst of the wounded who were not expected to survive or who had deteriorated since surgery were “specialled” by one of the nurses, usually at the far end of the ward and with as much privacy and dignity as possible. Matron applied for and was granted VAD help which helped boost the nursing numbers. Nell turned up, it was all Tilly could do to stop herself squealing with delight and hugging her friend in front of her senior colleagues. They had to wait until the end of their shifts, but then their delight at being together again sawed them hugging and laughing and talking at the same time whilst jumping about the room. Naturally, they were accommodated separately but sought each other out at every opportunity and requested off-duty time together. Nell had achieved her objective! Initially, Matron had reservations about a nursing Sister and a VAD being so close, but once she witnessed their professionalism and sheered hard work, she relented. Unfortunately, time off duty was limited, and every hour spent away from the horror was taken up with eating or sleeping.

The great joy of being able to make friends in such challenging circumstances was the support the friendship offered both parties, which could only enrich both lives. Matron envied this special relationship whilst at the same time mourning her own position. For someone of her standing, it would be absolutely inappropriate to fraternise with her junior Sisters, and she missed the close and personal relationships she had enjoyed with her contemporaries in times past. She still wrote letters to her friends from those days, most of whom were in a similar position to herself if they were still nursing. Some, of course, had married and had had to relinquish their chosen career. Writing a letter wasn't the same, though, as having a kindred spirit to pour one's heart out to after a difficult shift. No point in maudlin', though! Things to do, she thought and shook herself with a wry smile as she secured her veil, brushed down her dress, and headed back to the wards.

MOBILISATION

Henry received his movement orders just days after the start of the "big push." To say he was surprised was an understatement, as every surgeon was fully employed dealing with the overwhelming intake of casualties. They were all operating round the clock, and his Commanding Officer looked worn out as he ran his hands through his silvering hair.

"I'm sorry to lose you, Henry," he said as he handed the posting order over, "but it seems the Colonel of 44 CCS has been called home to his critically ill child. They are flat out and understaffed as it is. You leave in two hours" he shook Henry firmly by the hand.

"May God go with you."

It was time to make his farewells, and quickly at that. The orderly in charge of his billet had already packed up his belongings when he returned to change, ready for the transport out. A hastily sought-out meal gave him barely enough time to meet the ambulance, which was to ferry him closer to the Front and deposit him at his new Casualty Clearing Station. His driver was a young soldier who had already been on the go for nearly twenty-four hours, he said. The back of the ambulance had recently been swilled out with water and smelled strongly of disinfectant of some kind.

"Covered in blood and muck, it was Sir," explained the soldier by way of explanation. He engaged Henry in conversation, mostly in order to avoid falling asleep at the wheel. Henry was happy to oblige, tired though he was, and quizzed him on his experiences of transporting the wounded from the front line.

"There were two of us when we started," he said. "I just drove the wagon, and me mate sat in the back with 'em doing what 'e could, but soon there wasn't enough of us, and he had to go to be a driver himself, well that was something, and 'e wasn't 'happy about that I can tell ya! Still, if there's one thing the army teaches ya, it's not to argue! Insubordination, they call it, and they're shooting people for less, so I hear" he kept his eyes on the road ahead and did his best to avoid the many potholes and numerous obstacles. The road was barely passable in places, and the old motorised ambulance was somewhat lacking in suspension.

Henry drew his greatcoat around himself. Though it was early July, he felt chilled at this nugget of information so lightly referred to by the young soldier. It didn't surprise him, though. War was brutal in many ways, and here was another example of extremism on their own side. He glanced out of the glassless window at the surrounding landscape. Devastation as far as the eye could see. Buildings were reduced to rubble, trees splintered by shells almost beyond recognition as trees, and always the incessant rumble of the guns. Occasionally he was aware of the the troops passing to and fro, and of the walking wounded being assisted by comrades in arms. As a doctor, it was Henry's instinct to stop and help, but they were heading in the other direction. He knew the driver had another load of wounded to collect and transport back down the line once he had been dropped off at number 44. It occurred to Henry that many more men would be in need of their services, and those who already had help were better off than most. The young driver continued to chatter on, but Henry was only half-listening now. He reflected on his time as a Police Surgeon. Naively, he had believed he would in some way be prepared for battle-wounded soldiers. He hadn't believed that much could shock him. The reality was quite different. Uncomfortable though it was, the monotonous noise of the engine started to lull him toward sleep, a precious commodity. The frequent jolts and disturbances barely registering through the ripe language of his driver caused him a few sly smiles. When he next had cause to open his eyes, Henry was aware of a quite different landscape, and he blinked a few times to assure himself he was really awake. They were motoring through cornfields. He looked questioningly at the driver, who confirmed the vision.

"They are laying a railway through the fields, special trains for the wounded, gets 'em quicker to the hospitals," offered the young soldier "poor buggers."

Colonel Doig couldn't have been more relieved to see Henry as he entered the office on his arrival at the Casualty Clearing Station. He was already in full uniform with his suitcase at his feet.

"Captain Lascelles? Oh, thank God! Forgive me. My boy is very sick. I must leave, no time" he was shaking Henry's hand as he collected his suitcase.

"Major Kyle will show you the ropes. Good Luck," and with that, he departed, leaving Henry quite alone in more than just a physical sense. Somewhat bewildered, he turned towards the closed door, only to be aware of a loud knock.

"Come in," said Henry, and in came Private Wells, a rotund military looking gentleman of indeterminate age who proceeded to inform Henry that he would be his new Batman.

"Served the Colonel but happy to take you on, Sir, come this way, please." He opened the door for Henry to pass and briskly collected the remaining luggage whilst somehow managing to proceed Henry out of the room, beckoning him to follow. They journeyed down the corridor and out of the building to an outside path running between rows of tents.

"Soon have you settled in, Sir, then I've to take you straight over to the operating theatre, Sir, Major Kyle's instructions. He is very keen to make your acquaintance, Sir."

Private Wells kept up the line of one-sided conversation all the way to the billet, where Henry was able to deposit his belongings, relieve himself of his greatcoat and enquire as to the nearest point for ablutions. By the time he returned, somewhat refreshed, Wells had managed to rustle up a cup of tea and a biscuit, both extremely welcome.

"Matron says to call by her office first, Sir, so we'd better get going as soon as you've had your cuppa.

Been a bit busy these past few days, Sir. Poor lads were coming in thick and fast."

Wells shook his head as he proceeded to unpack and store Henry's few belongings, keeping up a barrage of chatter about the work, the nurses, and the "poor lads." Henry didn't even try to get a word in edgeways other than to utter his thanks. Despite the vocal barrage, Wells seemed like a decent chap, regular army, certainly, but he appeared kind and helpful and a mine of information. Henry looked forward to getting to know him better. Meantime, they soon set off in the direction of the Matron's Office. Wells, standing to attention even outside of the door, knocked loudly. A second knock was met with an equally mute response, so seizing the initiative, Henry suggested they might move on and promptly found himself briskly escorted towards the Operating Theatres. Some of it appeared to be tented, but he was ushered into a solid hut in which a gowned surgeon was thoroughly washing his hands. He had just been relieved of a soiled apron, and an orderly was preparing to gown him in a clean one. Private Wells slammed to attention, making Henry jump!

"Captain Lascelles, Sir!" he announced in a voice loud enough to wake the dead.

"Yes, thank you, Wells, that will be all," came the reply as Wells turned on his heel and marched smartly out of the room.

The surgeon dried his hands quickly and smiled as he shook Henry's hand and introduced himself.

"Martin Kyle, Major and acting Commanding Officer for my sins, may it be a temporary situation! Delighted to meet you, Captain. You are very welcome and much needed. Unfortunately, the niceties will have to wait. Our position is dire, and I need you to be operating immediately. We are already operating above our capacity, well beyond, in fact. The system is woefully inadequate, but we soldier on. Are you up for it?" At this, he raised his eyebrows, and his eyes were bright and hopeful.

"Losing Colonel Doig was a blow, I'll not deny it, but it can't be helped, a tragedy at home, you know. So welcome to the 44th CCS baptism by fire, I'm afraid. Are you ready for the gates of hell?"

"I am, Sir," replied Henry and received a pat on the shoulder in sympathy.

"Roberts! Get the Captain gowned up," he instructed, and the orderly appeared with a clean apron and another pair of gloves. Henry was gowned, masked, hatted, and gloved within minutes, and together they entered the operating theatre. There were two theatre tables side by side, and the patients were already under anaesthetic.

"New Surgeon," announced Major Kyle. "Introductions later. We need to get on," he turned to Henry briefing him about his patient.

"This man needs an above-knee amputation and shrapnel removing from his side" his tone became gentler and more concerned. "Will you be alright, Captain?"

Henry smiled reassuringly, but as his face was masked, he hoped it showed in his eyes.

"Yes, Sir," he replied.

"Excellent!"

Henry approached the operating table nodding to the doctor anaesthetising, and accepted a scalpel from the theatre nurse opposite him. The patient had already been cleaned of mud and debris, but his wound was shockingly infected. The bone shattered and exposed. Henry set to cutting above the damage in preparation for amputation. He extended his hand for the bone saw, having dropped the scalpel into the bowl. He expected the instrument to be placed into his hand. But when it wasn't forthcoming, he was forced to look up enquiringly at the theatre Sister. She stood at the other side of the table stock still, her eyes fixed on his over the top of her mask in shock and silence. She was just looking at him. His heart missed a beat, and he found himself staring into a pair of blue eyes he knew so very well. It could only have been seconds. He took hold of her wrist and extracted the bone saw from her gripped fingers when the anaesthetist cleared his throat.

"Is there a problem here? Any chance of getting this chap's leg off before he dies of old age?"

Immediately they both snapped back into the present as professionalism took over. The operation proceeded. The leg was removed, the shrapnel extracted, bleeding arrested, and wounds cleaned and sutured. Tilly and the orderly dressed the wounds and moved the patient off the table in readiness for transfer back to the ward as Henry left the theatre to de-gown and scrub up for the next case.

The theatre table was quickly scrubbed, instruments changed, and Tilly prepared herself for the next case. She found she was shaking. Oh my goodness, what if anyone noticed? She would be moved, and she might never get the chance to see him again. With some effort, she managed to calm her breathing right down to almost a normal rate and focused her mind on the next case. They had to move quickly and operate quickly. There were too many wounded, and they all deserved an equal chance. It was overwhelming. One case at a time, she told herself, concentrate on doing your best one case at a time. The next patient was already on the theatre table, struggling with the anaesthetist.

"Trust me, old son. You don't want to be awake for this one!"

The soldier had an abdominal wound and a fractured arm that needed setting. Tilly was ready. Henry reappeared, his eyes were smiling, and he raised his eyebrows at her. He had been briefed by the major and quickly took in the situation.

"Ready?" he asked, holding out his hand for the scalpel as he glanced at his colleague, confirming the patient was duly anaesthetised. He and Tilly both nodded in confirmation, and the operation proceeded. Tilly noted with pride that Henry was indeed a fine surgeon with steady hands, thorough, methodical, and quick. A fine warm feeling came over her simply watching him work. She was enjoying this! They were a good team, and they operated on into the night. Time seemed to disappear as the long list of cases never seemed to get any smaller. They ploughed on as the wounded kept coming. There was light in the sky before the rush began to diminish just a little. The Major at the next table had barely finished a difficult head wound case when he acknowledged a small lull in the proceedings and announced a change of shift was due, at last! Major Kyle stripped off his gloves and wandered over to Henry, peering over his shoulder.

"Good work, Captain, welcome to the team!" he slapped him lightly on the shoulder and disappeared out of the theatre towards the post-operative wards murmuring about checking on the night's work. Once the last patient had returned to the ward Tilly, her counterpart from the next table, and the orderly set about clearing up, sterilising, and restocking for the oncoming shift. Dropping her theatre gown in the laundry basket and washing her hands as far up the arm as she could reach Tilly had to admit, she was exhausted. She reset her veil and gathered up her cape, swinging it around her shoulders as she pushed open the door. Roberts, the orderly, called her back as she was leaving.

"Sister, before you go, the new Captain- Lascelles- wants to see you in the Major's office. Hope he doesn't keep you too long, Ma'am. You look all in" with that, he saluted her and left.

Tilly took a huge breath and let it out slowly. She was a little apprehensive but hugely excited as she knocked gently on the office door. It was thrown open almost before her knuckle had left the surface. She felt her arm seized, and she was pulled into the office as the door closed swiftly behind her, and she found herself wrapped tightly in Henry's arms. He smelled of soap and disturbingly of rubber, but he also had his own distinctive smell, pine? Musk? She had never been able to define exactly what it was, but it smelled delicious, warm and comforting, and she revelled in his touch. He was kissing her neck and her hair, basking in the smell of her as she was of him. Her veil was in total disarray, so she pulled back laughing and removed it. She had never felt more alive. It was as though every fibre of her being was awake and electrified. She put her arms around his neck and kissed him, holding him, wanting to be absorbed into him. He was murmuring into her ear and neck, "Oh God, Tilly, my darling, girl, I can't believe it," and she felt the same overwhelming love for this man who had appeared like an angel in the depths of hell.

"I love you so much I don't know how I managed to keep my hands off you for all that time!" he started to laugh, and her own tears turned to those of joy wallowing in his embrace and knowing she didn't ever want to let him go. Almost immediately, reality began to creep in, and she became fearful. Relationships between Officers and nurses were strictly forbidden. If they were discovered, they would be instantly parted, and she simply couldn't bear the thought of that happening, not now, so soon.

She pulled back a little to look at him,

"Oh, Henry, be sensible, please. What if we're discovered? Think, my darling, we must be so careful……. and quiet, please, Henry, don't let us be found out!"

Henry knew she was right, but he drew her to him anyway, kissing her deeply, and the world stopped intruding for the moment.

Tilly lay in her bunk, not so very much later, hugging her pillow to her, re-living the precious reunion. All previous thoughts of tiredness banished, and she found she simply couldn't stop smiling. It was a blessing her roommates were as exhausted as she had previously been, as none had woken as Tilly had made her quiet and speedy preparations for bed. It would be difficult, there would be difficulties ahead, and it wasn't something she could share. She would have to be vigilant, they both would, and relentlessly self-disciplined……… but oh, what joy to be in such close proximity after all this time. To know where he was and to be able to work with him, just to see him every day, was enough. She convinced herself it was enough. It had to be enough.

JACK

On arrival in France, Private Jack Dobson had found himself seconded to the newly formed Stretcher Bearer Corps. He was less than thrilled at the news, but no amount of complaining had got him any more than extra "jankers" – miserable army chores of the worst sort, the best of which were unsavoury and usually degrading. Jack wanted to be "in the thick of it," fighting, not retrieving the wounded. In years to come, he came to realise he couldn't have been more "in the thick of it." His service to his fellow soldiers and his ability to find, comfort, help, aid, and extract them sometimes from the very jaws of hell would afford him an enormous feeling of satisfaction and a job well done. How he had survived at times was a mystery to him. His faith in God had been severely tested. But once he came to realise that God really does work in mysterious ways, he set about his task with renewed dedication and determination. Jack's previous job as a farm labourer had kept him fit and strong, both attributes which singled him out for such strenuous and demanding work. He was also bright and quick to learn.

His first allocation to a Regimental Aid Post (RAP) had brought him together for the first time with his fellow bearers and their Regimental Medical Officer (RMO). They quickly became a close-knit team, and at the times when the pressures of battle allowed, the RMO would enhance what little training they had received on the initial, brief, and basic training course. They had each been issued with a handbook, small enough to fit into the tunic pocket, along with maps they drew of the trench network through which they needed to negotiate a stretcher loaded with its casualty. In battle, they had to amend the maps to account for collapses in trenches and alteration of the landscape. New maps were issued at the start of every offensive and were poured over by the stretcher bearer teams. Time was of the essence. The sooner they could locate the casualties and get them to medical help, the better the chance of survival. Each bearer carried a haversack with basic medical supplies, mainly dressings, so they could, at least, try to stop the casualty from bleeding to death before they could load and transport him to the RAP. The work was arduous, and during battles, very little rest was available to any of them. The weather became a constant factor, too hot, and the casualties were dehydrated and pestered with flies. Too cold, and they could freeze to death before they were found. Ultimately though it was the mud that became the greatest of all trials. Wading through thick mud, miles of sticky mud sucking the energy out of the already exhausted bearers. Fearing they would stumble and fall. Men had been known to disappear completely beneath its foul surface. Jack heard them tell a story of a bearer bending down to retrieve an Australian hat he believed had been dropped accidentally, only to be startled to find it was attached to a head and a pair of eyes staring pleadingly up at him. As the bearer hooked the man under his armpits in an attempt to haul him out, the soldier caught his eye.

"Steady on, mate, I'm on a horse!"

Such anecdotes would bring a smile on an otherwise difficult day, but Jack had his own thoughts about that and could well believe it was true. Sometimes they ran out of stretchers, and then it was a matter of hauling the casualty onto your back. The use of blankets and greatcoats to haul the casualties in was discouraged as bumping them over heavy ground would re-open wounds, and they could haemorrhage severely before getting help. Jack could never quite figure out why carrying a man on your back was less likely to re-open wounds than the use of blankets and greatcoats..... Maybe he would remember to ask the medical officer at some point?

Stretcher-bearers understood the weight of casualties better than anyone, and mud-drenched, they were heavier still. Heaviest of all were the "dead weights" unconscious patients couldn't respond to further pain or bleeding to alert the bearers, and they definitely weighed more. "Carry" after "carry" over treacherous battlefields, sometimes under fire, and back through manned trenches to the Aid Posts required almost superhuman abilities. Hands became shredded, backs and shoulders wrenched, muscles pulled, and just about everything ached by the end of the journey. It didn't stop there. Often the RMO was busy with other casualties, so the bearers had to help out to keep the Aid Post running. Each casualty had a medical field card which needed to be filled out with the patient's details, injury, and any medication he had been given. Uniforms sometimes needed to be cut away to expose the wound, which would need assessing by the RMO and re-dressing when he could get to it.

Hair needed to be cut away from head wounds, providing drinks if the patient was up to it, and comfort until he could be attended to. Despite the exhaustion and gruelling physicality of the job, after the first few weeks, Jack found he was interested and wanted to learn more. He read whatever was available, questioning his more experienced colleagues and, whenever possible, picking the brains of the Medical Officers. The bearers were constantly hungry undertaking such strenuous work, and food parcels from home became ever more necessary. Between battles, reorganising, restocking, and cleaning the Aid Post, Jack found time to write home, mostly to ask for food parcels. He kept the details of his work to himself, Assuring his mother he was getting "plenty of exercise" and regaling stories of his fellow bearers. The camaraderie was one of the best parts of the job. Their doctor was a Scotsman, Captain William MacLeod, fondly referred to behind his back by the men as "Willy Mac." He was a strict but fair man whom they came to respect highly, not only for his medical skill but for his kindness and compassion to the wounded and the unflinching defence of his stretcher-bearers. He wasn't above bending the rules a little and turning a blind eye when he felt it was justified. A "wee nip" of a fine Scotch whisky would be offered around the end of an especially busy period. It not only warmed the throat, but it also warmed the heart.

THE HOME FRONT

Like all mothers, Alice Dobson worried about all her children. Only Richard was still at home. The three of them would wait anxiously for letters and would devour the contents, sharing them with the wider family. Likewise, the daughters-in-law did the same and hastily rushed around with letters to share from their spouses, minus the more personal content. Alice herself wrote daily to at least one of her four children serving in France. She felt it kept her connected with them and part of their lives. Parcels were sent with food, socks, scarves, knitted jumpers, hats, mittens, and whatever else she thought could be of use to them. Nan and Meryl were equally vigilant in their concerns and would send letters and little luxuries for them to enjoy. The family at home fretted for their safety and well-being, scanning the papers for news and dreading the arrival of the postman bringing telegrams. Will was outwardly strong and positive in front of the others, but inwardly he too feared for them and shared his worries only with Alice. She knew him inside-out. It would have been futile to pretend otherwise. Despite the worry they lived with daily, the shared concerns brought them closer together in support of each other, and the positivity with which they were able to face the world had a positive knock-on effect on those around them.

Philip and Arthur were together in Northern France, Jack was doing sterling work with the stretcher bearer corps, and Tilly was at a CCS. Will scoured the papers for news from the Front, and he and Richard had a map of the area they had found in a newspaper, so they used it to plot the different areas and offensives as the war unfolded. Where the boys and Tilly actually were was, of course, classified, and sometimes the letters came with offensive black marks through the text, which everyone found upsetting and frustrating. As joyful as the receipt of a letter was, there was always a tinge of fear as the postman came to the door. Once the letter dropped onto the mat, the collective sigh of relief caused them all to laugh in acknowledgement of the previous tension.

Alice had decided that keeping busy was the answer. The cottage was cleaned within an inch of its life. She cooked, baked, wrote letters, looked after the Grandchildren, gardened, and volunteered for the Women's Voluntary Service. Along with her daughters-in-law, she would man a stall down at the village hall selling donated goods and baking to raise funds for the soldiers in France. Will and Richard, when he was not at school, found themselves in charge of the Grandchildren, which in itself was a full-time occupation!

Alice had also taken on the care of her elderly father. Since the death of Adelaide, there has been a rapid thawing in the relationship with Walter. He had welcomed the renewal of contact with his eldest daughter and was becoming acquainted with her family. He found he was interested in all their lives but quickly formed an especially close relationship with his youngest Grandson. He listened with great interest to Richard's descriptions of his brothers and sister, detecting pride in their achievements. He knew Richard had his heart set on joining up as soon as he was able, but Walter was gently able to advocate caution, appliance to his studies, and not adding to his mother's already considerable stress. Walter had missed Alice in the estranged years, and he deeply regretted condoning Adelaide's stance. Despite the lost years, Walter found no bitterness on Alice's part, and he was welcomed into the whole Dobson family with open arms. Will's parents were now also in their twilight years, and Walter found unexpected friendship in their company. Simple pleasures such as wandering down to the village pub for a pint with Will and his father, and sitting in the sunshine with Alice arm-in-arm on a bench Walter had provided beside Adelaide's grave. There was no need for words. He and his daughter would sit in companionable silence, knowing they were blessed. Walter loved Sundays now. He had returned to the congregation at the church he had known since his childhood and in which he had been both a choirboy and a Server. Nan would often visit, and at such times he felt his life was complete. He had resisted advice to sell the house and the offer to move in with the Dobsons, he still wanted his own independence, but privately he had been to see his Solicitor in York and had altered his will.

Alice couldn't have been happier than to have her father back in her life, and she was learning things about him she had never known. He was an avid stamp collector, for instance, a solitary hobby not approved of by his wife. He loved music, and he and Richard would spend hours in his study, indulging their shared interest. The purchase of a gramophone and some records caused them much enjoyment. Getting to know his Grandfather had given Richard a new purpose in life. He became a frequent visitor at the big house and was encouraged to use the library, borrowing books as often as he liked for as long as he wished. He played chess with the old man, honing his skills and determined one day to win! The two of them poured over maps of France following the progression of the war and identified places that became names of great battles. Walter was delighted when Richard showed an interest in Philately, proudly showing him his own fine collection, identifying countries on the stamps and locating them on the large globe which stood pride of place on the library table. Richard came to love the smell of leather, wood-smoke, and tobacco, which he would forever associate with his Grandfather and the library at his mother's childhood home. Aunt Nan had taken a photograph of the pair of them pouring over maps, engrossed in conversation. She had the photograph copied and framed, presenting one to her father, one to her nephew, and a third was enclosed in the next letter bound for France.

Nan and Meryl visited whenever their occupations allowed. The atmosphere in the house had completely altered. The formality had gone to be replaced with informality and laughter. No longer were they stepping on eggshells to placate their mother, and the sound of gramophone music completely lightened the atmosphere. Nan would arrange large family dinners when she was home, and the first Christmas since reconciliation was an extravagant affair. The staff had reduced somewhat to just a Butler, a Cook, and a housemaid. But as most of the house was now mothballed, it was proving a satisfactory arrangement. Walter's needs were easily met, and he had more than enough room with just his sitting room, library, bedroom, bathroom, and hallway. Mostly he took his meals in the library, but the dining room would be opened up for special occasions and could easily accommodate the extended family, and Alice would engage extra staff. Walter had a new lease of life. He and William had eased into a genuine friendship, and when he had expressed a lifelong ambition to travel on the footplate of an engine, William was delighted to be able to make the arrangements. Overalls and a cap were provided, not only to protect Walter's fine clothes but to enhance the whole experience.

They had returned home for tea covered in oil and soot like a couple of schoolboys. It warmed Alice's heart to see him so happy. Walter's death in the summer of 1916 took them all by surprise. Richard found him in the rose garden amongst his prizewinning blooms with what looked like a smile on his face. The doctor told Alice he had never before seen a happy-looking corpse. It seemed he had lived with a heart condition for years but had never disclosed to his daughters exactly what it was or that it could be life-limiting. The fact that he had managed to live so long was a miracle, said the doctor.

The funeral was well-attended on a hot summer's day in July. Much as he was loved and would be missed, he was an old man, and it was difficult to mourn too long when the news from the Front brought reports of the deaths of thousands of allied soldiers, most of whom were young men and boys. It was said that twenty thousand died on the first day of battle alone. Young men who would never know the joys of a long life, theirs having been snatched away so cruelly in their prime.

Alice and Will prayed harder than they had ever done before that their children would not be among the wounded or worse. The coolness in the church was a sharp contrast to the heat of the bright summer's day, and Alice became aware of the almost overpowering smell of roses. She knew it came from the arrangement on top of the coffin as they were from his own garden. The many tribute arrangements adding to the strong perfume. She had always loved roses and their distinct perfume, but now and from then on, she would always associate the strong, distinctive perfume with fear and anxiety. It was cloying, and it was a relief to leave the church for the burial in the graveyard.

Nan hooked Alice's arm as they walked slowly back to the house for the wake. Alice simply couldn't concentrate, and her unusual aloofness was attributed to grief for her father. Nan understood, and as she was the perfect hostess, it really didn't matter. Will exchanged a knowing look with Nan, who relinquished her sister to him, patted her on the shoulder, and told her to take her time.

"Come on, love," said Will as he slipped his arm around Alice's waist. "Let's go for a walk." The herb garden was overgrown, and the greenhouse was now in need of attention, but Will guided her to the bench on which they had first sat together and declared their love all those years ago. Neither mentioned it, they didn't need to, but both felt it as Will put his arm around his wife's shoulder and held her close.

BEYOND EXHAUSTION

Tilly was beyond exhaustion as she felt she was performing her duties like an automaton. Strangely, there didn't seem to be shifts anymore, just more work than she ever thought possible. The casualties just kept on coming and in such distress. It was now a luxury for a nurse to be at the theatre tables. The surgeons operated alone. Some days there were simply no beds, and the incoming wounded had to remain on stretchers. The nurses tended to them as best they could, but some of the men refused to be undressed by a woman. Most were riddled with lice, and they even refused to allow the nurses to remove their boots and socks, such was the state of their trench feet. The smell was overpowering. The poor orderlies were expected to be everywhere at once and couldn’t possibly be expected to do all they were being asked. Tilly had had enough. If they were well enough to argue, they were well enough for a few home truths. She gathered herself up in readiness between the rows of stretchers, grabbed a bugle from the boy in the stretcher at her feet, and blew it. Shocked silence immediately ensued, and before the noise level could rise again, she leapt into the moment to take advantage.

“Right, you lot!” she shouted. “Enough of your false modesty and particular ways. This is not a convent, and we are not nuns! We are all trained nurses, and we all have brothers. So whatever it is that you think you’ve got that is so private and special, I’m here to tell you it's not! We've seen it all before. It's been a difficult day for us all, and we can do without the Prima Donna behaviour. So shut up with your nonsense and let us get on with our work if you please!" she returned the bugle to the open-mouthed boy at her feet and indicated that the nurses should continue.

"Hear, Hear, Sister!" came a shout from the back. Slowly at first but with increasing intensity, the sound of clapping could be heard. Tilly shook her head and smiled as again she knelt down to check the "ticket" on the jacket of the next soldier before administering treatment. He had a bad abdominal wound, so she arranged for him to be moved directly to the preoperative area.

"By heck, but I wish you were my sister, Sister!" the soldier managed an appreciative smile as he was hoisted away.

Mostly Tilly was assigned to the post-operative ward, not to Triage as she was doing now. Post-operative nursing had its own challenges, and generally, she loved nursing post operative patients. Making them more comfortable was so satisfying, and seeing them improve had been a joy. They didn't stay long enough here to see any of the recovery processes. Moving them back to the base hospital was the priority in order to release the beds for the next intake of wounded. Here Tilly spent a fair amount of time waiting for the patient to wake up as she held his hand and tried to break it to him as gently as possible that he had had both legs amputated. It was nurses like Tilly who comforted and guided men to face themselves in mirrors, explaining that they wouldn't always look like that once the swelling and the bruising had gone down. They reassured them that wonders were being performed all the time in the hospitals at home for all sorts of injuries. Men cried in their arms, soaking the front of their uniforms, but Tilly didn't mind. She was used to physical contact, having hugged, and fought with four brothers. Some of the more "genteel" nurses found the physicality uncomfortable and emotionally distressing. Large quantities of handkerchiefs were carried as the nurses comforted, held, and reassured, occasionally telling little white lies,

"Of course, you will get better," "Your parents are on their way," or even "Everything will be alright."

As soon as it was safe to move them, the patients were moved back to the base hospitals. Some days the CCS could receive two hundred casualties a day. There was no time to eat or rest, let alone reflect. If it wasn't for the Padre who had taken it upon himself to go to the kitchens and make soup and sandwiches for the staff, they wouldn't have eaten at all. He was the one hooking up the sides of the tents, as it was sunny and warm so that a little breeze might waft through. Getting enough fluids down the men was a task all of its own and a particular challenge for those with facial injuries. None of the staff had ever experienced anything like it. Modern weaponry was decimating bone and tissue, which was particularly horrendous when it was the face. The nurses all made a concerted effort to control their facial features so as not to show horror to the affected men and to help the poor souls who may not have had anything to eat or drink for days. Tilly found some straws to at least help them to drink and possibly tolerate watered-down soup, which was the only nourishment they could manage. The danger of choking had to be measured against the danger of them starving to death. The surgeons, at best, could only secure the airway, clean, and debride the wound, ligate bleeding vessels, extract shattered teeth, and insert a feeding tube through which the men could at least be given fluids and nourishment without the risk of aspiration. Tilly prayed they would be moved on quickly and with compassion to hospitals at home where she had heard pioneering surgery was being performed.

She made a mental note to add those boys to her prayer list, which was already so long that she had to trust that God would know who was on it and take action without her having to mention everyone by name. Otherwise, she would never get any sleep! Oh, she dare not even think about sleep. There was far too much to do. Her spirits were lifted when Nell appeared with a cup of tea for her. Nell and some of the other VADs had taken it upon themselves to make up little packages of Morphine and dressings to hand to the men outside on stretchers still waiting to be seen so at least they could treat themselves as everyone was rushing past them. Initially, there had been some objection to this practice, but Matron had seen sense in it and given her approval once the numbers became overwhelming. In some cases, it was days before some of the men were seen by a nurse, let alone a doctor, by which time some would have died of their injuries. Despite the overwhelming numbers of casualties and the Medical Services' inability to cope due to severe underestimation, the medical and nursing personnel, together with orderlies, stretcher-bearers, ambulance drivers, X-Ray technicians, and catering staff, pulled together to do whatever was needed to help. Tilly had been amazed but gratified when the Padre had provided such welcome sustenance that the ward doctors would shave patients prior to surgery if they were the only person not immediately needed at that very moment. Teamwork. Exactly what was needed. No one was heard to remark that "it isn't my job." Even Matron became handy with the mop and bucket and could make up a whole line of beds with pristine hospital corners in no time at all. It was an unspoken rule that the men must not see the nurses cry. Cheerfulness and positivity were the orders of the day. The nurses would smile, and life would go on. At one point, Tilly thought her cheeks would never recover because she had smiled so much during that dreadful time. She saw very little of Henry, who was operating almost continually. They passed in the mess tent on occasion, and just the sight of him lifted her spirits. He would send her little notes or funny drawings on occasion, but time together was completely out of the question, and they both knew it.

Nell was a tonic, always cheerful, and enormously helpful. She had a knack for always being where she was most needed without the need to ask, and the patients loved her. Funny, kind, and a little irreverent, she would get the work done whilst keeping up morale and bantering with the men. The sound of laughter was rare and such a morale booster. But whenever it was heard, Tilly would have bet her bottom dollar that Nell was somewhere in the midst of it. Their shifts together were a joy and lifted Tilly's morale more than a little! Nell's talent for acquisition knew no bounds. Whatever the men needed or asked for, whether it be chocolate, cigarettes, tobacco, newspapers, or even alcohol, Nell was the nurse to go to. She kept her sources secret, but Tilly suspected a fair amount came from parcels requested from home. When they began to run out of the drawstring bags they used for the men's few possessions. It was Nell who was instrumental in acquiring the material necessary and inspiring (and bribing) the staff to use whatever time they had available to sew a fresh supply. Somehow a competition emerged between the huts, who could sew the most drawstring bags. She even persuaded the Commanding Officer to come up with a prize. Tilly found herself sewing drawstring bags during her time off and even caught one of the nurses doing it as she sat at a dying man's bedside. Naturally, she turned a blind eye. It was her hut, after all. A lot of the less seriously wounded men were equally commandeered to the task as they waited to be moved. The variety of material acquired was remarkable, from scratchy army khaki off ruined uniforms to what Tilly could only believe was silk. One soldier appeared to be working on a bag made from Matron's bright red bloomers. She only realised this, having witnessed their drying on the washing line the previous week.

Tilly decided she wasn't even going to go into that one with Nell! The staff and the men were only too happy to help if they could because they realised the importance of the little bags which were handed out as the men arrived in order that their few possessions could be kept safely hung on the bedpost behind them. A source of comfort and relief from stress, at least as far as their possessions were concerned. Tilly became aware that many of the men fretted about their families at home. Sometimes letters would cause upset and additional worries. Wives left without money at the end of the week, children without birthday or Christmas presents, and tales of hardship, if not outright poverty. Between them, Tilly and Nell, along with some of the other nurses, devised a plan to contact charities local to the families to ask for help for them, and funds from donations could be sent and distributed by the charities who would check up on the families at the same time. This could only be undertaken during lulls in the action, but it kept them busy and feeling useful. The response from the charities took time to arrive, by which time the men had moved on. But they forwarded the responses to the men and hoped they would have some comfort knowing their families were not overlooked.

RESPITE

By the Autumn of 1916, the last casualties from The Battle of the Somme were transported back to the base hospitals, hoping for their "ticket to Blighty." The staff of the CCS were completing their own tasks, both professionally and personally. Wards were scrubbed clean, beds made, and supplies replenished. More personal tasks of housekeeping were caught upon, most importantly sleep. At last, there was time to write letters home, read letters from home, and attend to personal laundry. During the mad rush, Tilly had rarely spoken to Sonia and Sally. They had passed like ships in the night, to and from shifts or occasionally at dinner. Now they were able to catch up in their spare time off duty, and the act of washing their hair together was such a luxury. Being able to sit at the door of the tent, brushing each other's wet hair and allowing it to dry in the sun, was such a simple joy. Tilly had often thought the burden of long hair was much overrated and had contemplated cutting hers short. Fashion and time had so far gotten in the way. Something that she would revisit, she felt.

Writing letters home and actually having time to read them properly was equally a joy. Tilly read about the reconciliation with Grandpa Wharton and regretted she didn't get the chance to meet him. Richard's letters were full of him, and his admiration for the old gentleman shone through. Mum wrote that Philip and Arthur had both survived the battle, and Jack had been granted leave following his heroic efforts of carrying the wounded to safety. He was expected home any day now. She could almost feel the excitement in the house. Tilly had declined the leave, though she didn't tell her parents this. She simply couldn't leave here whilst Henry remained. Though she had seen so little of him over the past weeks, just knowing he was occupying the same space as her made her spirits soar.

Sonia and Sally had invited her to join them that afternoon on an excursion into town. An ambulance was leaving with another batch of wounded for the port and would give them a lift. Tilly thanked them but declined. She savoured the opportunity to catch up on her correspondence in peace and quiet. However, a different opportunity soon presented itself with the appearance of Nell, who, with a knowing smile, pressed a note into Tilly's hand. All it said in typed lettering was:

"Meet me in the woods? Please"

Tilly's heart started to race, and she looked up enquiringly. Nell met her gaze, crossed her arms, pouted her lips, and then smiled. "Well? Do you plan on meeting the dashing Captain, or should I go in your place?" an eyebrow was lifted as she waited for the reply.

"How?..." started Tilly keeping her voice low enough so as not to be overheard.

Nell shook her head. "Well, it's hardly difficult to work out, at least for me, but then I'm cleverer than most and more perceptive. Fortunately for you, I can't resist a romance, and even though you haven't asked for my help (shame on you!) I am going to help you anyway. So get your veil on and tidy yourself up a bit, and we'll be going for a walk in the woods, I think?"

Tilly couldn't help smiling as she shook her head and made ready. She didn't have time to dress her newly washed hair, so she simply bundled it beneath the veil, pinched her cheeks, smoothed her dress, and joined Nell on the other side of the tent flap. Her heart was about to burst out of her chest. She had to slow her breathing and try to appear normal. It was a beautiful day, sunny and warm. Nell casually linked arms with her, and within minutes they were at the edge of the woods behind the tents. Tilly took another deep breath, held Nell's hands momentarily, and mouthed the words, "Thank you!" Nell smiled, tilted her head, and gently returned the pressure.

"I'm afraid I am unable to join you, as much as you may wish me to. But some of us are on duty this afternoon, you know!" she joked as she turned to leave. "Have fun, don't do anything I wouldn't do!"

Tilly had known the layout of the woods quite well prior to the recent battle. The Sisters had come when able to read and relax under the cooling canopy during their rest periods. She headed for an area of clearance she suspected would be good for a place to meet. She was right. Henry appeared instantly and enveloped her in his embrace. He looked tired but immaculately dressed in his uniform, thinner but so handsome. How good it felt to be with him like this. He then held her at arms-length and looked closely at her "Are you alright?" he asked, and she smiled and nodded her head, touching his face with the palm of her hand.

"God, it's been torture not seeing you," and he buried his face in her neck. She reached up and pulled off the veil shaking loose her long luxurious mane, now soft and dry after the hairdressing, completely and naively unaware of the effect it was having on Henry. He made a deep noise in his throat as he stood before her in wonder, running his hands through her hair.

"You are so beautiful, Tilly. I don't think I've ever told you that before?" and he guided her towards a clearing where he laid a blanket down on the ground for them to sit on together.

"I'm fine," she reassured him," but what about you? You look so tired, my love."

"We're all tired, Tilly, it's been hellish. But then again, we've saved lives, not as many as we would have liked. But everyone is someone's son or husband or brother. Despite the horror and the workload, I've learnt so many lessons I'll be able to take back with me to practice in civilian life. God, but you're lovely," and they fell into each other's arms. She couldn't kiss him enough, but she was shy, too, and he sensed it.

"I need to talk to you, Tilly," he said, and he gently extracted her arms from about his neck and sat up.

Tilly sat up too, facing him and holding his hands.

"That sounds serious," she said.

He took a deep breath and smiled at her.

"You know that I love you, Tilly? More than I can ever say, and you have to know that I want you with every fibre of my being, so much that it physically hurts."

Tilly could hardly breathe but gripped his hands and looked up at him, waiting.

"But it can't be. Apart from the fact that I'm married, I won't risk you becoming pregnant and shamed," now he was kissing her hands. She suddenly felt like crying. All the pent-up emotion of the past few weeks and the seeming helplessness of their situation now opened the floodgates. Tears streamed down her face, and she reached for him. He held her to him until she had no more tears to cry. They settled down on the blanket. He was behind her, cradling her in front of him, kissing her hair, and holding her until she settled. Time was of no consequence. She knew he was right. Having a child out of wedlock would be a disaster for them both. As much as she loved him and wanted to be one with him, she couldn't risk the consequences. She simply couldn't do that to her parents either. She loved him even more for his thoughtfulness and care of her. She started to tell him that she understood and glanced back over her shoulder only to realise he was fast asleep. She pulled his arms in closer to her and leant back into him, listening to him breathing. Her mind was far too active for sleep, so she tried to process all that had happened to her since she had come to France. The friends she had made and the casualties she had encountered. The letters she had written for them to their loved ones and to hers. Had she changed? She knew she had grown up. Some of the sights she had seen would never leave her. The courage, bravery, stoicism and sense of humour of the soldiers cemented in her a renewed love and respect. She would forever admire the skill, compassion, and professionalism she encountered daily, and she realised this was a moment in time that would never be repeated. The sharing and camaraderie she had experienced here would not survive the transition back into civilian nursing. The old hierarchy would be unchanged, and the multidisciplinary teamwork she had come to love would be no more. That perhaps was something for the future. For the present, however, this war showed no sign of completion. She wished she knew where Phil and Arthur were. She always kept an eye out for a West Yorkshire cap badge. Those she had come across so far had not known her brothers. She was so proud of Jack. She had developed an enormous respect for stretcher-bearers. She had seen them coming in with their "carries" in the most dreadful circumstances, sometimes covered in mud and grime with their poor hands which were raw and the skin shredded. She had attempted to pin the men down and dress the wounds when she could, but the men had no time for that as they dusted themselves off, accepted a quick cup of tea, whatever there was in the way of food, and headed back out for the next load. Whenever she had the time, like now, Tilly found she also worried about Jane, working on a hospital train. She had heard they often came under fire, and sometimes the journeys could take days as the trains could be shunted into sidings to allow the transporting of ammunition and fresh troops to pass. Obviously, a priority over the wounded, though Jane's letters were always bright and cheery and full of hope. Tilly recognised the sentiment. They had to have hope in order to continue to function, and maintaining morale was just as important for the nurses as for the soldiers. She absentmindedly stroked Henry's hand and felt him stir. He sat up suddenly.

"Goodness! What time is it?" a little disoriented. "I'm so sorry, my love, what a waste of your time off with me asleep!" Tilly smiled as he shook himself awake and ran his hand through his hair. "We need to get back."

"Don't worry, there's time yet," she reassured him. He helped her up to her feet, and she reset her veil, straightening her uniform as he did his. Despite the activity of the CCS so relatively close to them, it was remarkably quiet in the woods. Only a distant sound reaching them on occasion as presumably the direction of the light breeze changed. To her surprise, Henry then produced a flask of tea and some fruitcake his mother had sent. They sat again on the blanket side by side, consuming the cake and sharing the flask of tea. It all tasted delicious! Conversation recommenced, and Tilly found herself asking him about Peter, who would soon be turning three. Almost as soon as she asked, she regretted it. As such sadness came over Henry, she felt her heart would break.

"He's well, I hear. Thank you for asking. Very spoilt, I'm sure, but the apple of his Grandparents' eyes" He didn't elaborate, so Tilly just leaned in closer to comfort him. It seemed to work as his mood quickly lightened as he again stood and helped her to her feet, wiping crumbs from his lap, and packing up the picnic.

"Really, Sister Dobson, leading me astray like this! Whatever would Matron say?" Tilly smiled as she held his face in her hands and looked deeply into his blue eyes.

"Matron must never know Captain Lascelles," and she kissed him.

Tilly left the woods first, making her way back to her quarters. Henry strolled around for a short time and out of the other side of the woods, hopefully unobserved.

"Hello, and where have you been?" asked Sally as Tilly re-entered the tent.

"Oh, I just fancied a walk in the woods. It's such a lovely afternoon," Tilly replied, casually throwing her veil onto her cot. She made busy redressing her hair as Sally watched carefully, but whatever her thoughts, she chose to keep them to herself. They both made their way to dinner before returning to duty, Sally updating her on the visit to town. Much to Tilly's chagrin, it was Sally who had been allocated to theatres and not her. Tilly made her way to the post-operative ward, soon realising she would have missed the boys had she gone to the theatre, and most of them were almost fit enough to be moved on. Nell had just finished clearing away the patients' meal as Tilly entered the ward. Nell caught her eye and smiled wickedly. Tilly took handover from Sister Williams and began her rounds,

"How was your afternoon, Sister?" asked Nell, sidling up to her, the picture of innocence whilst balancing an armful of linen bound for the shelving unit.

"Very nice, thank you, Nurse Rodgers," Tilly replied in kind. "Aren't you off duty soon?"

"Yes, Sister," replied Nell raising her eyebrows, "but I'm happy to stay if there's anything you need to share?" she added cheekily.

"That's very kind of you, Nurse Rodgers," replied Tilly entering into the banter, "but I would hate to detain you when time off is so precious," and she turned on her heel, smiling, to continue with her rounds leaving Nell stranded and more determined than ever to discover just what was going on between her beloved friend and the dashing Captain.

The lull in activity brought the inevitable movement of personnel. The surgeons were the first to be re-deployed, their skills much in need both back at the base hospitals as well as at home in England. Henry was posted back to England to join a team pioneering facial reconstruction. Necessity being the mother of invention, the team had to devise ways of helping the men damaged in ways never before witnessed. Henry found he was excited by the prospect though leaving Tilly would be hard. Tilly had been expecting it, but she still felt a physical pain in her chest when she was told. She would be moving, too, back to a base hospital on the coast. At least she didn't have to remain once Henry had gone, and she still had her brief but beautiful memories of their time together at the CCS. It had been both the worst and the best time of her life. Nell had broken the news to her in private. How she had known before the news became public, Tilly had no idea, but she was grateful as it gave her some time to absorb the shock and prepare herself. Henry was equally stoic. "Fortunes of war, eh?" he whispered to her as they met in the mess hall.

SEPARATION

Tilly was absorbed in her own preparations, which kept her busy. There was never enough warning, but as luck would have it, they were both on the same transport for the rail head. Taking her leave of Sonia and Sally was heart wrenching. She hadn't realised just how much they had come to mean to each other in the time they had shared, but it was Nell she would miss the most. Tilly again felt bereaved as they said their goodbyes, trying to hold it together, trying not to cry, promising to write as they hugged each other tightly. Henry gallantly handed her up into the ambulance for the short trip to the rail head. He followed her up and sat down beside her as close as he could get without attracting attention, holding her hand beneath the folds of her cloak. The journey went all too quickly, and with no chance to talk as others were present. She felt herself start to panic that there would be no opportunity to say goodbye properly. But as they approached the noisy, bustling station, Henry looked intently at her, engaging her attention.

"Are you alright, Sister?" he asked, turning towards her in a very concerned manner.

"You look dreadfully pale," and he put his hand to her forehead, for which he had to face her directly, and he mouthed the word "Faint!" She felt him assist her to stand, and then he jumped down from the back of the ambulance, arms out to help her down. As her feet touched the floor, she slumped into his arms as though she really had fainted. Henry scooped her up, calling to one of the orderlies to collect their bags as he made his way through the crowds in the station to the small office with her in his arms.

"Make way, please, Sister unwell," he called, and the door was opened for them to enter. "Out, please, give the lady some privacy," and he shut the door with his foot behind the rather startled Station Master. The one small window was so dirty it was unlikely anyone could see through it, and it was all Tilly could do to stop herself laughing in relief as he gently put her down. Her arms went around his neck, and she kissed him long and hard.

"Thank God you are so clever," she told him from the safety of his encircling arms. They knew they had so little time, and sure enough, the orderly appeared with their bags, most concerned about Sister Dobson. Asking if there was anything else that he could do to help.

"Thank you, Pearce," said Henry. "She's still a bit wobbly. Could you secure us a carriage, do you think?"

"Yes, Sir!" replied Pearce. "Don't you worry about a thing Sir! Me and the lads will load your baggage and secure you a carriage. Sir, you take good care of Sister Dobson, Sir! She's a good 'un she is" with that, he snapped to attention, saluted, and hurried off.

Tilly caught Henry's eye, and they giggled like children.

Pearce was as good as his word. All too soon, the train was called, and Pearce saw them and their baggage safely loaded. The train was simply too full to afford them any degree of privacy, so they stood together in the corridor, ostensibly looking out of the window, making the most of the time they had left together.

"Do you think there will ever be a time when we don't have to part?" asked Tilly.

"God willing, there will be," Henry replied, nudging her gently with his shoulder.

"You be careful and write to me?"

"You know I will," Tilly replied, and before she knew it, the journey had reached its end for her. Henry had further to go to the port of Boulogne, but she was destined for Number 16 Military Hospital at Le Treport.

Henry handed her down from the train, organised a porter to help with her luggage and direct her to the transport leaving for the hospital. Already the whistle was blowing for imminent departure, so Henry pulled her to him and kissed her thoroughly, regardless of witnesses. Everyone seemed otherwise too occupied to be interested in them. In the midst of a surge of humanity, they were invisible. The train had begun to inch away as Henry hopped onto the running platform. He held on to the train with one hand as he placed the other over his heart and blew her a kiss. Tilly mouthed the words "I love you!" as he disappeared into the carriage.

There was no time to grieve, she was swept along the platform with the rest of humanity, but she did hear the call for:

"Anyone for number 16?" Tilly managed to step out of the surge towards the voice, raising her arm and crying out.

"Yes! I am!"

"Hop in, Sister! Are these your bags? Good, Good," and the soldier waved her into the back of the truck. Hands appeared to haul her in, and once settled on the bench, she realised she was in the company of seven others. Three of whom were VADs.

"Hello," she said, smiling and settling herself down. "I'm Tilly Dobson. Are you all for number 16?" The girls all looked nervous and nodded. One of them filled her in.

"We're new, just arrived from England. I'm Dorothy Forbes. How do you do?"

The others followed suit and shyly introduced themselves, keen to know where she had been so far. The other Nurses seemed just as interested but less chatty. They seemed very impressed that she had been at a Casualty Clearing Station, so she answered their questions as simply as she could with a minimum amount of graphic detail. No need to scare them.

Before she knew it, they had reached their destination and were disembarking from the truck. She promised to catch up with them once they were all settled.

"Don't look so terrified! You'll be fine. We'll look after you!" and with that, she gathered her belongings together and set off for Matron's office.

STIFLED

Jack felt mixed emotions as his leave came to an end. His mother and both sisters-in-law had spoilt him rotten, an unusual state of events, but now he had to admit that it was all wearing a bit thin. He was starting to feel suffocated. The attention of the family was usually diluted by the presence of his siblings. Being the centre of attention and having his every need met almost before he had even thought of it had lost its appeal after a few days. His father, he noted, had looked on in amusement and would occasionally rise to his defence:

"Ladies, please! Give the poor lad some room!"

Thank the good Lord for Richard. He at least took pity on Jack and provided the excuses he needed to extricate himself from the house. The brothers walked for miles, and Jack soaked up the familiarity of the clean smells and lush green grass so lacking in the hell hole he had so recently experienced. They fished in the river, lounged about on the riverbank, and generally kept out of the way. Slowly his hands had healed and hardened, callouses they called the hard bits. Alice had spent the first few days cleaning and dressing them, and once the flesh had healed over, she rubbed lanolin into them. Time spent like this with his mother was precious, he wanted her to know that. But he couldn't talk about his work or the conditions the men faced. He didn't have the words. Even if he did, he wouldn't have told her that was something he and his comrades would share only with each other, or maybe not at all. It was enough that they knew what the other had been through. He understood now why the army "beasted" the men into coherent groups. They wanted to fight for each other, not let their fellow soldiers down. Camaraderie was not a word Jack had known until France, but the power of it kept the men together, and supporting each other and fighting. Banter became as much of a lifeline as mail deliveries and the receiving of parcels. He missed his mates; he couldn't wait to get back. How odd was that?

Richard bombarded him with questions, all the innocence of youth! Jack felt older than the seven years that separated them. He cautioned his young brother about his enthusiasm for war with all the understanding of his own experience. He tried to describe some of the horrors without being too graphic but enough for Rich to see there was no glory in mass carnage. He spoke of the horrors of lice infestation and trench feet, always being hungry, and the monotony and blandness of the food when it did appear. He told him of the luxury of unexpected results of egg foraging or being given fresh bread. How the men would imagine their home-cooked meals and speak of them with such detail, the rest could almost smell it. He spoke of the heat and the sun and not being comfortable in either and the mud. Oh God, the mud and the sounds of men injured on the battlefield crying out to be rescued. Minutes passed between the brothers. There was comfort in companionable silence here in the safety of home.

“Stay well out of it, Dick,” Jack cautioned.

“Stick to your studies so you can get on in the world. When the war is over, educated lads like you will be needed to help us rebuild our lives.” The brothers sat side by side on the riverbank. The fish weren’t biting today.

LEAVE

Tilly's leave came through only two weeks after her start at the hospital. She had barely had time to settle in, but when Matron called her to the office to give her the news, she found she was excited. It was a while since she had been home and she suddenly realised it was what she needed. Ten days leave! She would go home to Yorkshire, to her family. Peace and rest and family.

The noise and bustle of the port and the excitement of the troops, also bound for home leave, were infectious. Tilly found herself swept along onboard the ship with many a comment of "thanks," doffing of hats, and respect from the men who recognised her uniform. They couldn't do enough to help her and the other nurses on board, finding them seats, and carrying bags despite protestations that she could manage! The good-humoured banter on the top deck was a contrast to the quieter decks of the wounded below. They would all have been delighted though, to have a "Blighty" ticket. There were rumours of submarines in the English Channel. Tilly knew ships were being targeted, but, like her, everyone was keeping a "stiff upper lip" and trusting it wouldn't happen to them.

Tilly sat quietly, watching the activity around her, listening to the chatter, breathing in the fresh, salty sea breeze. She pulled her cloak gently around her as she watched the men. Despite having been through hell in the past months and experiencing the deaths and wounds of many of their friends and colleagues, they were still able to function, sharing cigarettes, playing cards, and keeping up their spirits, thinking no further than the next two weeks' leave. Tilly felt proud of them, and tears pricked her eyes. She needed this leave even more than she had thought! The realisation made her smile. The breeze on deck and the taste of salt in the air suddenly rejuvenated her, and she felt glad to be alive. Her thoughts turned to her homecoming, unannounced, as there had been no time to send a telegram, let alone a letter. She was excited at the thought of her parents' reaction to her arrival. What bliss it would be to sit down in the chair by the fire with a cup of tea and later be able to sleep in clean sheets in her own bed.........

"Tilly!" came a familiar voice above the noise of the activity on deck and full of excitement. She looked up into the face of her brother, Arthur, rapidly advancing towards her. He hauled her to her feet and enveloped her in a huge brotherly hug. Tilly hugged him back fiercely, and the relief of seeing him alive and well really did cause her tears to flow. Arthur lifted her right off her feet and swung her round as she clung to his neck.

"Lucky bugger!" shouted one of the soldiers, and Arthur laughed, replying.

"She's 'me, sister! Our Tilly!"

Tilly was so full of questions they all came flooding out together, causing Arthur to slow her down.

"Whoa, Sis, one at a time!" as he directed her back to the bench from which he'd lifted her. He sat down himself facing her, holding her hands, and grinning like a Cheshire cat.

"I don't believe it, Art! I haven't known where you were…. Where's Phil?" and her eyes scanned the deck around them.

"Phil's fine, Tilly, leading a gun crew now, you know?"

"No! I didn't know! Tell me?"

So she and Arthur spent the remainder of the journey catching up on their news. He, too, was heading for home on leave. Philip was still in France, now a corporal. He and Arthur had been together so far.

"Hell, Tilly, I don't know where to start. You can't imagine it……. Oh, maybe you can, as you'll have been getting the poor buggers off the battlefield. I've never seen anything like it. They said the barrage of guns would take out the German trenches and cut the barbed wire, but it didn't, Tilly. Our lads going over the top were mowed down by their machine gun fire and left hanging on the barbed wire!" Neither of them spoke for some minutes, but then Arthur rubbed his hands through his hair, looked at her, and said:

"How could they get it so wrong?"

Tilly leant into him, and he put his arm around her shoulders,

"Me and our Phil were further back. He had the big artillery gun, and I was seconded to the Lewis gun. The noise was indescribable, Tilly. It'll be a miracle if we're both not deaf at the end of this. I can still hear it pounding in my head, day and night. Sent some of the lads mad it did. Listen, we can't tell Mam and Dad any of this. We have to keep it to ourselves. It wouldn't be fair, only add to their worry. God, I need a bath and a sleep. How long have you got? Leave, I mean?"

"Ten days," replied Tilly.

"Alright, for some!" he said, smiling. "I've got a week. At least we can travel together. Did you tell them you were coming? Me neither! A bit of a shock, I should think!"

She was so grateful for his safety and presence she tucked her head into his shoulder and hugged him, further warmed by the thought of their mutual homecoming.

Waking up in her own bed in freshly laundered sheets knowing there was nothing she absolutely had to do today, was a delight more precious for its rarity. For the first time in months, Tilly felt well-rested. She pulled the sheets up to her chin and turned onto her side, facing the window. The comforting sound of raindrops on the windowpane blended perfectly with the familiar sounds of the house wakening. Her father would be making the fire in the kitchen and putting the kettle on to boil. Mum would be performing her morning "toilette" – a term which made Tilly smile. She really was becoming "continental"! Mums' soft, gentle voice was singing as she washed and dressed. Art had made his excuses after dinner. He and a beaming Violet had made their way home, Vi clinging to him as if he were life itself. Tilly had settled for a while with her parents, but tiredness had soon claimed her. As her eyes drooped, Dad suggested an early night. She had hugged them both tightly, immensely grateful to be home. Mum had followed her up the stairs, turning down the bed and pouring water from the pitcher into the bowl for Tilly to wash. Mum took her hairbrush, and as Tilly sat at the small dressing table, she felt her hair released from its pins and cascading down her back. Mum set about giving it a thorough brushing. Tilly found it soothing, the rhythmic strokes of the brush so familiar in Mum's hands. Once brushed, it was plaited for the night, and she was tucked up in bed as if she were a child again. Mum kissed her forehead before blowing out the candle and softly closing the door.

Now it was morning. Tilly heard her Mum go downstairs, so she threw back the covers and began to make her own "toilette" in readiness for the new day. Her thoughts turned to Arts' warning that they should be selective with the details of their experiences. She knew he was right. She would be honest and truthful, answer their questions and share most of her experiences with them, if asked, but like her brother, she would protect them from the grim details of the carnage and suffering. The alternative would inflict unknown grief and double their worries for their children. Tilly couldn't do that.

Mum had been full of Jack's leave only weeks before. Tilly was sorry to have missed him. He had obviously spun a positive tale himself judging from the stories their parents regaled of his experiences.

"God Bless you, Jack," thought Tilly as she smiled and listened, sitting by the fire holding a steaming hot cup of tea.

2016

The operation has not been the success we had hoped for. The initial positivity didn't last, and now the shaking is as bad as ever. Of course, there was no guarantee that it would be completely successful, but it all looked so hopeful initially that now he is cast into a gloom of depression. The surgeon is trying to put a positive spin on it. Apparently, there are a few tweaks to try, and he is so keen to help.

He can't really help.

I'm trying to believe that he can, and I know my brother believes absolutely in his ability to do so. That's the problem. How to approach the conversation that perhaps all that can be done has been done? I don't think we're there yet, and contemplating the end of the road is not on my radar as yet!

I'm praying really hard, and I know others are too. His GP has started him on antidepressants, but we've been here before, and he gave up on them because he didn't believe they were helping him. The fact that these drugs take weeks to become effective seemed to have passed him by. So did the option of increasing the dose. Quite what the GP discussed with him is a mystery.

I'm finding it difficult, living so far away, because I know he relies on me. I'm really all he has to fight his corner, and I'm very aware of my responsibilities.

Worst case scenario – the disease is progressing faster than any had anticipated. I fear for his future, but I can't share that with him. He has to have hope.

BATTLE SHOCK

1917

"Have you seen much shell shock, Tilly?" Richard asks. The question came out of the blue one morning at breakfast. We were just finishing and beginning to clear the table. Dad had left for work much earlier, and mum was at the sink preparing to wash the dishes.

Richard was reading the newspaper. No, not reading it, devouring it! He had it laid out flat on the far end of the kitchen table, and he was devouring it cover to cover, as he did every day. I looked across at him.

"Some," I replied. "Why?" and I continued clearing away the dishes, tea towel in hand.

"It says here there's a lad being court-martialled. Cowardice, apparently, if he's convicted, they'll shoot him. The family says it's not cowardice but shell shock."

He looked up from the paper at me questioningly, and as I met his gaze. I suddenly felt a little hot and queasy. My mouth was dry. He had my full attention now.

"What's his name?" I asked instinctively, knowing what the answer would be.

"George something," he replied, scouring the article for the full name "George Marshall."

"Are you alright, Tilly?" he asked as the noise of his chair scraping back on the flagstone floor alerted mum to our conversation. I had turned pale and had apparently let out a small, strangled cry. He pulled out a chair and guided me into it as Mum approached, full of concern.

"What is it love?" she asked as she sat down next to me and covered my hand with hers scanning my face for clues of illness.

"Do you know him, Tilly?" asked Richard, his eyes lighting up at the possibility.

Mum stepped in.

"Right young man, off to school with you!" and she ushered him about his preparations to leave, gathering up his books and herding him out of the door almost before he'd finished speaking. He was doing his best to delay.

"I don't need to go yet, Mam!" he protested.

"Oh yes, you do!" his mother replied, "and if you're too early, you can drop those books off at the library for your Dad."

He knew he was beaten and accepted his fate grudgingly, muttering and grabbing the books along with his satchel on his accelerated way out.

The paper was still open, so I moved to sit before it and fearfully read the article for myself. It was small and did not have much detail, but it had mentioned a name. I had heard rumours, but this was actually in print. Maybe it was another George Marshall? I was grabbing at straws now. Mum busied herself making us both a cup of tea and then came to sit next to me. She put her hand on my forearm as I finished reading and looked up. Quietly I slid the paper across to her, and she read what had been reported herself. I sat with my head in my hands, feeling an enormous sadness mingled with fear which was rapidly turning to anger.

"I do know him, Mam. I nursed him last year." And I told her the details. How young he was, how shockingly affected he had been, and how he should never have been returned to active service. If nothing else, he was underage!

"It's not cowardice, Mam. He's ill. This shell shock is something we see more and more of. No one really understands it, so those affected are not being identified properly. If it's not recognised for what it is, then they won't get the right treatment. Not that there's much to offer other than rest and understanding and discharge from the bloody army!"

I could see Mam was shocked, not only by my use of a swear word, but she didn't reproach me for it.

"This is not right, Mam, it's just not right!" I could feel the anger bubbling up inside of me as I began to pace the floor, this was not an emotion I was very familiar with but one which was causing me to consider if there was anything I could do to help.

"Go easy, Tilly," Mam counselled. "Don't go off half-cocked. Wait until Dad gets home and talk it over with him" she could see how agitated I was becoming. The paper had said the Court Martial was to be held in

France. But when?? I still had four days of leave left, but I found myself planning an earlier return. How would I know where to go? How could I make contact with his defence lawyer? Or his family? All these questions kept popping into my head until I felt positively dizzy. Why would the testament of a mere nurse even be considered? Surely it would need to be a medical expert? Had they got one? Were there even any medical experts in shell shock who would be both plausible and convincing?

I found I couldn't settle or put my mind to any of the routine daily chores prompting Mam to exclaim:

"Oh, for goodness sake Tilly, if you can't wait for your father to get home, you'd better get your hat and coat. We'll go and see Robert Fielding in Malton!"

I must have looked non- plussed causing her to explain.

"Robert Fielding Senior was my father's solicitor. I believe his son runs the practice now. He's a good man, and he may know what to do in circumstances such as this."

Within the hour, we had caught the bus into town, presenting ourselves at the offices of Messrs. Fielding and Sindall.

Robert Fielding was younger than I had imagined him to be, more of my parent's generation than my grandparents. His father had acted for Grandfather Wharton, and when the time had come for him to retire, Mr Fielding Junior had taken over the business. He seems genuinely delighted to greet my mother, holding her hands and kissing her on both cheeks, rather an unusual greeting in Yorkshire! Mother, for her part, appeared to be blushing (I made a note to myself that we would have that conversation later!). Whatever discomfort she may have felt, she soon brushed it away as she introduced me.

"Robert, may I introduce my daughter Matilda? She has a dilemma about which we would value your advice."

I shook Robert Fielding's hand, it was firm and strong, yet his eyes twinkled as he greeted me formally.

"I am delighted to make your acquaintance Miss Dobson. Your mother and I are old friends" he still had hold of my hand, which, unexpectedly, he proceeded to kiss! I was a little taken aback but recognised gallantry and no little degree of charm.

"Thank you, Sir. Please call me Tilly. Everyone does."

He gestured for us to be seated and settled himself behind the large desk.

"Very well, Tilly. Now, how may I be of assistance?"

Once I started, I found I couldn't stop. Mr Fielding took notes and occasionally caused me to pause for clarification. But he listened intently as I poured out all my concerns for George Marshall, his youth, his illness, the injustice, and my fears for the outcome. Robert Fielding confessed to having heard of the condition but had no knowledge of the subject. That, he declared, was no great obstacle as he would make enquiries. He had colleagues he would consult, and we would decide, once all the information we had could be gathered and collated, what would be the best way to proceed.

Would I be willing to bear witness at the trial if that could be arranged? Military Courts conducted trials, of a kind, but didn't necessarily require a jury. This I found disturbing, but in a case that may result in a Death Sentence, it was intolerable. I assured Mr fielding it was certainly my intention to appear for the defence, but I stressed the urgency as we had so little time. Could it be organised at such short notice? Robert Fielding put down his pen, took off his reading glasses, and looked at me directly.

"If I'm honest, Tilly, I don't know. Nothing happens rapidly in the legal system, as a rule. I can see how deeply this is affecting you, and if you would be good enough to grant me a few hours to make enquiries and consult with colleagues, I may be able to answer you with greater certainty."

He then turned to my mother, who had been sitting quietly with her hands in her lap, taking it all in.

"May I suggest a spot of luncheon or a turn around town? Shopping perhaps? I can recommend The Lion, a very fine minestrone soup! We will reconvene at 3 pm to then decide on a plan of action."

He stood and moved to pull out the chair for my mother to rise.

"Thank you, Robert," she said kindly as we made our preparations to leave.

"Yes, thank you, Sir," I reiterated, shaking his hand again.

"Interesting morning Alice" he commented "It makes a change from conveyancing!" he held the door open as we passed out of the room, mother behind me, and I heard him comment to her.

"My congratulations on your daughter Alice, she not only has beauty, but she's feisty and passionate. Reminds me of you!"

We lunched at The Lion, and I tried to take an interest in the shops. I didn't even feel like interrogating her about the charming Mr Fielding. That could wait. Mam picked up small gifts for the grandchildren, but I couldn't wait to return to the solicitor's office to see what Robert Fielding had been able to discover and if we could have any impact on the miscarriage of justice I felt was about to occur. I was very, very conscious of time running out.

Mr Fielding was blunt:

"I think your best bet is to contact the journalist who wrote the article. Lawyers appoint a Council, and gathering evidence takes time, and it is the time we don't have. I'm sorry to say I doubt your young soldier stands much of a chance, but you may be able to prevent it from happening in the future. I wish there was more I could do, Tilly, but I do wish you the best of luck. You're a brave young woman."

There was a public telephone in the local Post Office, and that's where Mam and I headed next. It gave me a start, but the journalist wasn't in the office when I rang. I made an appointment to see him the following day, stressing the urgency of the meeting. The secretary seemed surprised by my insistence but promised to track him down. She was also kind enough to recommend suitable lodgings.

THE SPECIALIST

Henry Lascelles found himself frustrated with many aspects of army life. Lack of personnel and equipment he could understand, especially given the demands on the medical services, but military discipline was something else. Necessary undoubtedly, but nevertheless irritating in the extreme. There were times he felt an almost overwhelming desire to deck the jumped-up "Rupert" (as he knew the men called the officers) pontificating some nonsense Henry neither believed nor adhered to. On the positive side, the military experience afforded him unrivalled opportunities to develop his surgical skills to a degree unprecedented in peacetime. The development of teamwork and camaraderie, preventative medicine, sanitation, and inoculation. Blood transfusions were being used to great effect in the casualty clearing stations resulting in rapid replacement of body fluids, thereby combatting shock and saving lives. He was excited by the recent innovations, and he felt they were making a difference. Primarily though, he found himself drawn towards a new and emerging speciality. One which necessitated fine surgical skills, innovation, and a whole new approach to surgical repair. Going back to the basic anatomy of the head and face, and building on his knowledge both academically and in practice was stimulating. For the first time in years, he acknowledged his excitement at the possibilities before him. The war had thrown up injuries never before seen. Men were being blown apart and maimed by modern weapons. Surgeons had been faced with injuries they could never have imagined, and just about the worst of these were facial. Most men with such injuries died of course, especially if the injuries were multiple, but Henry had come across men whose only injury was a catastrophic hole in the face. Once the airway had been secured and a tube inserted into the stomach to feed and hydrate the poor chap, what then to do with him? If the men with such injuries made it back to the CCS alive, then surely, they deserved as good a chance as the next man? Mostly, they could only utter incoherent noises, and often they were also blinded. But if they could see through the swelling and dirt and mangled flesh, Henry had recognised a desperate plea in those frightened eyes. He was determined to do whatever he could to alleviate suffering and attempt a repair. It could only be basic at the CCS.

Resources were limited, and at first, the best he could do was clean up the wound and remove fragments of clothing, bone, and teeth. But some of the men were making it back to the base hospitals, and then something really did have to be done. These cases haunted him, it would be a huge challenge, and he knew he had a lot to learn before he could realistically help them. However, he was fortunate in finding he wasn't alone in his quest, and during lulls in activity and conversations with surgical colleagues, the subject of the facially injured soldier was much dwelt upon. Cross-examination of colleagues who had treated these cases and meticulous scouring of textbooks for what little information there was used up what little spare time he had. Word obviously got around, and his next posing was to Sidcup, the army's new" facial" hospital. His boss was a particularly gifted New Zealander by the name of Harold Gillies.

"Call me Harold. I can't be doing with any of that army nonsense!" he said enthusiastically, shaking Henry by the hand.

"I hear I may have a protégé on my hands?" Harold widened his eyes and winked. Henry was immediately put at ease, and he laughed.

"Oh, I do hope so, Sir!"

PHILIP

Philip Dobson was sick to death of soldiering. He'd been told by an old wag that it consisted of 99% boredom and 1% sheer terror, and he reckoned that was about right. He was desperate for the end of the war and had to stop himself from dwelling on thoughts of home, for there lay the road to madness. He was amazed at his former naivety, his enthusiasm to "do his bit" "For King and Country", and how he had ever thought going to war would be a bit of a lark. His only aim now was to survive, protect his men, and get home in one piece. Despite his weariness and reticence, Phil was a good soldier. He'd been promoted to corporal the previous year and had quickly gained his sergeant's stripes which he promptly lost, along with a day's pay, for decking a fellow sergeant for bullying the soldiers. He had no regrets, the bastard had deserved it, but it hadn't made life easy in the following few months. That was all passed now, and he had a good relationship with the boys in his platoon. They had lost their replacement sergeant in action, so he was technically the senior man, and the boys had no difficulty with that. He was respected and liked though he was no pushover. He worked them hard, but he was fair and supportive. Looking out for the younger lads in particular, some of whom looked to be barely out of short trousers. He rather suspected they weren't, but they were here now and had best get on with it. Phil didn't like to delve too deeply on that subject though he had had cause to take action when one young lad took fright and, on the eve of battle, had declared himself to be only fifteen. At the time, Phil could have decked him too, but he had younger brothers himself and had taken pity on the lad. Nineteen was the youngest any soldier should have been posted overseas. How the recruiting sergeants could mistake a child for an adult was clearly an act of indifference in the need to improve numbers. That these lads could then pass a medical as being nineteen was even more astounding. Phil shook his head and returned his attention to cleaning his weapon.

The West Yorkshires were in Flanders and had pushed forwards as far as the outskirts of the ruined village of Ploegsteert. The enemy had resisted the advance. But by means of rifle grenades and Lewis-gun fire, all objectives had been gained and the line of posts established. The battalion had lost one officer (killed) and two other officers wounded, along with twenty-six other ranks killed or wounded, including their platoon sergeant. The attack may have been small, but it was carried out with great vigour and dash, and congratulations had been wired to the battalion's commanding officer. Revelling in their success was short lived, however, as orders had been received for them now to form the advance guard of the Ninety-Third Brigade that night. Despite exhaustion, the column marched relentlessly along the Rossignol road until south of Messines. They came under heavy and accurate shell fire. Phil ordered his platoon to find whatever cover they could, and the Lewis guns were unpacked and mounted, and their transport sent back. Casualties were mounting up, and the order to don gas masks was given. As if conditions weren't hard enough, this was the last degradation for Phil. At fifty-yard intervals between platoons, the column proceeded to pass through the barrage with covering fire from the Lewis guns manned by Corporal Dobson and his platoon. After an hour the hostile shell fire slackened, and the battalion had passed through, heading East. It would be a long march. The guns had now to be carried, and ammunition was low. The men were tired before the action and could now barely find the energy to chew their meagre rations as darkness fell. Keeping up morale was no easy task, but the camaraderie between the men and their corporal made the hours less tedious. The loss of their sergeant was no great loss as Corporal Dobson was more than able to step up to the mark and, like Yorkshiremen everywhere, was determined to complete the task at hand with the best humour possible. Finally, being able to do without the hated gas masks had come as an enormous relief. The enemy was being pushed ahead of them but still had outposts of defence, "pill boxes" scattered about the countryside. Those outposts were still, occasionally, manned by one or two enemy soldiers left behind to cover the retreat. Phil's group of men came upon one of these in the early dusk. The gunfire was fierce, and he gave the order to take cover. Very little cover was available, and his men began to fall like heads of wheat before the scythe. The returning fire cracked behind them, but ammunition was running low, and they would soon be pinned down. Phil Dobson had had a trying day. He was tired and hungry, cold and wet, and more than a little pissed off. He feared for his men, and as he heard the screams of the wounded behind him, he lost it, and a great veil of red mist descended before his eyes. He snatched up as much ammunition as he could quickly lay his hands on. He called to the soldier nearest to him to "follow me," and stormed the gun turret singlehandedly whilst discharging his weapon and screaming abuse at the enemy. Davis, the young Private who followed him on his mad rampage, later gave the account of what had happened. Corporal Dobson had charged forward, rushing the German gun position and shooting the two soldiers manning it who were causing such destruction to his platoon. Davis reported that Dobson had seemed to possess almost superhuman strength as well as a great deal of luck. They then captured the guns and ammunition and returned to the road below to what was left of the column. He immediately took charge of the remains of the men, dead, wounded, and a few still able-bodied, and they saw to the wounded as a message was received to dig in for the night and await further orders. A miserable night was spent at the side of the road doing what they could for the wounded and laying out the dead. None were sorry to see dawn approach and new orders arrive. The wounded were collected, and working parties arrived to bury the dead. Phil's company moved on.

Corporal Philip Dobson was later awarded the Military Medal for Bravery in the field. By the time the letter arrived informing him of this, the war was over, and he had resumed his life at home. The letter arrived in the post with an invitation to Buckingham Palace, the King, it said, would present him with the medal. By return of post, Phil declined the invitation to the Palace. If they wanted him to have the medal, they could send it in the post.

This they did, and although the family knew he had it, he spoke of it only once, to his daughters, on condition they would never ask him again. He never spoke of his wartime experiences and forbade the family to ask him any questions about them. The medal was found, still in its box with the letter at the bottom of a trunk of his belongings, by his Grandchildren, after his death at the great age of eighty-six.

THE JOURNALIST

I boarded the train at Malton Station, having said my goodbyes to the family. Only Mam accompanied me to the platform.

"Go easy, Tilly!" she again advised.

"I know how worried you are, but give the man a chance to explain. You need to understand the full story. Don't go in all guns blazing! I know you. Once you know the facts, you can formulate a plan of action calmly."

I hugged her fiercely. She was right, I could be full of righteous indignation, but if I was to be a creditable witness, I must impress upon the male-dominated hierarchy my sincerity, professionalism, and inability to submit to an attack of the vapours!

I changed trains at York for the main line into London Kings Cross. It gave me time to reflect on what had happened so far and formulate how I might have a small say in blocking a shocking injustice. I had to keep my emotions and personal feelings out of it, or I would simply be discredited. Normally I relished travelling by train. I felt safe, cocooned in the carriage, lulled by the repetitive clickety-clack of the wheels on the rails. It was calming, but today I just wanted to be at my destination. The landscape outside the window rolled by too slowly, and every stop was a minor irritation. I ate my sandwiches which had been so lovingly prepared. I tried to read the paper, but my mind constantly returned to the thought of those young boys being shot and how on earth must the execution party feel having to perform such a distasteful task on boys and young men who could have been their brothers or even sons?

Passengers came and went through the carriage with a brief nod and a smile to acknowledge their arrival and departure, but I didn't encourage conversation. I wasn't wearing my uniform, safely packed in my suitcase, so another subject for conversation had been avoided. I looked out of the window with sightless eyes, willing the train to go faster. At some point, I must have dropped off to sleep as I woke suddenly to feel the train braking and the station signage come into view. Thank goodness.

If I'm honest, I don't recall getting across the city to the newspaper office, yet here I was, standing in front of an imposing front door with a suitcase in hand. People were passing me on both sides, going up and down the stairs in and out of the building. I felt invisible.

"Right, Matilda Dobson. It's now or never!" so I took a deep breath and proceeded up the stairs and into the lobby of the newspaper office. It was bustling with people. I felt a little overwhelmed and intimidated initially, so I briskly made my way over to the reception desk.

"Good afternoon, my name is Matilda Dobson, and I have an appointment to see Mr Samuel Leigh-Smith."

The receptionist checked her diary, greeted me pleasantly, and rose to direct me to a seat down the corridor outside an impressive-looking and highly polished wooden door.

The young lady receptionist had obviously been conducting a conversation with me, of which I was entirely unaware.

"I'm so sorry. Did you just ask me something?"

The young lady smiled and repeated her question.

"Can I offer you any refreshment, Miss Dobson?"

"Oh, yes, please. A cup of tea would be marvellous, thank you."

The young lady scampered off, and I sat patiently waiting, watching the activity happening all around me. I began to feel tired, as emotions can be draining, and it had been a long day. Just as my eyes were beginning to droop, the refreshment arrived, with two plain biscuits balanced on the side of the saucer. I accepted them gratefully and uttered thanks as the young lady excused herself, promising to return with news of the whereabouts of the journalist.

"Please wait here, Miss Dobson. Mr Leigh- Smith is most anxious to make your acquaintance."

"Well, that was reassuring," I thought. "At least I'm expected."

The whirlwind of the past day began to wash over me. Mam had packed my case and provisioned me for the journey, calming me with her determination and straightforward practicality. Dad had listened carefully to the explanation of my intent, nodding his approval but advising caution.

"Facts, Tilly, stick to the facts. Don't allow emotion to weaken your case."

Their support was unwavering and strengthened my resolve to do whatever I could. However little that may be.

It was late in the day now, and my usually cheerful spirits were beginning to flag. The thoughts of a hot bath, a meal, and a good night's sleep began to feel unattainable.

"Miss Dobson?"

I became aware of a splendidly polished pair of brown shoes standing in front of me. I looked up into the face of a very tall and solidly built gentleman. I stood up and held out my hand in greeting. He almost crushed it!

"Good evening, I am Samuel Leigh-Smith," he explained whilst balancing a pile of papers under his left arm. Some of the papers dropped onto the floor. I naturally bent down to retrieve them, unfortunately at the very same time as the large gentleman, and our heads banged together! It is no exaggeration to say I saw stars.

"I am so sorry, Miss Dobson!" He apologised as he tried simultaneously to rise, gather up the papers, and direct me back to the seat I had so recently vacated.

“Are you alright?” he asked, all concerned as I held my head, tears appearing in sympathy from my stunned eyes. I glanced up at him out of one of the stunned eyes and started to laugh. Tiredness undoubtedly was the cause, but also, the relief of tension I hadn’t previously acknowledged now caused me to laugh almost uncontrollably.

“I hope you are a better journalist than you are a juggler of papers?” I commented.

He handed me a freshly pressed handkerchief.

“I can assure you that I am!” he smiled and invited me to accompany him to the office.

“Come in, Miss Dobson, please do come in,” and he held the door open as I passed before him into a relatively private office. There were others present but not in close proximity, and the tapping of typewriters was not intrusive. Mr Samuel Leigh-Smith promptly relieved himself of the pile of papers he had been carrying under his arm, and once his limb was again his own, he used both hands to ruffle through his thick hair. He perched himself on the corner of the desk and indicated that I should sit in the chair before it.

“How may I be of help to you, Miss Dobson?” he asked.

I talked for what seemed like hours, and he listened without interruption, only moving to sit in the chair behind the large desk. He had his hands folded in front of him. Fingers entwined beneath his chin as his elbow rested on the surface of the desk. I guessed him to be in his early thirties, which caused me to wonder why he himself was not in uniform. Despite the activity occurring in the rest of the office, we seemed to be so focused on our concerns. I, for one, was completely unaware of them. I had so many questions I barely knew how to begin asking. As I contemplated the best approach, he suddenly rose and took off his jacket, hanging it neatly on the back of the chair.

"I expect you will have questions, Miss Dobson? First, allow me to request some tea, and if you don't mind, I have some questions of my own, so may I use a notepad?"

As the tea arrived and a notepad was found, he seemed less meticulous about the whereabouts of his belongings. He began to explain how the story had come about.

His brother was a junior officer in an artillery regiment and had been asked to represent one of his men accused of cowardice. He had no knowledge of the legalities involved and had represented his man in dire circumstances before a hastily assembled Court Martial. The panel of three serving senior officers had found the man guilty, and the following morning he had been put up against a wall and shot. The ideology was to dissuade others from the same action and to boost morale.

Really? I would have thought it would have had the exact opposite effect, but I didn't interrupt. Mr Leigh-Smiths brother had been quite traumatised by this process and, when next on home leave, had succumbed to an illness related to his nerves. He had spoken to no one until Samuel had been summoned home, and the whole sorry story began to pour out. Brother Harold had gained some relief from his nerves as a cathartic result, but Samuel had become aware of the horrific story and guessed correctly that this was not an isolated incident. As a journalist, he started to dig. It was not easy and involved a visit to the Western Front where he was denied access to information or personnel. But soldiers would talk, quite innocently answering questions put to them by a gentleman of the press. What he did find out shocked him intensely. His Editor was all for suppressing him breaking the story in fear it would have a devastating effect on morale in the armed services and an even worse response at home. His anger and frustration were soon replaced by an intractable determination to publish the story, and in doing so, he risked losing his employment. Journalists, he told me, can be like a dog with a bone. He just couldn't drop it. His Editor was an old school "Hack" coming to the end of his career. Despite his initial reluctance to believe the story, he knew a "scoop" when he saw one and ultimately backed Samuel to publish. Initially, very few papers would carry the story, it simply beggared belief, and if mentioned at all, it was cut down and relegated to a back page. The military was definitely hostile and dismissive, but that only made Samuel dig deeper. It was happening. Soldiers were being shot by their own side for many misdemeanours, not just cowardice.

If the Army thought this was a deterrent, they were sadly mistaken. Most of these young men and boys were suffering from something as yet unrecognised, and the public would not have it. He was now on a mission to expose the practice, but he was met at every turn by secrecy and subterfuge. Once an accusation was made, the accused was tried within days, and the sentence was carried out immediately or at least the next day. They had no legal representation, only their immediate officer to represent them, and no recourse to appeal. It was all done and dusted before anyone knew the details. The aftermath for the families was devastating. They would all be tarred with the same brush, so they didn't want anyone to know the true fate of their loved one for fear of being ostracised by their own communities.

I was horrified. Tears were rolling down my cheeks. I found the handkerchief Samuel had given me and used it. He had spoken so eloquently, and I was now making a fool of myself.

"Forgive me, Sir, I thank you for your honesty, and I apologise for my tearful response. What I really want to know is how I can help. People must know, and it must be stopped!"

"My dear Miss Dobson, whilst I applaud your intent and kind heart, you must understand that short of publicising the events, there is little we can do. We are at war, and normal sensibilities don't apply. The Army does what it sees fit, and any opposition to that is seen as unpatriotic. Discipline must be enforced, and justice has very little to do with it. All we can hope to do is keep reporting and shining a light into dark corners, lobbying politicians, and raising the awareness of the general public to these practices in the hope that change will come in time. Now remind me of the name of the young boy you nursed, and I'll see if I can find out any more about him."

He took the details down on his notepad and arranged for me to return the following day. I felt helpless and angry. Everything he had told me rang true about the Army and the lack of recognition for this new phenomenon, "shell shock," which was causing institutionalised murder. I had to see my own nursing hierarchy and start to make waves of my own. I could not be the only nurse, or doctor, with these concerns.

We shook hands and agreed to meet briefly tomorrow. I already knew the news about George would not be good, but I had to try to stop any other young man from being murdered as a result of an illness.

I returned the following day at the appointed time, and it was as I had feared. George had indeed been shot at dawn only a week ago.

I sat in the local church for some time to shed tears for my young friend, to pray for him and his family, and to compose myself. I took comfort only in that he was no longer suffering, but my resolve to prevent others from suffering the same fate only deepened. Yet I knew what Samuel Leigh-Smith had told me was the truth, and maybe he was right, the best way to approach this injustice was through the press, shame the authorities, and the public in their treatment of the mentally wounded soldier. I couldn't possibly have known it would take almost a century.

I lobbied my fellow nurses and spoke of my concerns to my superiors. All agreed it was dreadful, but "that's the army for you," and they shrugged their shoulders. Many agreed with me, but not many were prepared to stand up and be counted. I wrote letters to MPs and to the press, but as soon as this was discovered, I was disciplined about it and labelled a "troublemaker – bringing the service into disrepute."

WIMERAUX

I was frustrated and restless. I tried to concentrate on my new assignment, which was to the hilltop Hospital at Wimeraux, on the Northern French coastline. Again, I was posted into theatres, but as much as I loved the work, it reminded me of Henry, and I asked to be moved to the medical ward. The men were generally cheerful and lifted my spirits. They knew the shootings were happening but hadn't attributed it to illness. They felt it was justified, but it was not a subject they wanted to dwell on.

I missed Nell. Her letters, full of gossip, irreverence, and humour, lifted my spirits. I missed my family, I missed Henry, and I felt disjointed and ineffectual.

I needed a change.

"Tilly! Come quickly. There's been a crash."

I could hear footsteps running which was odd as it was quite early in the morning. I had just fallen asleep after the night shift, and everything seemed not altogether real. Maybe I was dreaming?

"Tilly! Get up. We're needed!"

That was my roommate and recently acquired friend. Her name was Wendy Wills, very Welsh, very efficient and very nice! She was heading back out of the door when I asked.

"A crash? Of what?" I asked as I pulled on my uniform and pinned back my hair.

"An aeroplane has crashed over the way; the pilot is being brought in now. Hurry up!"

"Why do you need me if only one pilot is injured? Surely the rest of this hospital can deal with one crashed pilot?"

"No, you idiot, he crashed it into the village. There are multiple casualties. I'll see you down in triage," and with that, she set off, adding to the sound of running feet still audible.

By the time I reached triage, everyone was standing around waiting.

"What's happening?" I asked, assuming someone would enlighten me, but they just shrugged their shoulders and waited.

"Has the equipment been checked?" I asked, "Have we enough supplies?"

"All done, Sister," replied a male orderly "Sister Wills has gone to see what to do," and sure enough, by the time I turned around, there was Wendy grinning all over her face.

"Stand down, everyone, false alarm. He crashed it into the village barn, fortunately, empty of livestock! He's broken his leg and dented his ego, but other than that, he'll be alright!"

Everyone departed, muttering under their breath, but I suspected silently relieved it wasn't as bad as expected.

"You go back to bed, love. You look all done in."

"Thanks, Wendy, I won't deny it. Do you think you can manage without me for a few hours?"

"Cheeky monkey! I'll see you later!" and off she set back to her ward, no doubt to charm the patients by telling ribald Welsh tales to aid their recovery.

My bed had never looked so inviting, and the next thing I knew, Wendy appeared with a cup of tea and a tall story involving the unlucky pilot who was not only a belligerent American but insisted that he knew me!

"Oh, my goodness! Neilan!" I exclaimed as I shot out of bed and dressed in record time.

"Where is he? Is he alright?"

"Calm down, woman! He's fine, had his leg set and his ego massaged, and now he wants to be fed and watered! Can you imagine?" she joked as I finalised my ablutions.

"I do expect a full report on the circumstances of your first encounter!" she shouted after me as I exited the room at breakneck speed.

"Slow down, Sister! You don't have the devil at your back, you know!" came Matron's dulcet tones behind me as I put the brakes on.

"I'm sorry, Matron," I apologised "it's just that……."

"Yes, I am aware, but he won't disappear if you don't arrive with smoke pouring from your heels!"

"Yes, Matron, thank you, Matron!" I smiled at her as we both continued in a more leisurely fashion towards the Wards.

I heard him before I saw him.

"What the hell is this? Can you get me something I recognise, at least? And a beer! What? No beer? You have to be kidding me!"

"Tilly! Thank God! Will you please tell these people I will not eat that, and if they do not feed me, it will be a diplomatic incident! Now come here and give your old mate a hug? Careful of the leg Tilly, wounded Officer and all that! I stoofed the crate in, did you know? Bit embarrassing, really!" Greg Neilan had undergone a transformation. The shy, retiring boy had gained the bravado and cockiness of the pilots of the RFC!

"Officer? You? Really? Were they that desperate? And yes, I did know. Got me out of bed thinking you'd killed the whole village!" and I gave him a hug laughing with him as I did so.

He was just the tonic I needed, and we talked incessantly until I had to eat and report for my next shift.

"You'll come back tomorrow, won't you? Don't leave me in the hands of these English ingrates who don't even know what a decent steak looks like!"

"You behave yourself," I warned jokingly, "or they will starve you to death, and with my blessing!" he groaned dramatically and threw up his hands in supplication as I left.

My spirits had lifted as Greg Nielan recovered. He would be moved back to convalesce in England. But until that happened, I spent most of my off-duty time with him and introduced him to my friends and colleagues at the hospital. He was a good raconteur, and it was good to hear laughter from the wards as he soon became a favourite. Like most Americans, he had an easy manner about him and could be charming as well as bloody-minded. He saved his very best charm for Matron, who, like many spinster ladies, secretly enjoyed the attention whilst scolding him often.

"Now don't you try that nonsense on with me, young man!" she would warn, but we noticed she visited the ward more often than had previously been the case.

"You cut me to the quick, Matron!" he would complain, placing his right hand over his heart. "You know there's only one for me. Get the Padre in here and marry me? You do know I can't possibly continue calling you Matron once we're married. What IS your Christian name?"

She stood at the foot of his bed, shaking her head and smiling, knowing the rest of us were loving it too, but she was far too proper to show it.

"Christian name indeed! You are far too familiar young man! Now don't you be a trouble to my nurses, or I will forbid you a visit from your Squadron friends."

We all looked to the door of the ward simultaneously, and sure enough, there were three handsome young men dressed in Royal Flying Corps uniforms. Matron beckoned them in, and amidst much whooping and back-slapping, they set chairs beside Neilan's bed.

"Thirty minutes, gentlemen!" Matron warned, "and if there is excessive noise, it will be a lot less!"

The three pilots stood rigidly to attention and saluted her as she left the ward, still grinning like a girl! They then settled down to visit Neilan, and we all returned to our duties. The men in adjoining beds and indeed in the whole ward were included in the banter, and though the noise level rose at times, we were tolerant as we all recognised the boost to morale the visit had brought.

I really dreaded the impending loss of my friend as he would be moved soon and possibly at a moment's notice. During one of our late-night conversations, he reminded me of the time he had told me about the formation of a new Royal Air Force. Well, now he said it was coming to pass. He spoke eloquently about it and the involvement of American Forces, which had changed the course of the war. He said he would "see it out (God willing) with the RFC," but after the war, he intended to return to The United States to join their flying services. Again, he stressed how many good nurses would be needed in the new British service, nurses like me.

Maybe this was the change I was looking for.

"Get your papers in early, Tilly, be one of the first!" was his advice.

I thought about little else in the following days, and even Neilan's departure didn't throw me into the gloom I thought it would.

"After the war, come to the States for a visit, Tilly? I mean it! You'll love it. I'll take good care of you! Are you still in touch with the little gobshite?... What was her name??? (As if he didn't know!) Bring her too. I could find you both husbands! I will be married to Matron, of course, so technically off the market...."

How could I not laugh? But he had given me food for thought on many accounts and a lift of spirits unexpected but very, very welcome. The war was coming to an end. Then I would have to move on professionally as well as personally. How exciting would it be to be instrumental in setting up a whole new Nursing Service?

DISCHARGE

2017

My spirits are high. My brother is being discharged today after weeks of repeated visits and tweaking of the electrodes in his head, juggling with the correct medication and rehabilitation. I have arrived to take him home. I find myself smiling, there is a spring in my step, and I savour the sunshine and the blossom appearing on the trees as I arrive at the hospital. I love spring. Always a sign of new beginnings and hope. Please, God, it will be for him. I'm very aware of the people milling around as I pass through the rotating door into the hospital's reception area. The lady in reception greets me with a smile and a wave. Over the months we've been coming, I've got to know most of the staff, even if only on sight. I'm comfortable in this environment and very grateful for the care and compassion all have shown to us over this time. I make my way down the long corridor toward the lifts, the cleaner is hard at work as I greet her, and she nods her acknowledgment. I don't smell cleaning fluid, so often I've heard comments about "hospital smells" of disinfectant, bleaches, and gasses….. But I've never experienced these myself, only cleanliness, though I'm aware of how powerful smells can trigger distant memories of childhood or people or even trauma. My own experiences are gentler. My mother's perfume, the smell of daffodils at our home, and freshly baked bread immediately bring to mind my grandmother in her kitchen, clapping her hands together in glee and dusting everyone in flour! But I digress.

I put my head into the four bedded ward and see Richard packing up his washbag. He's as excited as I am and hugs me briefly. He's not usually so demonstrative, so I'm a little surprised. We have to wait for his discharge medication to arrive from the pharmacy. He's not cured, Parkinson's disease is not curable, but he has improved. The DBS (deep brain stimulation) has helped, and in conjunction with the medication, his shaking is a lot less aggressive, making the possibility of coping at home so much better. He is now able to feed himself. Though at times the shaking returns unannounced for varying lengths of time, he now has periods without any shaking at all. I've noticed he's slower generally, mentally, and physically. The stiffness of the limbs associated with the condition is having an impact, but he seems accepting of that. It was primarily the shaking he couldn't cope with. The whole purpose of this journey has been to alleviate that unpredictable and debilitating symptom. He is disappointed not to have had complete success with the DBS, but there is no denying that the improvement has been well worth it. It's been tough on him, and I admire his resilience and perseverance. My job has always been to support and advise him and to love him, which I do.

He's chatting to the other men in the ward, and I stand by the window looking out over Sheffield gathering my thoughts. Positivity, hope, and thankfulness. He is going home to independent living, with a support package in place, to his own home. He's excited about that. His home is perfect for him, one level living in the same town he's lived in for forty years. The house was bequeathed by an Aunt, and we refurbished it together with just this scenario in mind. God bless her for her forethought.

I turn back to see how he's getting on, and I become aware of a man in a white coat leaning on the ward door, looking at me. For some entirely unexplainable reason, my heart skips a beat. Perhaps I'm mistaken, and he's not looking at me. I look behind myself to see if there is someone behind me, but no, there is only empty space. When I look back, he's gone, and I feel a shiver running down my spine. I'm oddly unsettled but deliberately concentrate on helping Richard fasten his suitcase. The nurse explains the discharge letter to us and once his medication arrives, we are free to go. She is busy, so I offer to go and see if it has arrived at the nursing station. The man in the white coat is standing at the Nursing station, which unsettles me more, but I make an effort to "pull myself together" and proceed. He sees me coming and looks quizzically at me as though he's trying to place me. I feel the same.

"Hello!" he says and offers his hand to shake "have we met somewhere before?" I take the offered hand, and I'm shocked as an electrical current seems to pass between us. I withdraw my hand automatically.

"No, I don't think so," I reply, though there is something familiar about him.

"You're Richard's sister, aren't you?" he asks.

"Forgive me. I should introduce myself, Henry Lascelles. I'm the Prof's Registrar. Are you sure we haven't met before?"

He's good-looking, and he has a wonderful twinkle in his eye. I'm feeling unusually flustered.

"No, I'm pretty sure I would have remembered!" I repeat …. But there is just something about him…..

"Well, that's a shame, Miss Dobson," he says, and his smile is dazzling. He's turning, and I panic. I don't want him to go.

"It's Milly," I say, and he turns back. Now we're both smiling, and I feel a rush of warmth all over. Whatever is happening to me? He seems just as puzzled, and we both just stand there, not wanting to break the connection. It can only have been seconds but time really did just seem to stand still.

"These are yours, I think," says the nurse as she handed me the bag of medications, "Richard's medication!"

"Oh, yes, thank you" I reply automatically, somehow unable to take my eyes off the face of Henry Lascelles. I feel foolish, good grief Milly! Get a grip!

"Well, that's it, I suppose, time to go home," and I shrug helplessly as I force myself to turn away whilst my whole being is crying out to stay.

"Goodbye"

I return up the corridor as if in a daze. Whatever is the matter with me? I almost feel bereft, we've been waiting for this moment for months, and now I don't want to go.

"Milly! Wait!" comes a voice behind me, and my heart almost stops.

"I know this is going to sound bonkers… as we've only just met…… but …. Well…. oh good grief Henry Lascelles just say it! I really would like to see you again! Look, I'm a doctor, I work ridiculous hours, I have practically no social life, I'm badly in need of a haircut, I play cricket very badly, and I'm even worse at cards! That said, I'm really a very nice man, and I would very much like to take you out for tea sometime."

How could I not laugh?

"Well, Henry Lascelles, as it happens, I'm a nurse, and I also work ridiculous hours! I love history, sports, cards, and dogs. I have a very annoying but strangely loveable brother, and that has to be the nicest invitation I've had this week! I would love to have tea with you!"

Suddenly everything seemed to fall into place. It's funny how that happens sometimes, isn't it?

Perhaps I'll leave the conversation about my serving with The Princess Mary's Royal Air Force Nursing Service for another day?

Printed in Great Britain
by Amazon

53264317R00178